It has been said that the primary role of the fiction writer is to entertain, for to bore the reader is the greatest sin. I believe the second task is to challenge, surprise and move the reader. Welcome to Jared's world.

Printed in Victoria, Canada

Published by Boudica Press, in Cooperation with Trafford Publishing.

Cover design by Tia Seifert

This is a work of fiction and any resemblance to persons living or dead in coincidental. The exception to this is information concerning Dachau and certain officers based upon research.

Note for Librarians: a cataloguing record for this book that includes Dewey Classification and US Library of Congress numbers is available from the National Library of Canada. The complete cataloguing record can be obtained from the National Library's online database at: www.nlc-bnc.ca/amicus/index-e.html

ISBN 1-4120-1419-0

TRAFFORD

Suite 6E, 2333 Government St., Victoria, B.C. V8T 4P4, CANADA
Phone   250-383-6864   Toll-free   1-888-232-4444 (Canada & US)
Fax   250-383-6804   E-mail   sales@trafford.com
Web site www.trafford.com   TRAFFORD PUBLISHING IS A DIVISION OF TRAFFORD HOLDINGS LTD.
Trafford Catalogue #03-1797   www.trafford.com/robots/03-1797.html
10   9   8   7

Dedication:

To my family and friends, and to my birth mother Linda whose gifted screenplays inspired my own writing.

Acknowledgements:

Thanks to family and friends who read and commented on drafts, to Sharon Crawford my editor, Jennifer and Andy for their help, and Tia Seifert for her cover design. Thanks to Mike Rowbottom for his constant encouragement with this project.

Chapter One

Why should people understand? Hell, they probably wouldn't even believe him. Jared had difficulty believing it himself, and as he lay in the hospital bed he wondered if maybe he *was* just crazy.

Crazy would be a relief. What happened was something beyond extraordinary and the explanation couldn't be so simple. Awake from a coma for just a few hours, Jared Clarkson's exchanges with the nurses remained brief and hazy. He thought he recalled one of the nurses saying that soon a doctor would come to see him and his mind pondered what *could* he say to the doctor that wouldn't sound like delusional nonsense, or outright fabrication? The Dachau experience was no dream, although it was, and wasn't, a nightmare.

The doctor would draw his own conclusions, albeit the wrong ones. It wouldn't necessarily be the doctor's fault. Medicine just didn't have categories for experiences like his. The Department of

Parapsychology might, but Jared doubted the doctor would consult them.

These thoughts, jumbled and intense, aroused Jared to a state of painful alert, and he felt so ill that part of him wished a return to the oblivion of the past three days. His mind continued to churn with thoughts of the recent past and fears of the future. In particular, he worried what the doctor would think if he told him the truth.

He'd probably call Jared nuts, or certainly think that. Hell, if someone told Jared a story like that, *he'd* think so. Truth wasn't particularly the issue.

Oh man, how could he feel so sick and still be alive? He felt ten times worse than the time he and Clarence drank two bottles of homemade wine. Was he dying? Well, maybe, but then wasn't that the idea? Thoughts swirled then shifted, like one of those Mobius strips where back changes to front and back again without taking pen from paper.

Jared looked up when he heard footsteps outside the hospital room. As the door opened, its hinge squeaked. A young doctor wearing Buddy Holly glasses and a white lab coat entered with a nurse following behind.

"Mr. Clarkson, I'm Dr. Schondale, the Psychiatric Resident in charge tonight. How are you feeling?"

What was with the mister stuff? This guy seemed hardly older than him.

The doctor leaned close to capture Jared's whisper.

"Headache, bad one."

"Frankly I'm not surprised your head hurts. Just don't ask me for a Tylenol, O.K.?"

Jared glimpsed a smug look flicker across the doctor's face and felt like smacking the guy.

"We were afraid we'd lost you. You took a serious overdose. We still aren't certain if there is damage to your liver."

Evidently he'd come closer to killing himself than he thought.

"Great job guy." Jared's eyes flashed. "Bring me back from the brink so I can die slowly instead."

The young doctor weathered the blast patiently, too patiently, and Jared felt guilty. Shut the fuck *up* Clark', he thought. The guy's just tryin' to help.

The mother of all migraines continued stabbing his left eye and Jared rubbed his temple. He thought about the guy on T.V. with cluster headaches. His temporal torture had reduced him to banging his head on the cement floor.

"Let's get him an ice pack." The doctor addressed the nurse. She hurried off, and he continued. "Once we're certain you're medically stable, we'll be transferring you to psychiatry."

Transfer? Jared figured he was already one of the cashews in the nut ward. Until then he hadn't noticed the wires attached to his chest, and the I.V. tube taped to his arm.

"Where am I?" His voice was low, muffled.

"You're in the intensive care unit at St. Joe's Health Centre. Someone found you unconscious in High Park and called an ambulance. Probably you don't feel much like talking right now, but I hope you'll be able to talk to staff on Psych later. Any family you'd like us to contact?"

At the mention of family Jared rolled away from the doctor and stared at a blood pressure cup sprawling from its holder on the wall.

"No. No one," He mumbled.

When the nurse returned she held the ice pack out to him.

Jared accepted it without comment and pressed it against his left eye.

"I'd like to give you something to help you relax. Would that be alright with you, Mr. Clarkson?" The doctor pushed back his Holly glasses.

Again with the Mr. Clarkson stuff? Who the hell called young guys 'Mister' in 1970? Jared remained quiet.

"We'll take that as a 'yes.' "

Jared didn't know what the doctor ordered and he didn't care, but in a few minutes he grew drowsy, then fell asleep.

A few days later, Jared was playing euchre with a young woman in the ward recreation area. A dangling tube ran from an I.V. bag overhead into her nose. At the sound of footsteps, Jared ceased shuffling the cards, and looked up to stare in amazement at the familiar man approaching. Jared's hands remained suspended in the air like some conjurer flash frozen amid a sleight of hand.

Jared greeted him with a mix of embarrassment and pleasure and stared at the fellow's hospital ID that read Simon Glassner, MSW Social Worker.

"Mensch." Images of the two of them sharing beers in Grossman's tavern came to mind. It seemed like eons ago.

"Heeey Clark'. How are you?" Simon reached out his hand. "Been awhile, eh?" Simon's face grew serious. "Guess you've been having a hard time lately."

Jared suddenly felt choked with emotion and unable to speak despite his mind crammed with things he wanted to share. All he could manage was a question.

"How come you always seem to show up when I'm in shit city?"

"Who knows?" Simon shrugged. "Maybe it's Karmic destiny

or something. I guess you're wondering what I'm doing here?"

"I assume from your badge that you work here."

"Yeah. I guess that's kind of obvious." Simon flushed. "I graduated last spring and started working here about two months ago." He lowered his voice. "Listen, can we meet privately to talk?"

"Right now?"

Simon nodded.

"Fine with me.' Jared gathered the cards and slid them into their box. "To tell you the truth, it's a relief to run into somebody I know." He pushed back his chair, then bid goodbye to his card partner.

"Better sign out, Clark'. The nurses hate it if I disappear with one of their patients and they don't know where they went.

Reflections From Shadow

Chapter Two

Jared remembers Derek, his younger brother, being delivered to the house as if it were yesterday. Well perhaps not *yesterday*, but he remembers it well – even if Jared was only three years old at the time. Jared had lived with the Clarkson's for two years already but he had no recollection of his own arrival. Derek's arrival was one of his earliest memories, the first of many events that would benchmark his life.

He remembers a warm spring day. It had rained earlier, and then he'd played outside on his tricycle. A knock came at the front door and when his foster mom Elizabeth Clarkson answered, a social worker stood waiting. She smiled at Elizabeth and Jared, who peeked from behind Elizabeth's skirt. In her arms the social worker held a baby, wrapped up in a blue and pink blanket and clutching a calico elephant in his hand.

Now one of the things that made the day memorable was that

Derek arrived through the front door of the Clarkson house. Only official people such as social workers or the minister knocked at the front door. Even the pesky Fuller Brush guy in the loud yellow and black check sports coat knew enough to use the side door.

Jared stood with his hands behind his back as he watched the social worker set Derek down on the blanket Elizabeth Clarkson quickly spread on the hardwood floor.

"My, my, what beautiful floors, Mrs. Clarkson."

Elizabeth's face shone brighter than the wood. She kept those floors gleaming with the help of paste wax from an ancient tin, and one of those old green electric floor polishers with sheepskin polishing disks. You'd only see them nowadays in garage sales, or maybe the day afterwards by the curb with the rest of the junk that didn't sell. Jared still recalls the wonderful grainy look of those floors and their woodsy cedar smell, and his sadness years later when wall-to-wall carpeting came into vogue and the Clarkson's broadloomed the main floor.

Baby Derek continued to sit quietly on the blanket playing with his stuffed elephant. Jared expected him to crawl away, but he didn't. He just smiled, waved his pachyderm, and gummed it's trunk.

From the first time he laid eyes on it, that toy elephant seemed fragile to Jared. It grew even more so over the years after endless washings, and being hung out to dry in the sunshine – one clothes peg holding each floppy ear. Eventually the toy barely held together, and only did so with the aid of the safety pins Mom Clarkson had placed in strategic locations along the seams. Jared wondered if Mom couldn't decide whether the elephant was worth fixing. She might have thrown the thing away, except that Derek wouldn't give it up. He clung to it the way the Clarkson's held onto their two chosen boys despite everything that was to happen.

Mom Clarkson and the social worker continued chatting and sipping tea from flowered china teacups. Jared stood near Mom, one hand on her knee, the other holding a homemade oatmeal cookie.

"The infant foster home thought Derek was such a good baby they were tempted to keep him themselves."

Elizabeth Clarkson wrinkled her face at the comment.

"Oh *no*, he's just the perfect baby for us, isn't he Jared? You'll have someone to play with when he's bigger, won't you?"

Maybe. Jared wasn't certain *what* to make of Derek's arrival. He didn't remember anyone telling him that another kid was coming from the Children's Aid.

There are few pictures of James, Elizabeth, and the two boys. In those days, photographs were considered expensive luxuries and only a few cracked black and white snaps remained in black pages of an album held by those little paper corner mounts. Invariably the mounts dried out, the picture came loose, and the photograph became damaged. Most of the snaps featured only the boys because Mom Clarkson didn't like having her picture taken, and Dad usually held the Brownie. Still, if not flattering, those few cracked images are revealing.

One of them showed Jared lined up against the house in a dirty T-shirt and his shorts. His face wore a miserable scowl as if he were some tiny inmate being mugged by the authorities at the start of a life sentence.

"You didn't smile for a long time after you came to live with us, Jared," Mom Clarkson liked to tell him. During the first year of his life he'd been shunted in and out of temporary foster care. Eventually, the court decided enough was enough, made Jared a ward of the Province, and placed him with the Clarkson's in long-term foster care.

James and Elizabeth Clarkson had always wanted children. However, faced with infertility since her only pregnancy ended in miscarriage ten years before, Elizabeth, now in her late thirties, had resigned herself to 'God's will', that she raise children born to others.

Chapter Three

Jared flopped down into a green plaid chair in Simon's office. The room, without windows, seemed more like a walk-in closet than a workspace, although Simon had tried his best to make it liveable. His newly-minted social work degree hung on the wall and a portrait of Malcolm X stood on the bookshelf. The picture was inscribed, *Tell me who I am*. Jared figured that the question applied to many people who entered this office, including himself.

"Get you a coffee or something?" Simon asked.

"No. Thanks. Just had one. By the way, that instant coffee you guys serve, it's really bad, you know."

"Oh, you mean the Maitre Dee? I think it's the cheapest stuff we can serve without getting sued. One cup was enough for me." Both laughed, then looked at one another in silence.

"Dr. Miller asked me to meet with you. Do you mind that we know each other outside of here?" Simon smiled at Jared.

"No, like I told you, I'm relieved."

"Why?"

"Because it's good to know somebody here. Besides, you've helped me out before. Course this is the first time you're going to get paid for it, eh?"

"Well, I guess that's right." The social worker smiled. "I would like to help you if I can, Jared. One thing though, can I ask you a personal favour?"

"Name it."

"Actually, it's two things. First, I'd appreciate it if you'd call me 'Simon.' I don't want people here starting up with the 'Mensch' thing."

"O.K. What else?"

"The other thing is that if we could avoid mentioning Cannabis, well, I'd appreciate that, too."

Jared had to smile, then shrugged. Mensch was lucky if keeping his pot on the backburner was his biggest concern in life.

"No problem – on both scores."

"Thanks." Simon resumed his usual relaxed self. "That will help me a lot. Now Dr. Miller asked me to meet with you to find out what's been happening, and how we might be helpful. Can you catch me up with what's been happening?"

"O.K. I'd be glad to, but I have to tell you – well, uh, it's pretty unusual."

"I'm all ears." Simon leaned forward and cocked his head to one side.

Where to begin? Figuring where to begin seemed like trying to find the start of the noodles on a plate of spaghetti. Jared decided to jump in with a mouthful.

"Until last summer, I was working in that fish and chip shop. I was fed-up and depressed with the job and myself for a long time. I was smoking way too much dope and drinking too much. And I wasn't sleeping well because I kept having weird dreams that made me edgy. I'd wake up in the morning not rested and feel spooked for half the day after those dreams. This went on for weeks."

"What were the weird things in the dream?"

"Prisoners and German soldiers mostly. Then I'd wake up with this sense that I was supposed to *do* something, or go somewhere, but I never could seem to figure out exactly what, or where, or why. Anyway, you remember that day I came to the bar really cracked and spilled my beer all over the place?"

"Yes, I remember." Simon nodded.

"Well, that was the around when I got fired from my job. Funny thing is, that although part of me was worried because I had very little money, another part of me didn't care. It was almost as if that lousy job was in my way somehow. Anyway, like I said, I had no idea how I was going to live, but it's almost as if I set myself up to get fired so I could get on with it."

"Get on with what?"

"With whatever was going to happen."

Jared began talking openly for the first time about what had happened to him in Europe, as well as his recent encounter with some thugs here in Toronto. Before he knew it, more than an hour had passed and he felt exhausted. He was amazed that Simon had listened quietly the whole time, except for the occasional question to clarify something. Simon was speechless, and when he did speak after an uncomfortable silence that went on far too long, it sounded to Jared as if Simon had to pry each word carefully from his brain.

"I hardly know what to say. It sounds horrible, and quite incredible."

"Yup. Germany was creepy from the time I got there because some places I went, and even some of the language, was familiar. And the stuff at the camp was, well terrifying. I wasn't sure I'd ever get out of there, and although I did get out, ever since then I've felt depressed and guilty as hell. Coming home to Canada didn't help much. Actually, I'm not even sure what made me think coming home would make any difference."

"And the guilt - is that why you wanted to kill yourself?"

"Yeah, I guess so. Well not only that, but mostly. Also I owed those guys a lot of money and had nothing to give them when payday arrived."

Another long silence ensued and Jared's anxiety began to escalate. Why didn't Simon say *something?* Jared began to panic, wondering if he'd made a mistake, told too much.

"You *do* believe me?"

Simon chose his response carefully. "I understand how real all this must have seemed. Can I ask you about your family? You haven't talked about them at all."

Now Mensch thinks I'm nuts too, Jared thought. He might have been angry, but right then he was too exhausted to care. Besides, could he blame people for not believing him? Jared stared into his lap.

"My family has nothing to do with this, or me. Can I go now? I'm really beat."

"Sorry, but I don't understand what you mean that your family has nothing to do with this?"

Jared shifted his gaze to the door and remained silent.

"Alright, we'll stop for today. Can you come in to see me

again tomorrow after group therapy?"

"Sure." Jared didn't want to, but he agreed to get out of there. What was the use of talking to people who didn't believe him?

That night, dreams of Clarence's suffering tormented Jared. He awoke tired and grumpy and didn't appreciate the nurse who insisted he get out of bed to eat breakfast.

After group therapy he occupied himself in his room but finally ran out of busy work and reluctantly made his way to Simon's office. He knocked on the door.

"It's Jared. Sorry I'm late."

Simon opened the door.

"Hi there. Does being late have anything to do with what we talked about yesterday?"

"Not really." Jared stared at the floor.

"Well, come on in." Simon lit a cigarette, took a puff and indicated a chair with his cigarette. After Jared sat down, Simon shifted forward in his seat.

"The way you say 'not really,' well it sounds like you have lots to say but don't want to talk about it."

"You're the expert." Jared felt embarrassed and annoyed.

Simon paused to take a thoughtful drag.

"Are we going to struggle today or are we going to do some serious talking?" He exhaled smoke.

Jared glowered.

"You and Dr. Miller think you know everything, don't you? Well you guys don't know *shit* about me."

"I can't speak for Dr. Miller, but as far as I'm concerned,

Jared, you're probably right. Thing is though, I won't understand anything if you won't talk to me."

Simon waited for a response but when Jared remained silent he continued.

"Seemed like we were getting on fine yesterday until you finished telling me about your experience in Germany and then I asked you about your family. Did you notice that?" Simon lit another smoke as he waited for a response. "Well?"

"I don't think you believe me and I'd rather not discuss my family."

"Sounds like it's important that I believe you and you're pissed because it seems that I don't."

"Yah, well you're the expert."

"Look, don't think you can avoid stuff with that 'you're the expert' crap. If I'm not right it's alright to disagree, you know."

"O.K., I guess so." Simon rolled his chair closer.

"What do you mean you 'guess?' "

"I mean, you're right." Jared stared back.

"What part of it is right?"

"That I'm pissed because I don't think you believe me."

"O.K. And why is talking about your family so difficult?"

"Because I did stuff to my family that wasn't great. I haven't had any contact with them in nearly two years." Forced to blink back tears, Jared swiped at his eyes with his sleeve. "O.K. I miss them, but—"

Simon moved closer. Now they were face-to-face.

"But what?"

"I dunno." Jared reached for a tissue from the lamp table.

"I've really fucked things up for myself and them."

"I guess it's lonely to be in this situation like this all by yourself?"

Jared became quiet and looked away.

"Aren't we all lonely?" He wiped his eyes. "I mean, don't we all go through this life alone when you get right down to it."

"Maybe so, but perhaps it will be more helpful if you would speak for *yourself?*"

"Alright."

"I have to wonder if having such an unusual experience in Germany that other people have difficulty getting their head around it makes things even more lonely?"

"I guess." Jared whispered.

"Let's talk more about that next time. Anyway, the hospital does require some information about your family. You know, next of kin and all that. Is that O.K.?"

"Whatever." Jared filled out the information on the sheet, then handed it back.

"Thanks." Simon got up to signal the end of the session, then sat down again, as if having second thoughts. "Ever read Plato's Allegory of the Cave?"

Jared shook his head. "Never heard of it."

"O.K., forget it."

"No, tell me."

"It's just a story in Plato's book, *Republic.* It's about a guy who has been chained in a totally dark cave all his life with some other guys. None of them have ever seen light before. One guy escapes his chains and wanders in the dark for awhile, then discovers light and the open world. He rushes back to tell the others, but they can't comprehend what he is talking about, or they just don't believe him. Well, I just thought it sounds a bit like your situation."

"Yeah, except that what I experienced wasn't sunlight. It was a helluva place that I wish I'd never seen."

Chapter Four

Three-year-old Jared held the top rail of his crib and stared down the smelly, empty hospital corridor. It smelled like the scary dream he kept having – the one where he was alone in a tall narrow dark room with ugly red and black colours flowing down the walls like candle wax all around him. That dream stank, and something in the hospital smelled the same. Frightened and feeling sick to his stomach, Jared rattled the crib and began crying.

Where were those green people? The green people that kept taking him in and out of the big room where they laid him underneath that big light, then sat him on the toilet, over and over. One of the green people got upset with him.

"Don't say you *went* if you didn't!" She hissed.

He *thought* he went.

He looked over at the Teddy bear sticking his paws through the crib rails. Jared figured Teddy wanted out of there as much as he did.

Where was Mommy? All Jared remembered was a big pain in his tummy that made him cry. Next thing he was running down the hospital corridor screaming, then banging on the two big elevator doors that swallowed Mommy.

Jared shook the crib so hard it banged against the wall. One of the green people appeared and picked him up.

"What a dear child you are. There, there. It's alright. Don't cry, dear one. I'll stay with you. Would you like a Popsicle?"

Jared locked his arms around her neck and snuggled into her chest.

Chapter Five

"We've two new people in group today," Nurse Clarisse announced. "Bill and Nancy. Please help them feel welcome on the ward." She adjusted the easel so everyone could see. Across the top she had written, *The best things about me and my life.* "Who wants to begin?"

The group members looked at one another but no one spoke. Finally nurse Clarisse tried to fix eye contact with someone.

"How about you, Charles? Can you share one good thing about your life and yourself?"

"My wife kicked me out two years ago and now the court won't let me see my kids," an overweight balding middle-aged man said.

"Charles, can you try to think about something that's going *well* for you?" Nurse Clarisse smiled.

"Nothing." Charles folded his arms across his chest.

"What about that? Charles says he has nothing that's going well for him?"

"I know what he means, I feel the same," said a weathered lady layered with too much makeup. "And being in this place isn't helping."

The nurse remained calm.

"Can we hear from someone who has noticed something that's going a little better for them?" She looked toward Jared.

Jared turned to Crystal, the anorexic young woman he liked to play cards with. She looked as bored as himself and Jared was surprised when she spoke.

"I am eating more now, and I haven't hidden food for two days. Still, I worry about my weight. When I look in the mirror, a part of me still worries I'm going to look like an elephant." She frowned.

Nurse Clarisse looked relieved to get a response.

"Sometimes we can't trust our own judgment when we are ill, Crystal. That's when we need others to help us out. Notice any changes in your thinking?"

"I'm learning that sometimes I get hung up with my problems and forget the things in my life that are good, like my parents and boyfriend coming to see me every day, and my friends from work sending me flowers and a get-well card. I'm learning it's important that I look for whatever good things are happening."

"That's easy for you," Charles said. "You're young and have your whole life ahead of you. My life's in wreck bay and it's going to be there from now on."

"Have you absolutely made your mind up about that, Charles?" Nurse Clarisse asked. "Maybe you have a *choice* about whether you spend the *rest* of your life in wreck bay?"

Charles remained quiet.

Mary, a tidy short woman with straight black hair spoke up.

"We can't change what has already happened but we have choices about what's going to happen from now on. I've decided that if I'm going to live for another fifty years I'm going to try and make it as good as possible. I know there will be difficult periods with my depression, and I'm going to stay on medication and use whatever help and support I can get. Most of all, I want to, have to, get back to my teaching. It's a very important thing in my life."

"Do you have a family?" Jared asked her.

"Yes, a husband and two lovely little girls."

"Maybe that's why you feel more hopeful. Some people don't feel they have anybody, you know."

After group ended, Jared continued to think about his life. It hadn't been very good so far, and after what had occurred at Dachau he wondered not only whether good things would ever happen again, but also whether he *deserved* good things to happen. When he met with Simon later that day, Jared was ready to talk, but uncertain where to start. He sat nervously manipulating a set of worry beads he snatched from Simon's desk while pacing the room. Simon watched quietly, then offered him a cigarette.

"Thanks."

Simon helped himself to a smoke also.

"You mentioned the other day about the loneliness you feel."

"I've always felt lonely, even when I was a kid at home. Like I didn't belong wherever I was, whether it was home or school. Or even this planet."

"And what planet *do* you belong on?" Simon asked. Before

Jared could reply Simon raised his hand and smiled. "Just kidding."

Funny guy, Jared thought, but what he didn't tell Simon was that in reality, nothing of that sort would be too much of a surprise given what had happened to him in the camp. After being silent for a moment, Jared waxed philosophic.

"Kids who are taken from their parents *are* sort of like aliens – dropped from one world to another world where no one looks like them, or acts like them or even thinks like them."

"You mean you feel that way? Speak for yourself instead of speaking generally." Simon took a puff of his cigarette.

"Maybe, but somehow it's easier to talk generally." Jared groaned.

"Easier? Yes. As helpful to you? No."

"O.K., *I* was lonely; I'm lonely now. Being away from my real mother is part of it, and being away from my foster family is another part. In a way, though, even those things don't seem to be the main thing. I mean, well, what do I mean? It's just this feeling of being unconnected to things in this world, as if I'm on FM, and the rest of the world is on AM. Sometimes I feel more like I belong when I'm stoned, as if I'm experiencing the world the way it really is somehow. But the experience at the camp; if that's reality—" Jared's voice faded.

"If that's reality, then what?"

Jared lit a smoke and took several frenetic drags before looking at the social worker to continue. He felt himself tearing up.

"Then I don't know whether I want to live."

That night, Jared lurched from his sleep with a shout.

"No!" Sweating he fumbled and turned on the light in a vain attempt to wash away his surreal nightmare of Clarence lying in the ice tank, his face blue with cold, staring up at him and whispering, "Why?"

A nurse opened his door and poked her head in.

"Are you alright Jared? We heard you yelling all the way from the nursing station."

Jared sat on the edge of his bed shaking. He wondered if he would ever sleep in peace again. He remained up although it was only five a.m., and all that day he felt guilt branding his gut.

Jared continued to meet and talk with Simon most days, and sometimes with Dr. Miller. Dr. Miller was nice enough, but simply too busy carrying the workload of three doctors to spend much time with him, or any other patient. It was just as well, though, because Jared sensed that Miller considered his story about the camp as little more than the pigments of a colourful imagination. Although Miller's scepticism was understandable in some ways, Jared thought it frightening if shrinks only saw the world from the medical, scientific perspective. Other realities apparently didn't really exist for them Monday to Friday, although Jared suspected that many of them went to Church on Sunday to worship an unseen, unproven God, yet they thought nothing of the inconsistency. He figured it was a good thing there were no shrinks around during Biblical times; Moses might have been locked up after disclosing his discussion with God in the burning bush.

During his first days in the hospital, Jared periodically heard the screams of people restrained in the locked ward and he felt sorry for them. Criminals had access to lawyers and trials; the fate of these souls was primarily at the behest of the medical staff. Be quiet, co-operate. Yes, doctor. Yes, nurse. Don't ask any embarrassing questions about the drugs or the effects of ECT. Get away from the nursing station.

Moses wouldn't have stood a chance.

Simon was *more* accepting of Jared's strange experiences, but in the long run that didn't matter. Miller had the power, and if Miller labeled him psychotic, they might never let him out. Not that he had any place to go, or that he even wanted out right now with those thugs on the lookout for him.

Jared dozed off in the day room, leaving his bummed Pall Mall to smoulder, then crumble in the ashtray.

Chapter Six

Large snowflakes settled onto the boys' tongues when they gazed up into the sky. Christmas would arrive in three weeks, and the family was out on a Sunday afternoon to find a tree.

Dad pulled the toboggan and Elizabeth, hands behind her back, walked alongside him. The couple gazed at one another, then the boys, and smiled in the manner of parents captivated with most anything their children did.

A few minutes later, Jared spied a prospective conifer.

"Here's one?"

"I think we'll walk a bit until we get to an area where the trees haven't been picked over," Dad said.

Jared wondered what "picked over" meant. Shortly Dad stopped, let go of the tow, and looked around at the boys. Jared wondered why they had stopped.

"Jared, how about you walk for a bit?"

The sun and mild temperature had made the snow wet, and pulling them proved more work than James anticipated. Jared clamped onto the ropes running down the sides of the toboggan and began yelling.

"NO! I wanna ride with Derek."

"Daddy is tired." Mom took him by the hand and pulled him to his feet. "You walk with me a bit; you can see the trees better if you're standing up." She pulled two candy canes from her pocket and handed one to each of the boys. Jared had it in his mouth before Derek could remove his mitt.

"Ummmm. Peppermint." Jared's favourite, next to chocolate.

Mom unwrapped Derek's and handed it back to him.

"Where's mine?" James asked.

"Sorry," Elizabeth replied. "I only brought enough for the boys."

Families and groups of young people laughed and shouted as they wandered about the tree farm. A group of teenage guys made snowballs, then chased their girlfriends around the trees. The girls shrieked with a combination of excitement and annoyance until finally, one girl bent down and scooped some ammunition of her own. Shortly all the girls gave a good account of themselves.

"What kind of tree were you thinking of, Beth?" James asked. He didn't sound as if he cared. He had learned to leave such decisions to his wife; then he didn't have to take the blame or feel responsible for her grumbling if something went wrong.

"I don't know James, probably one with soft needles so the guys won't get hurt when we decorate it. Maybe Balsam?"

"Whatever you say, Beth." James smiled and nodded.

After twenty minutes of walking, the family reached the back of the farm where the trees grew closer together and the groups of people were farther apart.

"There's a nice one, Jared," Mom said, pointing.

Jared broke away from Mom's hand to see the tree in question. Partially blocked from view behind two other trees, it seemed skulking to avoid detection.

"How about this one, James?" The six-foot Balsam exuded a distinctly seasonal fragrance.

"I like it!" Jared began jumping up and down. Derek joined him and they chased one another around the tree.

"Well, what do you think, James?" Beth asked.

"It might prove a chore to stand up." James face appeared uncertain as he studied the tree's crooked stem. "Guess it'll be fine." He pulled a small bucksaw from his pack, locked its jagged blade into business position, then knelt on the toboggan to keep himself dry as he made the cut.

"I wanna' help." Jared said.

"Alright, but we have to do it together." James took a breath, then sighed. "This saw is very sharp."

James placed his hand over Jared's and they began. Despite their best joint effort, the sawing motion proved awkward.

"I want to stop." Jared withdrew his hand.

James quickly completed the cut on his own before Derek thought to ask for a turn. Elizabeth and the boys grabbed the tottering tree and lowered it onto the toboggan. The wind had picked up and the temperature had dropped.

"Let's head back and get some hot chocolate," Elizabeth said.

"Yeah," the boys cheered.

Mom and Derek strolled on ahead while Jared stayed behind

to help Dad pull the toboggan. After a short distance, Jared let go of the rope and stepped away to watch the tree slide by. He started to whimper. James looked over and saw the troubled look on his face.

"What's wrong, son? Too tired to walk?"

Jared shook his head, then looked up at his dad with a pleading expression.

"When Christmas is done can we put the tree back where it was?"

"No, I'm sorry Jared, but once a tree is cut . . . well, that's *it*."

"You mean it's *dead*!" Jared panicked and started crying. He snatched Dad's sleeve and pulled it hard. "Put it back, Dad. Put it back now. Maybe it won't be dead."

James crouched down to Jared's level.

"Sorry Jared. No can do."

Elizabeth had turned around to look.

"What's wrong?" she called.

"Under control, Beth. I'm handling it. Come here Jared." James pulled his son towards him and sat him on his knee. "Jared, these trees here are specially grown for Christmas by the people who own this farm. Next summer they'll plant a baby tree for every one that's cut."

Jared seemed unmoved by this logic, his attention focused on this particular tree's plight.

"C'mon big guy, we've got to go now."

James took Jared's hand, and they walked along in silence. Jared swiped at his face with his mitten as he tried to comprehend this sudden glimpse into the circle of life and death that apparently never stopped.

Even during the happiest time of the year.

Chapter Seven

"How were things for you growing up?" Simon rocked back in his chair and draped his leg over the arm, but remained attentive.

Jared wondered how the guy could pay attention without yawning.

Simon's voice penetrated Jared's meandering thoughts.

"What are you thinking?"

"Oh, nothing much. Just wondering how you can listen to this stuff all the time. Don't you ever get bored or tired of listening?"

"Sometimes, but that's why they call it work. Is it easier for you to wonder about me being bored instead of focusing on your own stuff?"

"No . . . well, maybe it is easier. What do you want to know again?"

"What do you need to tell me?"

"I don't know. Things weren't really too bad for me until I started school." Jared reflexively placed his right hand over the birthmark on his face. "That's when kids started teasing me, about my birthmark. After the first while I'd get into fights and stuff over the teasing. Mom told me to ignore them. She'd say 'sticks and stones will break your bones,' and that kind of stuff but I never understood that because the teasing hurt like hell. Later on there were a couple of those guys I wanted to kill." Jared looked away. "I'd rather not talk about this anymore."

"Why not?"

"No point."

"You never know what the point might be. What do you think will happen if you *do* talk about this?" Jared remained quiet. He knew, but he couldn't say. He just wanted to be alone.

"I need some fresh air and a smoke. Can we take a break?"

"Sure , I guess . . . but that's kind of contradictory isn't it?"

"Whaddya mean?"

"Fresh air and a smoke – kind of an oxygen-moron."

They each decompressed with a laugh, then Simon continued.

"Look, you can take a break whenever you need to, but I'm not sure that's really the thing right now. Sometimes when we don't *want* to talk about certain things . . . well, maybe that's exactly the thing you *need* to talk about. Know what I mean?"

Why was this guy always right? Jared thought. It was getting to be annoying, but he relented.

"Alright, maybe I'll just smoke here and forget the fresh air." When he opened the package he noticed he only had one cigarette left. Ought to quit. He had no money to buy more. His pocket money from welfare was gone and he wouldn't get more for another week.

"Outta smokes?" Simon observed.

"Yeah, until I get some money."

Simon reached for his own Rothman's and withdrew half the deck. "Take these." At Jared's hesitation, he prodded. "Don't worry, I've got a carton at home. Just keep it to yourself, O.K."

"I'll pay you back when I get my money."

"Forget it, it's nothing." Simon waved him off.

"O.K. Thanks, Mensch." It was the first time in days that Jared had referred to Simon that way, but it seemed appropriate to the moment.

"Now, you were saying about your birthmark and being teased?"

Jared lit his cigarette, took a puff, then sighed.

"There was this kid at school, Walter Tompkins . . . used to call me 'Shitface.' " He felt a lump rising in his throat.

"The guy sounds like a real prick."

"Yep. The worst." Jared tried to swallow the tears welling up. He brushed his sleeve across his face then took another drag. After exhaling, he gazed at the rising smoke then ploughed the ashes about in the ashtray. "School was another place I just didn't belong. I never told anyone this before. Once when I was around eight years old I tried to hang myself from a nail on the wall with a string. Damn thing broke." He smiled weakly.

"Good thing it broke. Anybody ever ask you how you were doing in those days?"

"I don't remember. Probably Mom tried but I don't know. It was like being in some hole. I could see and hear others but just couldn't quite reach out."

"And nobody knew you were in the hole?"

"If they did, I guess they didn't know what to do about it."

Simon reached out to touch Jared's arm.

"It's good you can talk with me about that stuff now." He rose to signal the end of the session. "Catch up with you tomorrow. Same time?"

"Sure. See ya. Ah, thanks again for the smokes."

"No problem. See ya."

Jared walked away down the corridor to join group, just getting underway on the ward.

Chapter Eight

Jared squinted in the sun as he, his best friend Robby from next door, and Robby's older brother Don, waited outside for the school taxi. Jared wore his red "Perry Como" cardigan, and proudly carried the Superman lunch box he admired the previous week at Woolworth's. He was ecstatic when Mom had bought it for him on the spot.

"Smile, guys." Robby's Mom aimed a Brownie camera, then snapped a picture. She held up her hand, flipped over the camera, and wound the film.

"One more, guys."

Today was Jared's first day of school. He'd been excited for weeks waiting for this day to arrive. Don, who was in Grade three, carried himself with the cockiness of an old pro. A yellow taxi pulled up, and when the driver climbed out, he reviewed a clipboard.

"Don, Robby and Jared? That you guys? He asked.

"Yup," Don replied.

"Well hop in."

Mom gave Jared a final hug and Derek began to pull away from her hand and cry. "Me, too. Me going, too." Derek's protest made everyone laugh.

Jared walked over and gave him a hug.

"Don't worry, Derek. I'll be home later and tell you all about it."

In the front seat of the cab sat a lady with gold wire glasses, grey hair, and a shawl. She grinned at the boys as she massaged her hand.

"Hello Donald, is this your brother?"

"Yes, Miss Vickers."

"I'm in Grade One." Robby's chest swelled with pride.

"I know that," Miss Vickers said. "It's nice to meet you, Robert. I'm going to be your teacher. And you must be Jared?" She smiled at him.

"Yes, ma'm." Jared looked down at the ground.

After Robby received one more kiss on the forehead from his Mom, the three boys piled into the back of the cab. As the driver pulled away, Jared turned to wave out the back window and watched their moms and Derek, grow smaller and disappear. What's that funny feeling in my stomach, he wondered.

A few minutes later, the cab arrived at the ancient red brick schoolhouse and turned into the gravel parking lot. The schoolyard boiled with children standing, playing, shouting and catching up on the summer's news. Jared scrambled from the cab and stood there taking in the sights and sounds.

"See you soon, boys," Miss Vickers said. "We're going to do some fun things today."

She seems nice, Jared thought. He hoped he would like school.

Don and Robby rushed off together, and although Jared could join them, he decided to stay by himself and watch things from a distance. A few minutes later, another teacher with gray hair stepped out the front door of the school and began ringing a large gold bell. The children hustled to line up.

Robby called Jared into line. Behind Jared was a girl with black pigtails; she wore a red cotton print dress. In one hand she held her lunch pail, and in the other, a wooden pencil case. The pencil case had a removable lid that doubled as a ruler.

"Neat lunch pail," Jared said. "Felix the Cat is one of my favourite cartoons."

The girl smiled and put her finger to her lips.

"Thanks. I don't think we're s'posed to talk in line," she said in a whisper. She smiled. "I'm Alice."

Chapter Nine

Jared stared at himself in the bathroom mirror. He scrunched his face and rubbed the birthmark on his cheek. He called it, "the thing."

Until he turned six, "the thing" hadn't bothered him much; probably his family and the kids in the neighbourhood hadn't noticed, or if they had, they seldom mentioned it. But now that Jared was older and away from home more, he found people noticing. He'd sense people looking at him strangely, whispering and snickering behind his back as he walked away.

Jared usually avoided mirrors but today was different. Today, the longer he stared at himself, the more fixated he became upon "the thing." *It's just a stupid mark*, one voice in his head tried to say, but then another voice in his mind interrupted. *Who are you trying to kid? It's awful.*

He wondered if anything could be done about the mark.

Maybe a doctor could take it off. Yeah, right, take it off then leave a hole in his face.

The longer he stared at it, the larger the mark loomed in his mind.

Why did everything about him have to be different? Other kids lived with their real parents. Jared hadn't seen his real mother for a long time. He could hardly remember her now; even her face was a blur. He recalled that she screamed a lot. The social worker said he'd never see her again. Clarkson's were his family now.

"I'm adopted . . . sort of," he'd tell people if they asked. Truth was, he didn't know why he still had his old name legally even though most of the time he went by Clarkson. Mom Clarkson took pains to explain that they were not well off, and needed the agency's money to pay his expenses, but Jared found the whole situation difficult to understand. The deal with Derek was the same, but he was too young to care. Jared's real name felt like a thread connecting him someplace else. He just didn't know where.

He felt different in other ways, too. Unlike Robby, Jared had no aptitude for sports. He couldn't throw the baseball, let alone hit it. And forget hockey; he had trouble staying up on skates even with ankle supports. The main thing he did really well was read and write stories. But the most painful difference between the other kids and Jared was that they looked normal; he on the other hand was ugly.

Someone pounded at the bathroom door.

"Open the door, Jared. I gotta pee." Derek said through the door.

"Go pee behind the house. I'm busy."

"Mom. Jared won't let me in the bathroom and I have to go . . . *bad*."

Now Mom rapped on the door.

"What *are* you doing Jared? You've been in there a long time.

Let Derek in, it's an emergency."

"Alright, alright."

Derek burst in and dashed to the toilet, his fly already unzipped. Jared felt Mom's eyes upon him as she guided him from the bathroom to give Derek some privacy.

"Are you not well?"

His burst of tears was unexpected and unwanted; he wiped his face with his shirttail. He hoped Mom wouldn't notice, but of course she did.

"Jared, what's wrong?" She had a look of concern on her face.

"Nuthin." He tried to squeeze past her, but she reached out and blocked his escape.

"Hold on there. I want to know what's the trouble."

"Whaddya mean?"

"You know what I mean. You've been moping around the house all morning. Aren't you feeling well? Let me feel your head."

"I'm not sick." Why did she always have to feel his head? He tried to brush her hand away. "I'm not sick. I just want—"

He couldn't continue, partly because he had no idea what he did want, except that he didn't want to blubber like a baby. He stared in silence at the floor.

"I don't belong." As soon as Jared said it, he felt mortified. He felt his face turn hot and he considered running downstairs to feed himself to the monster under the cellar steps.

There is no monster stupid, the first voice in his head chided. *Oh yeah, how do you know?* The second voice said.

Jared had no idea of what would happen if the monster actually grabbed him, but he thought about it. Maybe just one bite, or whatever it was that monsters did, and all of his troubles would be over. Mom's voice called him from his thoughts. Strangely, she seemed far away.

"Jared. Are you listening to me?" She placed her hand on his shoulder and looked into his eyes. "How about you and Derek come and have some Kool Aid? I have some cookies fresh out of the oven."

Jared wasn't hungry until that moment, but suddenly the idea of having something to eat, as opposed to being eaten, sounded good.

In the kitchen, while Mom mixed the drink, the boys kicked one another under the table. It was just a game, but sometimes it escalated into a fight. When the snack arrived, they stopped to grab cookies.

"One at a time, guys. There's enough for both of you."

Jared bit into the cookie and washed it down with a gulp of cherry drink. Mom's cookies were the best. Soft, chewy, and tasty, not like those cardboard things from the store. He noticed Mom smiling. What was it about kids eating that adults found so interesting? Adults didn't look very appealing when they were eating.

In fact, Jared thought it was downright disgusting the way some adults ate. At family get-togethers he hated sitting near one uncle who sprayed chunks of food when he ate. Jared figured if the guy were a kid, someone would tell him off or pull his ear. Kids didn't get away with that kind of stuff; rules were different for adults.

Jared downed his drink in two gulps, then wiped his brow with his shirt.

"Phew, sure is hot today. Can I have another glass?"

When Mom returned, he caught a reflection of himself in the smiling pitcher as she poured.

He grimaced and covered his cheek.

"Why is your hand against your face, Jared?" Mom asked.

"No reason."

"Yer coverin' your mark." Derek snickered.

Jared's face flushed like the emperor in the parade. He glared at Derek and kicked him.

"Shut up Derek. Am not."

"Mom, Jared's kickin' me under the table."

"That's enough, Jared. Derek, I'd like you to take your drink and cookie outside. Jared and I need to have a little talk."

Derek's chair screeched against the floor then he strutted out carrying a cookie in his mouth, a police car in one hand, and his drink in the other.

Jared felt Mom looking at him. Waiting. Waiting for him to say something.

"Want to talk about it?"

"What?"

Mom gave him her 'I'm waiting' look. Jared decided to try a run for it.

"Gotta call on Robby."

"Hold on there. Robby can wait till we're finished talking." Mom sat kitty-corner from him, her hands clasped together on the table. "You're not very happy today, Jared. What's wrong?"

Jared stared down into his lap and squirmed in his seat.

"I hate being different," he said. "I just want to be like everyone else."

"What do you mean you're different?"

The question annoyed him. Why did she have to ask? She knew, everybody knew about his mark. Why did he have to *say* it?

"Do you mean the birthmark on your face?"

Jared replied with a half-nod, but continued staring into his lap. He couldn't tell Mom what Walter and Roy called him at school; that was profanity. In his mind he could hear their voices calling him "Shitface." He looked at Mom.

"Mom, how come God makes people with things wrong with them?"

Mom sighed and took his hand.

"Jared, some things about God are very hard for us to understand. Sometimes God sends trials to make us better people."

"You mean like Job?" Mom seemed startled by the question.

"Yes. Yes. I guess like Job."

As far as Jared was concerned, when he'd heard that story at Sunday school, Jared thought it mean for God to let the devil pick on Job like that.

"We'll never understand all of God's mysteries, " Mom said.

"Do ya think God could take away my mark if he wanted too?" Jared asked.

Mom answered with hesitation and a frown.

"Well, yes, yes I guess he could."

"Well why *doesn't* he? I've asked him lots of times in my prayers?" Jared narrowed his eyes, and they flashed.

Mom said nothing. She moved her chair closer and pulled the child to her breast and began stroking his head.

"Where *do* these questions of yours come from, Jared? There are a lot of smart people who have tried to understand questions like that. Maybe we expect too much from God. He gives us life and a world to live in, but maybe even God can't make a perfect world. And even if he could, maybe it wouldn't be a good thing."

At this, Jared pulled away.

"Well, I don't think it's fair I have to have this problem." He pushed his chair from the table and hurried outside. This time Mom let him go.

Chapter Ten

After winding the steam locomotive with its large metal key, Jared carefully placed it onto the track. Hooking the train cars together, then keeping them on the track proved difficult, and when the spring ran down, he had to do it all over again. Maybe an electric train would be nice but he knew it wouldn't be the same. Jared loved his windup train, his most favourite thing Santa ever brought.

One day years later that train set just disappeared from the house. Jared recalled he had moped around the house feeling derailed when he realized it was gone. He knew what had happened, Mom had figured he was too old for trains and gave it away. There was no use mentioning it, he knew that's what she'd say. What's done was done.

Derek showed up and watched as Jared cut up a shoebox to make a railroad tunnel.

Jared enjoyed making things. He loved the music of scissors

cutting construction paper; the sound somehow soothing and reassuring.

"Wanna play cowboys?" Derek asked.

"Not now. Makin' stuff for my train."

The tape, scissors, and other items he needed were spread about him on the floor.

"Ah, come on, Jared. Robby's outside and he's got a new gun."

New gun, eh! *That* grabbed Jared's attention.

"Alright, I'm coming." He leaped up from the floor to dash out of the room and stepped on one of the shoebox tunnels he'd just completed. He shook his head in disgust.

As they ran next door, they could see Robby standing in his backyard. He wore his imitation leather cowboy vest and posed in a comical bowlegged stance as he attempted to spin the plastic Colt 45 on his pointer finger. With each movement, the fringe on his vest bounced around. Despite his best effort, he couldn't get the gun to spin even once before it toppled to the ground. Robby looked up when Derek and Jared entered his backyard.

"Neat gun, Robby. Lemme try." Jared reached out, but Robby pulled it away.

"Nope. Can't. Just got it, and my dad said not to let anyone else use it 'cause my last one got busted." He shoved it in its holster.

"C'mon Robby, lemme try. Aren't I your best friend? I'll be careful." Jared reached out again with positive expectation. Robby fidgeted and frowned, then looked around.

"Well, alright. But just for a minute."

Jared slapped his friend on the back, then accepted the pistol.

"Thanks, Robby. Got any caps?"

"Yep, five packs."

"Get out!"

"No, really." Robby dug into his jeans to extract the evidence, pulling out his pocket lining as well.

"Neat. Can I try some?"

"Nope." Robby shook his head.

"C'mon, Robby. I'd give you some if I had some."

Robby wasn't paying attention; he was too busy trying to stuff the caps and the pocket back where they belonged.

As Jared watched Robby's efforts, it occurred to him that fixing stuff usually proved more trouble than messing things up to begin with. When he finished, Robby looked over at Jared.

"We'll shoot some later," he said.

Jared turned over the new firearm marveling at its gleaming silver and pearl plastic handle engraved with Wyatt Earp's signature. Jared knew it wasn't really Wyatt Earp's signature, but he still thought it pretty neat. He tried twirling the gun, but succeeded only in pinching his finger. It looked so easy when Marshall Dillon or the bad guys on *Gunsmoke* did it. Then Derek spoke up.

"Lemme have a turn." Quiet and patient to that point as he watched a group of ants carrying a leaf, Derek suddenly stood and seized the barrel of the pistol. Jared shoved his hand away.

"Buzz off, I'm not done yet."

Robby intervened and took the gun.

"Thanks Derek!" Jared gave his brother a disgusted look.

"You can have a turn with it later," Robby told Derek.

At this, Derek began to shriek. His shriek, with a volume and pitch reminiscent of a catfight, elicited a shout from Mom who poked her head out the window.

"What's going on? Why is Derek crying?"

"Derek's being a *baby*."

At that, the wailing jumped an octave, and Derek began to stomp his feet. Finally, Robby had enough and took his hands from his ears.

"Alright, alright. Take it."

Little brothers were a pain, Jared thought with annoyance. Why couldn't he have a big brother instead? Yeah, a big brother that could stick up for him at school.

With gun in hand, the flow of tears stalled in the middle of Derek's cheeks, and a smile erupted across his face like one of those rainbows that show up just as the thunderstorm ends.

"Don't think you can get whatever you want by acting like a baby." Jared scowled.

At this, a cloud drifted over the rainbow and Derek stuck out his tongue. He pointed the six-shooter carefully at Jared and pulled the trigger.

"Yer dead."

"Am not. Ya missed me."

"Did not miss. Yer dead."

"Well if I'm dead, how come I'm still standing and talking, *stupid?*"

Fed up watching them argue, Robby pushed between them.

"Shut up, Jared. Are you guys going to fight or are we going to play cowboys?"

"Alright, alright." Jared stared at Derek and narrowed his eyes. "If yer going to act like a baby, then yer not playing."

Derek appeared as if he might start crying again, so Robby put his arm around the little guy's shoulder.

"Shut up, Jared, or *you'll* be the one not playing. Right, Derek?"

Derek gave his four-year-old freckled face a resolute nod, handed the pistol back to Robby, then withdrew his own battered weapon from its leather holster and commenced waving it about. Half of the plastic handle was missing but Derek didn't mind.

Robby pulled some caps from his pocket, and tore off a roll for each of the guys.

"Go get your gun, Jared."

"O.K. I'll be right back."

A moment later the screen door slammed behind Jared and he prepared to race downstairs. Gotta run fast, he reminded himself. Running fast was the only sure way he knew to avoid being grabbed by the monster that lived under the cellar stairs. It had worked so far.

Jared spied his rifle stock just visible under the couch in the rec room, snatched it and next thing he knew, he was outside again.

How did I get back here so fast? He wondered. He couldn't remember running back up the stairs. It was as if he'd arrived magically. Sometimes this happened and it caused Jared to wonder if maybe he had some special power to think himself from one place to another.

That's *stupid*, one voice in his head said. Tis not, the other voice said. You don't know *everything*.

When Jared returned to Robby's yard, he found that Robby's brother, Don, had joined the group. Don didn't have a pistol of his own so Derek had loaned him one.

The only weapon Don owned was a ray gun. Don was a space nut and kept the ray gun nearby while he read his Tom Swift books. He owned nearly thirty titles in the collection, and claimed to have read each volume twice. Jared admired Don's knowledge of all things scientific.

"Hi, Don,' Jared said. "Gonna play cowboys with us?"

"Sure. Nothing else to do."

"Great. Listen guys; I've got an idea what we can play. How 'bout Don's a bad guy that's broke outta jail, and the rest of us are the posse that hav'ta catch him."

"Yeah, sounds good to me," Robby said.

Derek and Don simply shrugged.

"Don, we'll give you a count of twenty-five to get away," Jared said.

"Alright. What boundaries?" Don asked.

"Hey, why don't we play in the bush?" Robby suggested.

"Yeah!' Jared nodded, but first he had to check it out with Dad. The bush was out of bounds without permission. Jared ran over to where Dad was engaged in a battle of his own clipping an overgrown honeysuckle hedge.

"Dad, can we play in the bush?"

"Well, I suppose so. Are you taking Derek?"

"Yeah, he's playing with us."

"O.K., but be sure you keep an eye on him."

"Sure. Thanks, Dad." Jared wheeled around and shouted, "Hey Derek, we're ALLOWED."

Now the wooded area across the street from the Clarkson house was an ideal venue for kids to play. Large enough to engage childish imagination, it was small enough to facilitate the work of parental search parties when kids lost track of time. Best of all, a creek deep enough for swimming and fishing meandered through the property.

The four boys clambered over the rusty wire fence and ran through the tall grass to the tree line. A thunderstorm earlier in the day had soaked the grass, and in seconds Jared and Robby's shoes and pants were drenched. Wearing rubber boots Derek fared better.

The air in the wood was laden with that kind of hazy dampness that, depending on the wind and sun, could seem either warm or cool from one minute to the next.

Jared stepped into a clump of bushes to relieve himself.

"Hey Jared, I can see your dick!" Robby said.

Derek and Don laughed.

"Soooo? How cum yer looking anyway?" Jared looked over his shoulder and stuck out his tongue at Robby who then stepped up and gave Jared a playful shove. Jared turned towards him and peed on the toe of his running shoe. Robby looked so funny as he jerked his foot away then hopped around trying to wipe his shoe clean on the weeds that Jared shook with laughter. Don stood grinning with his hands on his hips, shaking his head at the two of them.

"Are you guys going to horse around, or are we going to play cowboys?"

"O.K., O.K., Don," Jared said. "We'll close our eyes and you take off. We'll give you a count of twenty-five."

Don scurried away, snapping twigs and swishing branches as he scrambled through the wood.

"Twenty-three, twenty-four, twenty-five. Ready or not here we come," Jared said. "You follow him towards the creek, Robby, I'll try the other side of the trees. He might try doublin' back to get away behind us."

"I want to go with you, Robby," Derek said, emphasizing his preference with his pointer finger.

Jared didn't care; he knew the creek area was more interesting. Besides, if Derek was with Robby, it saved him from holding the branches out of the way for Derek.

"O.K., Derek. You're with Robby."

Jared set out alone to track Don's path through the brush and tall grass. Soon he realized that Don must have doubled back towards the creek and as he prepared to alert the others, he heard Robby shouting.

"Jared! Don! Derek fell in the crick."

Jared's heart pounded in his ears, and he ran fast as he could. Immediately the voice in his head began the accusations,

Yer supposed to be watching him, stupid. You know he can't swim very well. If anything happens . . .

Ignoring the sting of branches against his face, Jared continued to run and broke into the clearing where the creek twisted in an oxbow around two large willows. There, just upstream from the swimming hole, he could see Derek up to his waist in the water, struggling to remain upright as angry brown water churned around him.

Robby reached out to Derek but the riverbank was too high and eroded to get close enough. When Derek tried to seize Robby's hand, he slipped and the water carried him downstream closer to the swimming hole.

"Ahhhh!" Derek stumbled and fell backwards into the water. Trying to regain his footing, he yelled and thrashed about.

By now, Don had joined Robby on the bank and they tried extending a branch but Derek was too upset to notice. Jared threw down his rifle, kicked off his shoes and jumped into the cold water.

Derek immediately seized him around the neck.

"Leggo' Derek; yer breaking my neck."

Derek refused to let go and a moment later the two of them toppled sideways. Jared scraped his lower back on a large rock, but at least Derek's grip was broken and Jared righted himself. He grasped his brother by the jacket and dragged him backwards to the riverbank where Don and Robby took hold and hauled him up the bank, managing in the process to smear river muck all down the back of the kid's wet clothes. Don then held out a branch assisting Jared from the creek.

The breeze quickly chilled the boys.

"S.s.s.sorry J.j.j.Jared." Derek hung his head. His teeth chattered and he began to cry.

Don removed his jacket and wrapped it around Derek's shoulders. At least Derek was O.K, Jared thought. Still, the both of them were a muddy mess. Worst of all, one of Derek's rubber boots was missing. Jared tried to calm Derek.

"It's alright. You're O.K. Everybody falls in the creek or gets a soaker once in a while, right guys?"

"Yeah, sure!" Robby and Don said together. Jared put a protective arm around his brother.

Don spied Derek's missing boot and fished it out downstream. He looked in it, wrinkled his nose at the creek smell, then poured out the water. At least the boot wasn't lost. Jared hoped Mom wouldn't give him a licking for not looking after Derek. He wished there was some way to clean up a little before going home. He worried Mom and Dad would ground them from the woods.

At that moment Mom came tearing out of the brush with her jacket flying behind her. She took one good look at Derek. Her face was pale.

"What in the *world?*"

Derek plastered a weepy look on his grimy face then ran to meet her. She gathered him in her arms and checked him over, then stared at Jared.

"You were *supposed* to be watching him!" Her stare chilled Jared beyond the water and cold air.

"Sorry. We were playing separately and—"

Mom interrupted, her eyes flashing.

"For goodness sake, Jared. Sometimes I think that when God gave out the brains." Perhaps it was the crestfallen look that swept across Jared's face, but Mom took a deep breath. "Come *here*, Jared."

He approached her with the hesitance of a nervous puppy. She heaved a big sigh, then gathered both boys to herself. She put her own warm coat around the boys and they all hurried home.

Later that day, after warming up in a hot bath with Derek, Jared donned his cozy flannel Maple Leaf hockey pyjamas and returned to solitary play with his train. He wished he'd spent the whole day alone as he'd planned.

Alone wasn't always so bad; it was easier to stay out of trouble that way.

Chapter Eleven

Without any doubt, Sunday was Jared's least favourite day of the week, and it became less so with each passing year. It seemed the Clarkson's spent half their life inside the tiny white frame Baptist Church attending one service or another. Jared came to the conclusion that religion was like salt; a little was fine, maybe even good sometimes, but too much and you wanted to spit it out. Or gag.

There were some things about going to Church Jared didn't mind; indeed certain things he actually liked, such as feeling he was part of a large family. Or those times when the Sunday school held contests.

With his tremendous memory, Jared easily won prizes for memorizing Bible verses or reciting the books of the Old Testament in order. Once he had won a large plastic boat with *John 3:16* printed on the sail. Winning it had become an obsession after he saw another boy get one.

He had also corralled Robby and Don and invited them during the annual Sunday school roundup, earning himself a balsa plane model. He wasn't sure that the Sunday school people were pleased to have Robby in their group though, for if Jared found it difficult to sit still, Robby found it well nigh impossible. He constantly chewed gum, looked at hockey cards, or talked to Jared.

Jared found Sunday school boring, but not because of the teachers. They were actually quite nice. Most of them were older teenagers, or young adults who hoped they would someday receive the "call" from God to study at Bible school and become ministers or missionaries. Sunday school class constituted their first "call." Anyway, Jared would much rather be outside riding his bike, or sledding, or at home reading a book than going to Church. When Christmas fell on Sunday, Jared hated Church most because the Clarkson's insisted they had to go to Church first before they could open their presents. Jared felt guilty because he knew Christmas was Christ's birthday, but all he could think of was getting out of Church so he could see his new toys.

One cold winter Jared's Sunday school class had to meet in the Church's furnace room due to overcrowding. The room oozed so much heat it reminded Jared of hellfire and repentance before he even sat down.

Sometimes amusing things happened in Sunday school. For instance, there was the student minister who knew magic. The guy would pour a jug of water into a newspaper cone, roll the paper into a perfectly dry ball, and then toss it at the children – all the while prattling on about the mysteries of God.

Jared didn't always understand what the guy talked about; indeed he wondered if the guy understood it all himself, but Jared thought his magic tricks were at least as interesting as stories about loaves and fishes or the parting of the Red Sea. Jared wondered if the guy knew any good card tricks.

Course not, stupid, the voice in his mind said. Cards were sinful; Pastor Ronson said so. They were among the most devious of Satan's tools, along with movie theatres, dancing, and pool halls. Jared never found out if the guy did know card tricks because after a month or so he returned to Bible College and that was the end of Sunday magic.

One particular Sunday, Jared and Robby sat together at the back of the class with their chairs tilted against the wall to dangle their feet.

Lars Olufsson, Jared's teacher, lead the Sunday school with his usual sing-song version of Nordic English.

"Velcome to Mishonary Shunday."

Jared ears perked up, he'd forgotten this. In his mind, Missionary Sunday was *good* . This meant they would likely see interesting slides from Africa or some other neat place at the evening service, instead of listening to another sermon.

Jared loved listening to the missionaries talk about distant lands, and peoples. He privately made up his mind that when he grew up he wanted to visit some of those places himself; although not as a missionary. Jared felt a special affinity with the African people often depicted in those slide shows. While poor in a material sense, Jared noticed they seemed to have something that this part of the world lacked – they seemed happy, always smiling or singing. Sometimes as he sat in the dark Church watching the slides change, Jared felt a pang in his heart and wished he'd been born in one of those places. Maybe then he'd feel as if he belonged somewhere.

Anyway, lost in his thoughts, Jared didn't notice that everyone else had stood up to sing. Robby gave him a poke. Kids turned around and snickered as Jared and Robby kicked their chairs forward and the metal legs banged onto the cement floor. They stood up just as the ancient pump organ began to groan and screech. Jared thought it sounded like a set of bagpipes with indigestion.

"Jesus loves the little children, all the children of the world. Red and yellow black and white all are precious in his sight, Jesus loves the little children of the world."

Jared refused to sing those songs any more because they seemed childish to him, but he listened and thought about the words. He wondered whether Jesus would still love those children if they turned out to be Hindus, or whatever else there was to believe in? Pastor Ronson didn't seem to think so. He said Jesus was *the* way, *the* truth, and *the* light. That didn't leave much room for other religions but it made little sense to Jared why other religion's people couldn't go to heaven if they were good. Sometimes trying to figure stuff like this out made Jared want to hit himself in the head. Why did he think about stuff like that? No other kids seemed to think about such things; or if they did, they knew enough to keep it to themselves. Not Jared. One day in Sunday school, Jared asserted it wasn't "fair" that only Christians went to Heaven. The kids in the class just stared at him and giggled. Even the teacher gave him a peculiar look, and Jared wondered why.

Other times, usually at night in the dark, Jared worried about entertaining such thoughts. Maybe God was angry with him. Pastor Ronson said God knew our every thought, but that also made no sense to Jared. Why would God be so interested in every one of our thoughts, especially the dumb stuff kids thought about most of the time? He figured God had a lot more important stuff to do.

When Sunday school finished Jared looked for Derek and spied him across the room. Derek carried a crayon picture he'd drawn in class. The picture showed three people in a car. Jared took it from Derek's hand to review it.

"What's this supposed to be?"

"God's driving Adam and Eve out of the Garden of Eden."

Jared leaned into his brother's face.

"Don't be so *stupid* Derek," he whispered. "They didn't even *have* cars in those days."

Derek seemed unperturbed.

The guys made their way upstairs to where Dad stood at the entrance to the Church sanctuary greeting people and ushering them to their seats. Dad winked when he saw them and pointed them in the direction where Mom knelt, lost in prayer, with her forehead resting on the back of the pew in front.

Jared, already fidgety, reviewed the Church bulletin as he waited for the service to begin. He wished he could sneak in a comic book. When the organist started to play, Jared lifted his head from the bulletin and watched Pastor Ronson step up to the pulpit. The pastor paused then raised his hands.

"Please rise and join in the singing of the doxology."

Doxology? What was that anyway? Jared wondered why this particular hymn had such a weird name.

"Praise God From Whom All Blessings *Flow*." Jared joined the congregation in song, and felt peaceful. Was that God's peace? It felt like God was with them sometimes when they sang, but how could God be there? There had to be millions of Church services going on at that very moment. How could God be everywhere?

"Please be seated. Welcome to Missionary Sunday. Today we welcome home the Baileys who are home on leave from Ghana.

They will be speaking to us this evening about their ministry, and showing us slides of their work."

Christians sent people to "evangelize" other countries. Pastor Ronson said to evangelize meant to bring "the good news." It was Christ's commandment to "go ye into all the world and preach the gospel."

Fine, Jared thought, but he had to wonder why Christians got so upset when the Jehovah Witness people knocked on *their* doors. Maybe those guys had some "good news" of their own to share. Maybe what they had to say was right but nobody would listen. None of this made much sense, and worst of all, Jared seemed to be the only person who thought so.

Chapter Twelve

"You understand that your story about the concentration camp is . . . well . . . *unusual,* to say the least. And we have to remember that you and your friend were doing a lot of drugs at the time." Dr. Miller appeared noticeably reserved as he spoke to Jared. "Any other strange things ever happen to you?"

"Whaddya mean 'strange things?'"

"Hearing things or seeing things that weren't there, special messages for you on the radio. Anything like that?"

"You're asking if I think I'm crazy?" Jared felt his fist clench. From the jukebox of his mind, he suddenly heard the song, 'They're coming to take me away, ho ho, hee hee, ha ha.'

"I'm not saying that Jared, just trying to understand what's been going on with you. Hallucinations often seem very real."

Jared shook his head "This was no hallucination. I can't say what it was, how I got there, or back, but I know it wasn't just something my mind made up."

"Any similar strange experiences in your life, like voices that weren't there or seeing things that weren't there."

Jared took a minute to think.

"No, well, maybe when I was a kid. Sometimes I'd imagine stuff, or wonder how I'd gotten from one place to another. I probably was distracted, but that stuff is completely different from what happened in Germany."

Dr. Miller leaned forward. "Any other really bad stuff happen to you when you were growing up?"

"Whaddya mean 'Bad stuff?' "

"I don't know . . . it could be anything." Dr. Miller pursed his lips. "What's the worst thing that happened to you when growing up?"

Jared grew silent and flushed. He knew the answer to that one. He hadn't thought about Ed the pervert for a long time. Indeed, he'd tried hard *not* to think about him. Dr. Miller noticed his angst.

"What are you thinking about right now?"

"Well . . ." After fidgeting in his chair, Jared told Dr. Miller what Ed the pervert had done to him, how upset he'd been; and how he'd become angry with his little brother afterwards. "Mom smacked me around good that time." He clenched his teeth and hung on tight to the arms of the chair. He felt beads of sweat forming on his face.

"Did it happen more than once?" Miller's face looked blank and calm.

"Which thing?"

"The stuff Ed did."

"Just once." Once was enough.

"Did you tell anybody at the time?"

"No, I was too frightened. He said he'd find me and fix me if I said anything."

"O.K., and what did you start to tell me about your Mom?"

"You mean her hitting me. She beat the hell out of me a few times but I don't really blame her. She thought it was the right thing to do and I was a pretty rotten kid."

"Kids can be really difficult sometimes." Dr. Miller agreed. "But that doesn't make it alright for their parents to beat them."

"I know, I know. It's just that, well, I don't think she really meant anything bad by it. I know that sounds weird."

"How do you feel about your mother?"

"I miss her, in a way, but not the fact she could be so nice, then so mean when she got angry. But no one's perfect, eh?"

"Perfection isn't the issue, Jared. Why did she hit you that time?"

Wasn't this guy listening? Jared wondered.

"It was right after the thing happened with Ed. I shoved my little brother and he got cut."

"And what about the other times?"

Jared remained quiet and fidgeted. Talking about this stuff was hard.

"There was another time was when I got kicked out of school for fighting. There were other times too, but these were the worst."

"What did she hit you with?"

"Usually her hand, or Dad's belt. The worst was the time with the stick."

"How come she hit you with a stick?"

"That was when I got kicked out of school for fighting. She

locked me in my room for a few days."

"What was that like?"

"Boring mostly; I slept a lot." Jared's face went blank as if he remembered something.

"What are you thinking about?"

"When I was locked in the room, I think that was the first times I heard that German guy's voice."

"What German guy?"

"Just a voice I heard. It scared the hell out of me. I looked all over the room and in my closet to see who was talking. It was my German toy soldier. I know that sounds crazy."

"I see. Do you remember what it said?"

"I don't recall exactly, but I think it told me to look for something in the room."

"What else did it say?" The doctor stroked his chin and leaned forward.

"Not much really. All I remember was that it called me 'Kinder' and told me to look under my bed. My Mom had taken everything out of my room but she missed a couple of things."

"So what happened?"

"I looked under the bed and found out the voice was right. There *was* stuff under the bed. It was damn creepy but I sure was glad to have something to play with besides the soldier."

"And why didn't you have anything else to play with?"

Aren't you *listening*? "Because the bitch took all my stuff out of the room. Everything except one plastic German soldier and some blocks."

"Ever hear voices that weren't there after that time?"

"Not that I recall."

"Alright Jared, it sounds as if you are a guy at risk for strange things. Maybe it was partly related to shock from what happened with Ed. Time's up, but I'd like you to continue talking with Simon while you are with us in hospital. That O.K.?"

"Yeah . . .fine." Jared shrugged. He was in no rush to leave the hospital. If he returned to the street those thugs were waiting.

Chapter Thirteen

"Come here Jared, I need you," Mom called from the kitchen.

After throwing down his Superman comic, Jared jumped up to see what she wanted. On the way down the hall, he forgot to avert his eyes, caught a glimpse of himself in the mirror, and scowled.

"Jared, would you mind going downstairs to get me a jar of peaches from the fruit cellar."

Yuck, not the fruit cellar. Jared hated going there.

"Ask Derek. I went last time."

"Derek's outside. It will just take you a minute. I'd go myself but I am up to my elbows in flour."

And she was too. Just like every other Saturday morning, she was baking tarts, cookies and pies to last for the coming week. Jared marveled that Mom could make so many yummy things at one time.

"Alright, alright." He didn't mind helping out, it was just that the fruit cellar was the creepiest place in Jared's world, next to the monster that lived under the stairs. He knew that he shouldn't be afraid of monsters under cellar steps or spooks in fruit cellars, but he was. Excursions to those places provided ample ordinance for the canons of his imagination. The first voice tried to reassure him, *just run fast and you'll be okay.* Jared steeled himself, but worried this might be the time he'd be caught.

Jared took a breath and opened the cellar door. It squeaked. He leaned forward and listened for any stirring beneath the steps; then he tore down the cellar stairs, grabbed the doorframe, and swung right past the laundry room.

That's when he heard the voice. It was low, and not one of the usual ones that argued in his head, but it was definitely a voice. Jared skidded to a stop and listened.

"Psst. Over here."

"Derek," Jared whispered. "Is that you?" He knew Derek was outside, but he had to ask. His heart beat fast and he felt faint.

"Over here, kid."

Jared's neck tingled and he wanted to scream but for some reason he didn't dare; screaming was bad luck. He tried telling himself that it was nothing, that there was no such thing as a monster under cellar stairs, or *was* there? *Somebody* talked. After a few minutes, he decided to pretend nothing had happened and he took off at a clip, his heart still pounding and the cement floor stinging his feet until he entered Dad's workshop.

The fruit cellar opened off one end of the workshop. Jared closed his eyes, seized the dilapidated wooden door, and started to open it. As it scraped across the floor, Jared shivered. The door open, Jared forced himself to gaze into the musty murk beyond.

At least the fruit cellar contained a light, albeit a single bulb with a pull string. Jared took a deep breath, then immersed his arm into the darkness to locate the string. He hoped the last person who turned it off hadn't yanked it and sent it flying. He found it right away and gave it a tug.

The fruit cellar was just an oversized closet with perpetually damp block walls and ancient dusty wooden shelves, but to Jared it was a dim space containing who knows what. Jared looked at the rows filled with jars of preserves, then let his eyes wander down to the bottom shelf where a wooden bin filled with potatoes sent spouts into the dark looking for a place to root. When he encountered the sprouts in the dark, Jared imagined they were monster fingers. The still air was stale and foul. Jared imagined giant spiders lurked behind the jars waiting to bite anyone who ventured near.

With the light on, the fruit cellar appeared less spooky in some respects, but worse in others, because now the swinging naked bulb caused shadows to dance across the contents. Jared shivered and made a fast examination of labels on jars. Jam, pears, fruit cocktail, tomatoes. Oh, no. What was he supposed to get? He stepped out and shouted at the top of his lungs.

"Mom."

"What is it Jared?"

"I forgot what you want."

"Laws, Jared, your mind is like a sieve! I might just as well do it myself. Peaches, Jared. *Peaches.*" Oh yeah, peaches. What did she mean, 'mind like a sieve?' He grabbed the closest jar of peaches, snapped off the light, and pulled the door shut. He prayed that the door scraping on the floor would be the last sound he heard down here. He wanted to run all the way back upstairs but managed to restrain himself.

If I drop this jar . . .

Chapter Fourteen

Blazing sunshine reflected into Jared's eyes from the bicycle wheel as he sat on the grass polishing its rims with a rag and compound. If only he didn't ride through those puddles. Oh well, that was O.K. He didn't mind polishing his bike.

Every few minutes he took a break to stare at the puffy cumulous clouds in the blue summer sky. He smiled at their constant evolution from one thing to another, each moment producing fresh fodder for his imagination. Hey, look, it's old Mrs. Rogers, well, at least her big nose. He tried to stand up for a better look, but pins and needles shot through his leg.

"Ouch." He rolled back onto the grass to massage his leg and heard the screen door slam. A moment later Derek leaned over him.

"Whatcha doin' Jared?"

"Planning a trip to Mars! Whatsit look like?" The sting in Jared's leg had migrated to his tongue. *Shut up.* What did I say that for? "Sorry, Derek. My leg hurts. I was cleaning my bike and my leg went to sleep. I hate that."

"Uh huh," Derek said. "Me too. What's that feeling, Jared?"

"I dunno. Somethin' to do with your blood, I think."

"Whatsit got to do with your blood?"

"How do I know? Do I look like the Encyclopedia Britannica?"

"Oh." Jared's tone caused Derek to be quiet. He changed the subject. "Can I clean my bike, too?"

"Yeah, fine, but make sure you put all the stuff away when you are done or Dad will murder us."

"Can you help me?"

"I knew it! Do it yourself Derek! You know how." Yeah, yeah, Derek knew what to do, but Jared also understood that he liked someone with him anyway. Like the time Derek cried in the night and told Mom he wanted someone to stay with him.

"You have your Teddy with you," Mom told him, but Derek told her he wanted somebody who 'talked.' Jared gave in.

"Alright, Alright, I'll help you. Go get your bike."

"Thanks!" Derek turned to leave, then stopped. "Jared?"

"What *now*?"

"What's a 'cyclopedia?'"

"A bunch of books full of information. Look, hurry up. I don't want to spend the whole day at this."

"O.K."

As he watched him leave, Jared figured that Derek wasn't a bad kid for a brother, even if he did ask a lot of dumb questions. He lay back on the grass to review the cloud patterns. Mrs. Rogers' nose had broken off from the main part of the cloud, and now it resembled one of Bo Peep's lost sheep.

"Hoi there! Jared, Derek." Dad's voice came from the front of the house.

What did Dad want? Jared wondered. Usually when Dad called it meant mealtime, a chore, or he had landed in trouble of some kind. Because Jared didn't think he had done anything bad in the last few days, and they had just eaten lunch, he figured it was chores and he took his time.

Dad stood waiting for the boys in the front yard. He wore his "paint clothes." Jared had only seen him use those clothes for painting once or twice. Mostly he used them for gardening. Why didn't he call them his garden clothes? *Who cares what they're called*? Jared wished he'd been born with a switch to turn off the voices in his head, and his big mouth.

Derek, who had already arrived, was talking to Dad.

"How 'bout you guys bring me a big drink of water from the house. You can get yourselves a Popsicle while you're there."

"O.K. C'mon, Jared."

The boys raced into the house and soon returned with a tall red metal tumbler of ice water, and one Popsicle. Jared set the Popsicle against the edge of the front step and whacked the back of his hand against the Popsicle, deftly breaking the treat in half. Jared was proud of his Popsicle expertise.

Dad downed most of his water in one gulp then splashed some on his face.

"I'm driving over to Uncle Ted's this afternoon. You guys want to come?"

"Yea, the farm!" Derek said.

Memories of tractor rides, baling hay, collecting eggs, and watching farm animals doing weird stuff filled Jared's mind. Uncle

Ted's farm was just about the coolest place in Jared's world.

"Alright, then. Put your bikes away and make sure you put *my* stuff back where it came from. By the way, I didn't appreciate finding my 3/8 box wrench rusting in the grass the other day.

"Wasn't me," Derek said.

"Well it wasn't *me*," Jared said. "I always put stuff back."

"Right guys; it's never anybody. Rinse your hands under the tap before you get in the car, O.K?"

The family station wagon lurched in and out of the potholes as Dad drove up the laneway of Brookside Farm. Jared found potholes mysterious. Where did they come from, and what determined their size? Why did they occur in that particular place instead of another? When the car jolted through a particularly large pothole, Derek banged his head against the window. Dad reached out to soothe the sore spot.

"Sorry Pal, I'll slow down."

Lassie, the farm collie barked and ran beside the car.

"Look," Derek said. "Lassie's smiling, she's so glad to see us.'"

"Dogs can't smile, son," Dad said.

Jared wasn't certain Dad was right about that. Some dogs scowled.

Dad pulled the Rambler to a stop under an immense Maple tree in front of the white frame farmhouse.

The farmhouse had green trim and a big covered veranda on three sides. Comfortable wicker seats with colourful cushions invited one to sit down out of the heat to sip ice tea and eat fresh baked squares and cookies. The wicker loveseat, suspended on chains, was the boys' favourite. They erupted from the car and raced for it. Jared reached the loveseat first and sprawled out. Derek squawked in protest, then began swatting Jared until Dad intervened.

"Sit up there Jared and make some room."

Aunt Mary pushed open the creaky Victorian screen door, and stood there wiping her hands clean on her bright pink gingham apron while Dad nipped the disturbance.

"C'mere you two scallywags and give Aunt Mary a hug!"

The boys bounded from the swing into her open arms. Jared thought Aunt Mary smelled good. She always smelled good whether it was fresh hay from collecting eggs or some yummy thing she was baking in the kitchen.

Dad glanced about for Uncle Ted then raised his hand to Mary in greeting.

"G'Day Mary."

"Hello James. Come and sit down; Ted's in the barn. You boys go find Uncle Ted and see what he's up to. We're having a tea party later with apple pie and ice cream."

"C'mon, Derek." Jared took Derek's hand and the two boys headed for the barn.

"Watch out for cow-pies," Jared advised.

Each of them had new running shoes, and Jared wanted to keep his pair looking like new, at least for a week or two.

The boys entered the barn and found Uncle Ted grooming Frisk, the chestnut mare. As the boys drew closer Frisk snorted and shifted about in her stall.

"Whoa, girl." Uncle Ted rubbed her chin, then turned to the boys. "She's a tad skittish today for some reason. How you guys doin'? Whoa, there Frisk. Come round this way boys and give 'er a pat."

Jared noted the horse's disposition and held back, but Derek stepped forward with enthusiasm.

"Can we have a ride on Frisk?" Derek asked.

"Sure can. We'll bring her outside to the corral."

"Yippee." Derek hopped up and down.

Jared wandered off and occupied himself looking around the barn. Uncle Ted watched him, then laughed. "Looking for treats there, Jared? Just got a load of chocolate bars t'other day. Most of 'em t'ain't even broke. Let's have a ride on Frisk and then we'll get you guys stocked up, eh?" When Uncle Ted shelled out, he meant business. He bought discard candy by the barrel to feed the pigs. Much of it was still edible for people and the guys always returned home with bags full of the stuff. Best of all, Uncle Ted shelled out year round. After cinching the saddle on Frisk, and leading her out to the corral, Uncle Ted turned to the boys.

"O.K., who's first?"

"Me, me." Derek jumped up and down..

"Go ahead, Derek." Jared said.

Uncle Ted scooped Derek and placed him in the saddle.

"Hol' tight to the horn there lil' buddy."

"Giddap Frisk," Derek said. "Good horsey." His short legs hardly extended over the saddle, making his attempt to spur the horse with his feet as fruitless as it was comical. Uncle Ted stood in the centre of the ring holding Frisk at the end of a rope. He gave the rope a shake, made a clicking sound with his tongue, and Frisk began trotting in a circle.

Derek looks good up there, Jared thought. Too bad he didn't bring his western stuff with him. After several circles of the corral, Uncle Ted reined in the horse.

"Whoa there, Frisk, Jared's turn now."

Jared ignored the cue and began scuffing the dirt with the toe of his runner, forgetting his resolve to keep his shoes clean. Derek slid off the horse so fast that Uncle Ted barely had time to grab him by the shirt and break his fall.

"Your turn Jared." Uncle Ted smiled.

Jared felt Uncle Ted's eyes upon him. He'd get on the horse if he had to, but all he could think of was being up so high and he shook. Jared hated heights of any kind, but had lately decided that riding a horse was the worst. Unlike ladders and trees, horses had minds of their own. He stared at the ground.

"Ah, no thanks."

"You don't have to be scared. Its fun," Derek said, causing Jared to blush.

"I'm *not* scared. I just don't want to ride now. You take my turn."

Uncle Ted's puzzlement further lined his tanned face.

"What's wrong there Jared?" he asked. "You used to like riding Frisk."

"Yeah, I know I did . . . and I still do, but . . . ah, I dunno." He felt his stomach turn over just thinking about being up on the horse.

"Right, then," Uncle Ted said. "Another ride for Derek." He hoisted Derek back onto the saddle for a few more loops around the corral.

Jared wandered back into the barn alone.

Why am I acting so stupid? It's only a dumb horse. Uncle Ted wouldn't let anything happen. Sure, people always said that, but you never knew for certain. Like two weeks ago when Jake, one of the farm kids from school, let him ride his pony.

"Nobody ever falls off," Jake said. Naturally, Jared was the first. When he climbed on the animal, it suddenly twisted, throwing him off, then headed back to its stall. Jake stood there laughing like crazy.

Derek on the other hand, was seldom afraid of anything. He even climbed high in the big Maple at home with Robby and Don, while Jared sat on the bottom branch.

Maybe I'm just a chicken, he concluded.

"Hi Jared." Uncle Ted tapped him on the shoulder, then led Frisk back to her stall.

"Oh, Hi Uncle Ted, uh, where's Derek?"

"Gone up to the house for tea. You comin'?"

"Guess so."

Uncle Ted put his arm around Jared's shoulder as they started back. "We'll have some tea, then get some candy for you guys. Horse got ya spooked, eh?"

"Guess so."

"Well, don't worry none 'bout that Jared. T'ain't nobody that ain't 'fraid of somethin' at one time or another, lessen a course he's a liar or a durn fool. The thing though is whether yer going to let that fear control ya and keep ya from doing what ya want to do."

Jared didn't quite understand what Uncle Ted meant but he nodded his head. That usually satisfied adults.

"Now the thing about somethin' like riding a horse is not whether ya *like* to ride or not, the thing is being able to get on the horse when *you* want to. You with me on this one, Jared"

Jared thought over Uncle Ted's words; he sort of understood, but he still wasn't getting on any horse today if that's what he had in mind.

Chapter Fifteen

Vivid television, such as *The Outer Limits* and the news, were all too real to Jared. While part of him wanted to leave such things alone, another part felt drawn to the strange and frightening. Today was one of those times. Jared sat alone, down in the basement, his eyes and mind fixated on Norman DePoe, the CBC newsman , on their black and white T.V. screen.

"The next twenty-four hours may tell us whether the Russians will stand down their warships that are most certainly en route to Cuba. We will shortly learn the outcome of the most dangerous superpower confrontation since World War II."

For the past few days Jared had been following this story on television and radio. At his age, listening to such news was unusual, and Jared didn't understand what it all meant except that he felt petrified, and worried they were about to die. Any hint of death stirred terror.

The wages of sin are death . . .Your good works are as filthy rags .

. . I am a jealous God . . . Then comes the judgment, the Bible said.

Pastor Ronson said Judgment Day might be "at hand," and that we lived in the "last days" when there would be wars and rumours of wars. Maybe the Pastor was right. Khrushchev and Kennedy seemed ready to fire nuclear missiles and destroy the world. Pending destruction preoccupied Jared's waking and resting hours. Rumours of war, actual war, and imminent final judgement filled his mind.

Jared wanted to be good, but felt so weak. Yes, God forgave sin, but he expected you to refrain from committing the same sin over and over again. Even when he managed to be a good boy, Jared shouldn't brag about it or even *think* he was being good. That was the sin of pride. Jared's nocturnal fears and resolutions faded with the light of day and he'd be at it again, using bad language, being mean to Derek, or "borrowing" a story idea from some book he'd read and incorporating it as his own.

Pastor Ronson said it was up to each man to do good or evil. Mankind had 'free choice' but it didn't seem like much of a choice to Jared. Do what God said, or burn in hell?

"Vengeance is mine," saith the Lord. One way or another, Jared knew God would have his way with him. He imagined an angry God reading out a litany of his sins from a big black book on Judgment Day. God would frown at him then say,

"Depart from me Jared Clarkson . . . I never knew you."

Jared sat up in the dark. The sheets and blankets twisted around him and the sweat poured down his face. He thought about the imminent end of everything. He wouldn't have to wait until he reached old age to die and face judgment if Kennedy and Khrushchev blew up the world.

Jared untangled the covers and pulled them around his head. He wished he'd never been born. He never asked to be born, at least as far as he knew. Eventually he drifted into a restless sleep until he awoke at dawn, his bed soaking wet. He found a towel to cover the wet spot, and changed into dry pajamas.

How could he ever stop sinning? He couldn't even stop wetting the bed.

Even Derek didn't wet the bed anymore.

Jared looked Simon in the eye then laid his cigarette down.

"Most people think that childhood is an innocent time, but that's bullshit. At least it was for me. Nobody knew what was in my head most of the time when I was a kid, and no one bothered to ask. I'm sure I didn't really understand half of the stuff I thought about, but it sure scared the hell out of me. Once I went to the cemetery with my parents – it's kind of funny now when I think about it – I didn't know where I should walk. I was afraid of walking on the graves, and too embarrassed to tell anyone I was afraid. Childhood sucked."

Chapter Sixteen

Distant spikes of lightning confirmed an approaching storm. The lifeguard blew her whistle.

"Everybody out of the water," she said.

Robby and Jared complied and headed to change quickly, then waited outside the pool for Derek. He was taking forever to get changed. They watched as the sky darkened and felt the turbid air turn to chill. Robby slapped down a nickel on the snack bar counter for a grape Popsicle just before the pool staff slammed down the shutter for the duration.

The storm crept closer. The first splashes of rain caused smoke-like tufts to explode from the dust.

"What's taking your brother so long?" Robby grumbled.

"How do I know? Think I got X-ray glasses?"

Robby had turned his attention to the sky and when Jared looked up he realized they wouldn't make it home before the storm.

He had an idea. "Let's go to Main Street and wait in Brand's Variety. We can read comics till the rain stops."

"Alright." Robby nodded.

After Derek joined them, the trio set off pedaling at full tilt with Robby on the point. They wove through the laneways behind houses to accomplish the shortcut.

The temperature continued to drop and the rain pelted faster. The hot sticky weather of a few minutes ago was a memory. The blackened sky seemed to turn day into night. Soon the rain falling in torrents soaked the boys. Derek wore only a T-shirt and shorts and his teeth chattered. Robby forced his bike to a stop in a tiny dry place under the portico of a large building. Above the portico a sign read *Render Casket Company*.

The brief shelter from the elements ended when the wind shifted, forcing the boys to the building's rear to huddle beneath a small overhang. Bored, and cold, Derek fiddled with a door handle.

"Hey, look here guys," Derek said. "It's open."

"Get out . . . Lemme see." Robby grabbed the handle to give it a twist and it turned.

"Hey, yer right, Derek!" Amazed, Robby turned to Jared. "Let's go in."

"Yeah, ins...s...sside," Derek said. "Maybe it's warm in there." He rubbed his arms.

"Sure, Robby,' Jared said. "And what if someone's in there?"

"There's never anybody in there on Saturdays."

Jared considered that Robby might be correct because sometimes the guys would stand in front of the window of the factory and watch the men build the caskets. He didn't recall ever seeing the workmen there on weekends. But why would the door be open?

"Even if there is someone there, we're just getting out of the rain," Robby said.

"But why would it be unlocked?"

"I dunno . . . Maybe they just forgot to lock it, or maybe someone is working. We'll just tell them we're cold."

"Well, you go on ahead, if you want Robby." Jared scratched his head. "I'm not going' in there . . . at least not first."

"Be a chicken then," Robby said. "But you're coming with me aren't you, Derek?"

"I'm sooo cold." Derek looked towards his brother.

Jared worried the kid might turn blue.

"Alright," he said. "You guys go in and see if it's O.K. I'll keep watch out here. Lemme know when the coast is clear."

Robby pushed the door open a crack, and he and Derek slipped inside, leaving Jared alone with the storm. After a short wait and hearing nothing, Jared decided to join them.

Inside the factory, heat and humidity choked the air. As Jared's eyes adjusted, ghostly outlines of caskets in various stages of construction emerged from the dim. Bottles standing on top of one of the caskets across the room resembled sentries guarding a distant rampart.

"Derek. Robby. Where are you guys?" Jared whispered.

"Right here." Robby's voice was right behind him.

"Jeez, Robby! You nearly scared you know what out of me. Where's Derek?"

"Next door playing with the staple gun. Come and see; it's really neat."

The guys had often watched the workers using the power staple guns to tack the satin lining into the caskets. It would be neat to try one; Jared thought they were almost as cool as real guns.

They joined Derek, firing staples at the wall. Phsst, Phsst, Phsst. Most of the staples ricocheted onto the floor, but a few stuck into the wallboard. Robby stepped up.

"Lemme' try."

He held out his hand and Derek gave him the gun. After only has a few shots, it started to go click, click, click.

"Oh sure," Jared said. "You guys use up all the ammo before I get a chance."

"Relax," Robby said. "There's tons of ammo." He held up a cardboard box filled with staples.

Jared grabbed the staple gun to reload when they heard a noise. A wooden bang followed by a groan. Or was it a moan? The boys stared at one other in terror.

"Let's get out of here!" Jared threw down the staple gun, grabbed Derek by the hand and began running for the exit.

By now the storm had passed and sunshine streaming in the windows illuminated particles of dust floating in the air, giving the room an eerie glow. Jared tried not to look at the caskets as he scooted past, and kept reminding himself that coffins couldn't have ghosts or vampires in them until *after* they'd been used.

They had almost reached the exit when Derek froze in place and shrieked. Robby crashed into Derek, then the three of them collapsed into a jumbled heap. When they untangled themselves and dared to peek, they observed just visible above the open lid of one of the caskets, a hand rubbing the side of a head. The head shouted.

"Who's there?"

The person tried to climb out of the coffin, then something smashed on the floor, the report sounding as if one of the bottle sentries had been shot. The three boys crouched behind a workbench and watched a man stand up and wobble to his feet.

"That's no ghost,' Jared whispered. "He's one of those bums that hang out under the old railway bridge. I've seen him sometimes when I'm fishing."

"What're you kids doin' here? How'd ya get in here?" The man hiccupped, then farted loudly.

The combination sent the boys into nervous gales of laughter. Now that the scare had passed, Robby had found his usual smart-ass self.

"What are *you* doin' in here?" He yelled.

"Why you little brat." The man started to move towards them, but after a couple of steps he slipped on the broken glass.

The boys bolted outside, snatched their bikes, and pedaled like spit.

The air outside was hot again, but the boys hardly noticed. As they raced home, Jared didn't know whether to laugh or cry the way his heart pounded. Although he had the feeling they did something wrong, he couldn't help smiling.

The spooky house at the Toronto C.N.E. was nothing compared to this.

Chapter Seventeen

Brands Variety stood last post amid a platoon of derelict buildings, each a sad monument to prosperity evaporated from Beacon's main street shortly after the town's first strip plaza opened in 1958.

The new plaza, a novelty at the time, contained big stores with large windows and lots of parking. In reality, the plaza was a retail Trojan horse that sucked shoppers, money, and finally the merchants themselves from main street. Those shoppers remaining were mostly old people, or those on fixed incomes living in apartments above the shops. Or teenagers hanging out. Nevertheless, Brand's Variety had survived and Jared loved to hang out there reading comics, selecting treats or buying fire-crackers around May 24th. The store was run by Ed, and part-timers from the high school. This day, Jared dropped in to check out the newest Superman comic. The weather was cold for

October, and Jared had difficulty closing the door against the wind.

"Hey Kiddo," Ed addressed Jared that way each time he entered the store.

" Ah, Hi Ed. Are the new comics in yet?"

" Yeah. Just put them out yesterday." Jared dashed to the comic rack and began leafing through the new ones. A few minutes later a Popular Science magazine with a picture of a flying car on the cover caught his eye. As he looked through the magazine, he heard a child squeal with delight. Looking up, he saw that Ed was doing one of his magic tricks, pulling a silver dollar out of a little boy's ear.

" W...w...w...wow! Ca...ca...can I keep it?" The child inquired.

Jared had to laugh, every kid asked Ed that question - once.

" Do...tha...tha...that again." As always Ed refused to discuss the issue and returned to his work re-stocking the cigar case.

A bugle alert from the Marconi in the corner caused Ed to raise a finger to his lips, to "Shssh" another child about to speak. He hurried over to the Marconi and turned up the volume, tilting his ear close.

" This is Darryl Wells with the results of the fifth race at Woodbine."

Now Jared never heard race results on anyone's radio except Ed's but every fifteen minutes, at the bugles cue, Ed would rush over as if he were Pavlov's dog.

" Quickstreet, a long shot the winner at 14 to 1. Try Harder second paying 5-1 and Sarah's Revenge third paying 2-1." A smile pursed Ed's lips and he turned down the volume and returned to the cash register where a man waited to purchase cigarettes.

Jared returned to the article about the flying car. The article said that that flying cars like this one would be commonplace by the year 2000. Jared felt excited with that idea. Wow, by 2000 he'd be all grown up, maybe even have kids of his own and certainly one of those cars. That was if the world didn't blow up of course. Jared imagined travelling any place he wished in that magic carpet of the future.

In no time, the bugle sounded again on the radio and Ed rushed over to hear the sixth race results.

At the news of Barnstorm paying 6-1 in the Exacter, Ed's face tightened like a circus clown whose make-up has cracked. He opened a notebook near the cash register, reviewed a page, then shook his head in disgust.

Jared wanted to ask about a special edition Batman but decided to wait until Ed was finished serving line-up of customers. Ed looked at his watch, as a teenage boy hurried in.

" Yer supposed to be here by 4. It's 4:20." Ed growled.

" Sorry, I missed the bus from school and had to walk."

" Well, hang up your coat and take over here."

When the young man took his place at cash, Ed walked to the back of the store where a curtain separated a store room from the front.

Jared took advantage of the opportunity to ask him about the comic he wanted.

" Ed, do you have any more of those special edition Batman comics you had last week.?" Ed stared at him in thought.

" Think they are all gone but I might have one left in the back. Wanna come with me and see?"

" Sure!" Jared had always wondered what was in that storeroom.

" Well come on then." Jared walked in then Ed pulled the curtain closed behind them.

The storeroom was mostly filled with stacks of pop, snack

foods, and boxes of cigarettes. To one side, behind the merchandise was a small seating area with two chairs and a small table.

" Sit down there Kiddo – I'll see if I can find that Batman for you."

Shortly he returned with it. Jared was thrilled.

" I was going to keep this for myself but how bout' I give it to you instead?"

" WOW. Thanks." Jared was so excited he felt like dancing – that comic was worth fifty cents - his whole allowance.

" Alright then, but first I want to show you a trick I know." Was it a magic trick, Jared wondered. He knew that Ed could pull silver dollars out of kid's ears – what else could he do.

Ed sat down in front of Jared, leaned forward, and whispered in his ear.

" Anyone ever suck your lollipop kid?"

Suck my lollipop – what was the guy talking about? Jared didn't like the sound of it.

"Whaddya mean?"

Ed didn't respond except to reach out and pull the child towards him. Jared tried to pull away but it was too late, he was caught in the man's vice.

With a free hand, Ed undid Jared's fly.

" Hey." Jared tried to pull away. He felt dizzy when Ed seized his dick. He began to shake and cry softly. He had a bad taste in his throat as if he were about to throw up.

" I, I don't like this." He whispered. He tried to push the man's hand away but at this Ed shook him and snarled,

" Shut the fuck *up* kid. I'm going to suck your lolli' then you can take your comic with you."

Jared didn't want the comic anymore, he just wanted to be out of there but he couldn't move. He felt the man's breath between his legs and then strangely found everything grow calm, and he felt himself floating. Floating near the ceiling and looking down at a man and a boy. The boy seemed familiar. It felt like one of those times when he was younger and seemed to arrive from one place to another without remembering, and whatever was happening didn't seem to be happening anymore, at least not to him.

Suddenly, it was all real again and he felt Ed sucking his dick. It felt weird, kind of nice, but also scary and embarrassing. He heard the man grunting and breathing hard doing something to himself with his free hand.

When he was finished, Ed said, " O.K. Kiddo, put your lollipop away. This is going to be our little secret. RIGHT. I'm going to give you that comic and you are going to keep your mouth shut."

"I...I don't want any comic..." Jared stammered. He tried to twist away but Ed squeezed his arm tight until he winced and stopped pulling away.

"This is our little secret Kiddo. If you *ever* tell anyone I'll find you Kiddo. I'll find you and *cut it off*. Do you understand me – I'll cut it *off*."

"I...I promise. Can I go now." Jared whimpered.

"Alright, you take your comic but *remember* what I said."

Out on the street, Jared felt suddenly ill and threw up on the sidewalk. He walked home in a shocked daze.

"Get *out* of my room!" Jared shoved Derek backwards causing him to trip on the crumpled area rug. As he went down, he banged his face on the doorframe causing blood to flow down his cheek. At the sight of blood, Derek started to wail. Jared tried to console him. He grabbed a tissue and pressed it to the wound.

"Derek, I'm sorry. Are you alright—?"

He had no time to finish because Dad arrived, scooped up Derek, and carried the screaming child to the bathroom. A moment later, Mom was there, puffing and red-faced from her dash from the basement. Seeing James swabbing Derek's cut with a facecloth she confronted Jared,

"What's going on? Did you hurt your brother? I've told you to keep your hands *off* him."

Jared backed away and tried to explain.

"I . . . I told him to get out of my room, but he wouldn't leave."

Jared knew what was coming. He backed onto his bed and curled his legs against his chest.

"I'll teach you to hurt your brother!" Mom grabbed his arm and yanked him forward to receive a smack.

Jared ducked just as she swung. Instead of his backside, she landed a stinging blow to the back of his head. At this, the day's bilge erupted from Jared in a flood and he commenced screaming, swearing, and kicking out towards her. Shocked by the ferocity of his reaction, Mom backed off and began to shake and cry. Jared threw himself into a foetal position on the floor near the wall and slammed his head against the floor.

When James returned, he tried to make some sense of the situation.

"Look after Derek, Beth. I don't think Jared meant to hurt him."

Mom took a breath to calm herself and knelt down beside Jared.

"Jared, I didn't mean to hit your head." Her voice was restrained only for a second. "But you've no business hurting your brother."

"Get away. Get away from me." Jared sat up and kicked out towards her.

"I'm not taking this from you Jared." She tried to grab him, but James shoved her from the room.

"That's enough, Beth! Go see to Derek."

He shut the door, then returned to kneel on the floor beside Jared who had resumed banging his head. Dad reached out to place his hand between the boy's head and the floor.

"O.K. son, that's enough. We all lost it here. I know Mom's sorry and you are too." He tried to pull the child towards him but Jared shoved him away.

Chapter Eighteen

"What's wrong? You've been daydreaming all period instead of doing your math?" Miss Vickers whispered into Jared's ear.

"Oh yeah, sorry Miss Vickers." The boy's tone was flat but obedient. He continued staring ahead. In his mind all he heard was Ed's threat.

"…find you and cut it off." Over and over.

Miss Vickers placed a hand on his shoulder.

"Jared, I'd like you to try to do some of your math; you don't want to get behind the class."

Jared still didn't look at her.

"O.K," he replied numbly.

At lunchtime Jared pulled on his snowsuit and Toronto Maple Leafs toque, then proceeded outside to sit alone in the apple tree beside the school's former driving shed. The first snowfall of the season had left the October landscape looking like December. Jared climbed up the tree and sat on a branch wondering what happened to nuclear fallout in the snow. Soon he heard Alice calling to him.

"Psst, Jared, what are you doing?"

Jared looked down and saw two other girls with Alice.

"Nuthin' . . . just sittin'."

"Want to play with us?" One of the girls asked.

Sure, some dorky game like Duck Duck Goose? Jared shook his head. He didn't mind if Alice stayed, but he wished the others would leave. Alice seemed to read his mind.

"You girls go play without me." Then she climbed up to join him.

No sooner had she settled down beside him when the other girls returned with snowballs, and began to chant.

"Jared and Alice, sitting in a tree, K-I-S-S-I-N-G."

"Get lost," Jared growled.

After the girls threw more snowballs, they laughed and ran off.

For a while, neither Jared nor Alice spoke. Alice pulled a sketchbook from her coat pocket to show him what she'd been working on. Alice loved drawing horses, and Jared admired her skill,

"This one's great." Jared pointed to a sketch of a horse rearing up.

"Thanks. So was your story the other day."

Jared didn't really hear her. He felt suddenly jealous of people who could draw.

"Yeah, I guess my stories are O.K., but I can't draw anything."

"Your poster for fire prevention week was good." Maybe, although Jared figured he had as much chance of winning the five dollar prize from the Ladies Auxiliary as the man in the moon.

Lots of people said they thought his jingle on the poster was really good, but he knew the drawing stunk.

"How come Miss Vickers was talking to you?" Alice asked.

"I dunno . . . said I wasn't paying attention . . . sleeping in class."

"Well you *were* sleeping Jared. I poked you twice."

"Thanks."

"Are you tired?"

"Yeah, tired." Mostly tired of stupid questions. Alice was beginning to get on his nerves. "You O.K., Jared? You don't seem very happy lately. I thought you'd be happy with Walter away from school with Chicken Pox." At the mention of his nemesis Jared hoped the guy would develop a thousand itchy poxes in places he couldn't reach.

"It's nothin' to do with Walter." Jared's face grew wistful. Part of him was bursting to tell someone what had happened with Ed, but that threat . "Can you keep a secret, Alice?"

"Sure I can. Cross my heart and hope—" Jared held up his hand. "O.K., but don't tell anybody. Last week when I was at the store . . . well, the guy did a sick thing to me."

"Whaddya mean?" Alice sounded concerned.

"He touched me."

"Yeah…touched you…I don't get it?" Alice leaned towards Jared.

"It's *where* he touched me."

"Oh, I didn't think that stuff happened to boys. My uncle did stuff like that to me one summer when I stayed at his house for a week. My Mom said he's a 'funny uncle' and I shouldn't pay any attention; just stay away from him."

"The guy doesn't sound too funny to me. Anyway, when I got home I was really mad and pushed my brother down. He cut his face when he fell so my Mom smacked me around pretty good."

"Did you tell your parents what happened?"

"Are you kidding? The guy said he would come after me and hurt me if I told *anybody*. I shouldn't even have told you . . . that's why you can't tell anybody."

Maybe he should let her 'hope to die.' Talking about what happened made him feel sick to his stomach again just as the bell rang them back to class.

"Hey, Alice." He found it hard to look at her but she turned around and made eye contact.

"Yeah."

"Thanks for sitting with me."

"That's O.K. But we better go now."

"You go. I'll be along." He mumbled because he could already taste what was coming. He managed to delay throwing up until she left, then rinsed his mouth out with fresh snow.

When he arrived at the door, Alice had held him a place. She waved him into line. Alice was one of the few reasons Jared could tolerate school at all.

Chapter Nineteen

November 22, 1963 was a school P.A. Day, so Jared and Derek stayed home. Earlier they played outside with Robby and Don, but clouds and rain chased them indoors. When Jared flicked on the T.V. in the afternoon, he found all three channels broadcasting the same terrible news. An assassin had shot John Kennedy, the American President, in Dallas. Jared was stunned. He liked President Kennedy because Kennedy had proposed that the U.S.A. land a man on the moon in a few years.

Too little to understand much about these events, Derek amused himself, but Jared remained transfixed to the television. As the hours passed, his mind grew more confused and upset. By late afternoon the CBC news anchor Norman DePoe announced that the president had died. That night in bed Jared's mind churned with speculation about the assassin's identity. What if the Russians did it? If they had, this could be it – the end of the world. Maybe this was what Pastor Ronson meant when he talked of wars, and rumours of wars, in the "last days." Finally Jared drifted into sleep, but he continued tossing and turning, consumed by fitful dreams.

"Schnell, schnell!" German soldiers shouted and waved their rifles at the prisoners. When one of the workers stumbled and dropped the rock he carried, one of the soldiers began to kick him. The man struggled to get up but kept falling back because the rock had broken his foot. The prisoner on the ground looked like President Kennedy. Every time Jared tried to wake up, the injured man's face flashed before his eyes.

Over the next few days Jared thought about little else but the President. He somehow got the idea that the President's hearse would pass by their house. This terrified him, although he didn't know why. He figured a way to protect himself by making a scrapbook of the assassination and the funeral. James just shook his head watching his son cut up the papers to record the morbid event.

Chapter Twenty

Early spring was one time that Jared actually looked forward to school. It was as if something inside of him came to life again. Maybe it had to do with the longer days arriving after the hard winter, and the mountains of snow reduced to a few icy patches in shady places. The waxing sun at mid-day heated the concrete steps enough so the children could sit with their coats undone. Winter seemed on the ropes, and spring poised to burst.

It amazed Jared that certain things just seemed to happen at specific times of the year. The Crocuses the children had planted last fall already had popped yellow and blue flowers throughout the schoolyard. But Jared's favourite reason to enjoy spring was marbles. Just like the Crocuses, one day in mid-April, suddenly everyone had marble bags at school, and the games began.

Unlike his ineptness at most sports, Jared was a whiz at marble games. For as long as Jared could remember, he, Derek and Robby had collected and played marbles. Jared had amassed a fantastic collection of cat's eyes, crystals, and biggies. Robby's Mom had sewn each of the three boys a special marble bag with his name embroidered; those bags garnered the envy of every child in the school. Also, this spring was unique because Jared still possessed *the* marble, Walter Thomkins' prize sapphire crystal that Jared had won last year in a murderous game of Closies. Since then Jared had kept that marble safe at home in a drawer, away from the bulk of his collection. It wasn't because the marble was his favourite, although it was indeed a fine specimen, but rather because losing it irritated Walter and Jared had derived great pleasure refusing him any opportunity to get it back. Not getting it back wasn't from lack of trying on Walter's part.

Walter was a bigger boy who from the first day of grade one had taken a dislike to Jared. He called Jared names and shoved him around. But when he lost his prized marble, Walter switched tactics and offered amazing trades, and even pretended to treat Jared like his friend. But Jared saw through all of it and refused to budge. Although Pastor Ronson preached that someone could be born again, Jared agreed with his Dad who often commented that leopards didn't change their spots. For once, Jared had Walter firmly in his grip, and he wasn't letting go. Eventually, Walter dropped his nice guy tactics and returned to his usual obnoxious ways.

One afternoon after school, Jared and Alice were walking home and had barely stepped off school property, when Walter confronted them.

"Hey, Four Eyes, what's with you and your goofy girlfriend?"

Jared was in no mood for Walter's nonsense today and tried to do what his Mom always recommended – that was to ignore the brat. Alice, however, seemed to have other ideas, as she stood with hands on her hips glaring at Walter.

"Why don't you go down the drain with the rest of the drips?"

"Sticks and stones . . ." Walter stuck his tongue out at her, then turned to Jared. "Hey, Shitface. Ya' need yer girl to stick up for you?"

Fuming, Jared turned toward Walter and reflexively made a fist. Alice latched onto his jacket sleeve.

"C'mon Jared, he's not worth the bother."

Jared shook her off and stepped up until he stood eye to chin with Walter, who sneered, then shoved him away. Jared kicked him in the leg, then took off with Walter in close pursuit.

"You can't outrun me, you little fart," Walter cried.

Maybe not, but Jared had an idea. After a few moments of zigging and zagging, Jared stopped dead and crouched. Walter kept going and tumbled over him, allowing Jared to get in the first lick, a powerful right to the side of Walter's head. However, Jared forgot Walter's hard farm boots and one caught him full in the stomach. Winded, Jared fell down and struggled to catch his breath. Walter stood over him to gloat.

"Stop it Walter; that's enough," Alice said. She tried to squeeze between the two boys, but Walter warned her off.

"I'm going to make your boyfriend cry."

Walter stepped over Jared, and crouched down, pinning Jared's shoulders with his knees. He grabbed one of Jared's ears, ready to pull it if Jared dared to move, and busied himself working up a big batch of spit.

Jared, still pinned and winded, could only wiggle and watch in disgust as slime from Walter's ugly puss oozed in a stringy mess down onto his face.

"You bastard," Alice said. She stood up close to Walter, who shoved her away.

"Stay out of this Alice, before I forget you're a girl and do the same thing to you."

Jared's face flushed red with anger and embarrassment. Had he the means right then, he would certainly kill Walter. Finally Walter jumped up and dashed off across the field. Jared could hear his laugh long after he disappeared behind some trees.

Alice removed a tissue from the pocket of her jacket and handed it to Jared. He stood up and took it without comment, then turned away, struggling to contain tears of rage as he cleaned himself.

"Are you O.K.?"

Jared nodded, but remained silent. Alice didn't press him, and she carried the conversation the rest of the way home. But Jared wasn't really listening and only caught some of her news about quilting at the 4H Club. His mind was busy creating a stew of revenge, and bringing it to boil in his mind.

At home Jared put on a brave face and tried to sneak past Mom in the kitchen but he had arrived late, and she was waiting.

"O.K., what's happened this time?"

"Nuthin'. Just a scrap with Walter. I'm alright." Before she could ask for details, he called out, "C'mon Derek. Let's go out and play."

Next day at lunch, Robby found Jared alone behind the school. As if in a trance, Jared kept throwing a large stone onto the ground.

"What are ya doin'?"

"Practicing." Jared slammed the rock down a few more times until finally he smiled with satisfaction. The rock was landing precisely where he wanted.

He hoped his plan would work. Course it would work. He had considered everything.

He figured that getting the rock to land in the right place formed only part of the problem; it was just as important that his target didn't skitter away. He needed to brace the target and finally decided on using some clay from the creek near the school. Clay would work well because it provided stability, but also would give way under force.

Jared practiced the entire procedure two more times with practice targets until he could execute perfectly. Robby scratched his head as he stared at Jared.

"Why ya doing that?"

"You'll see in a minute." He was almost ready for what Ed Sullivan liked to refer to as, 'The really big shew.'

As usual, Walter and Roy were making mischief at the other side of the school chasing two little girls and threatening to tie their shoelaces together. Jared made certain he had everything in place, then stepped around the corner.

"Hey, Walter, Roy," he said. "C'mere and see this new marble game I invented."

They took their time coming.

"Whaddya want Clarkson?" Walter asked suspiciously.

"I brought your fave' marble to school, Walter. I've decided to put it into a game. Interested?"

"What kind of game?"

"Just this."

Jared stepped aside and behind him sat Walter's marble perched in a lump of clay on the sidewalk. Before Walter could speak, Jared snatched the large stone, raised it over his head, and hurled it down onto the target.

Walter moved to kick the marble but was too late. The stone

hit the marble dead centre, shattering it with a distinctly satisfying crunch. Jared laughed as he stared at Walter's reddening face.

"You can have it back now, Walter."

"Yer going to pay for that Clarkson," Walter said, shaking his fist at him.

Maybe. Maybe he would, Jared thought. He didn't care. Where Walter was concerned, Jared always paid.

This was payback.

Chapter Twenty-one

Six months had passed since the horrendous events of the previous fall and Jared began to feel more like himself. The stuff with Ed seemed long ago, the Russians hadn't killed Kennedy so the world didn't blow up, and Walter was being no more than his usual belligerent self. Jared was enjoying himself and had even resumed writing stories for fun.

One morning Miss Vickers sat at her desk holding a bundle of student work in her hand.

"Grade fours, I've read your English compositions and some of them are very good. I'll pass them back, but first I'd like to read you a story I think is especially good. It's Jared's story about time travel. Would it be alright if I read your story to the class, Jared?"

When everybody in the classroom looked at him, Jared flushed. That story had percolated in his mind for a week before he wrote anything down.

From two aisles away, he sensed Walter and Roy whispering and staring. When Miss Vickers turned away, he looked over and stuck out his tongue.

"Jared, may I read out your story?" Miss Vickers asked again.

"Ah sure, Miss Vickers." Jared shrugged. Alice smiled and Robby gave him a wave. The teacher began reading.

"Sounds of whirring and flashing red lights filled the capsule as I took off in my time machine for the year 2050."

Jared closed his eyes and visualized hurtling into the future. When it came to stories, his imagination went that route – he'd see it all in his mind, then write down what he saw. He applied that same imagination to other subjects, for example, the stories of exploration during social studies. While Miss Vickers talked about the voyages of discovery, he'd stare at the map of the world on the wall beside his desk and imagine Magellan's ships tossed by the angry seas in the Cape of Storms during their circumnavigation of the world.

Today, Jared's vision of the future glowed in his mind's eye. He imagined the people's surprise when the globe-shaped time machine suddenly materialized in front of them as they sat enjoying a concert in a beautiful tropical park. The concert, provided by instruments of strange appearance and sounds, was most surprising because these instruments played themselves.

He imagined this city of the future as large, but clean and quiet. He foresaw people wearing simple old-fashioned tunics as they walked on pathways meandering through gardens of strange iridescent flowers, ferns and trees. Only when he heard the applause of his classmates did Jared open his eyes and return to the present.

"You make the future sound very appealing," Miss Vickers said.

"Thank you, Miss Vickers." Jared smiled.

When the hands on the big clock at the front approached noon, anticipation filled the classroom. Miss Vickers always let the children out right on time, but she expected them back and ready to work just as promptly afterwards.

"You're excused," she said, just as the three hands lined up on the twelve.

Jared approached Miss Vicker's desk to collect his story and smiled at the red A++ she'd written on the bottom of the last page. He placed the story carefully inside his desk. He could hardly wait to show Mom and Dad.

Kids hurried past him out into the sunshine but he decided to eat in the cloakroom so he wouldn't have to carry his lunch pail around. After lunch, he strolled outside. Everyone seemed busy at play and he found himself alone. In the distance, he spied Robby organizing a game of Move-ups with the other boys, but Jared didn't bother to join in. It took too long to get up to bat, and he'd seldom be up to bat for more than a minute before he was out. Either he wouldn't hit the ball at all, or if he did hit it, he might let the bat might go flying. Or maybe a guy on the sideline would yell, "swing," then everybody would have a big laugh at his expense. Jared didn't bother with team sports much.

Small groups of girls were scattered about the schoolyard. One group, including Alice, skipped Double-Dutch. They would let him join in if he wanted, but his skipping was even worse than his batting; he'd be tangled up in seconds and just spoil the game for everyone. So he wandered about the driveway, scuffing the dirt and gravel, watching the little clouds of dust, or examining the types of stones.

At one point he wandered over to observe three girls playing Cat's Cradle on the school steps. String games like that fascinated Jared. He wondered how far the game might actually go if played by experts. He thought he saw someone make five turns once. And who had invented the game, anyway?

Wondering about how things were first discovered or invented fascinated Jared. He'd spend hours pondering mysteries such as how people first got the idea of cooking things. After giving that particular problem considerable thought, he decided that cavemen probably got the idea after eating an animal caught in a forest fire. When they found it tasted good, they linked it to the fire and that was it.

"Pretty dumb story."

Jared spun about to find Walter and Roy, standing there. He tried to ignore them.

"Ya probably copied it," Roy said.

"Ya that's it Roy, he copied it. From one of the *girls*." Both of them laughed, then Walter reached forward and shoved Jared backwards over Roy's extended leg.

Jared's eyes narrowed, and he began to breathe fast. His temper was like nitro-glycerine, quiet when left alone, but it didn't tolerate much shaking.

News of trouble brewing traveled like wildfire through the schoolyard and kids began streaming in to see what was going on. Behind the thumping in his ears, Jared heard the muffled excitement of spectators closing in around them.

One mousy little boy kept repeating, "Fight, fight," as if he were flogging dailies on a busy city street corner. Jared remained on the ground with Walter standing over him, hands on his hips.

"Whereja' get such dorky glasses, Clarkson?" Walter mocked.

Jared's guts churned, and images of his fist slamming into Walter's face flashed through his mind even though he had to agree with Walter on that point; his glasses were dorky. He hated them and would have thrown them away except he was almost blind without them. He regarded them as the 'ugly pink things,' and figured they were the cheapest ones the Children's Aid Society could buy.

"Leave him alone." It was Becky, one of the grade eight girls. She pushed her way into the circle of children and grabbed Walter by the shirt.

Becky Robertson was taller than the teachers, and more than fit from seasons of pitching hay and mucking stalls on the family farm. Her pretty tanned features bore the confidence of children who carried adult responsibilities long before their time, and Becky had no patience for bullies. When Jared stood to dust himself off, Becky gave him a sly wink. She knew enough to let it go at that.

"Ouch." Walter protested when Becky gave his ear a punishing twist. The painful squawk from one of the school 'tough-guys' drew howls of laughter from the crowd. Then the bell rang.

It was the end of round one.

Back in class Alice leaned over to Jared and whispered.

"Becky showed him, eh?"

"Guess so." Jared wished he'd 'showed' Walter himself.

Miss Vickers called the class to order.

"Grade fours, please take out your math books and turn to page one forty-eight."

When Jared lifted the lid of his desk to retrieve his math book he noticed something missing - his story. He twisted around to see Walter and Roy, their hands in front of their faces stifling their mirth.

They must have stayed behind at recess and taken my story. Jared clenched his hands and his face grew hot as Miss Vickers droned on about fractions and wrote on the blackboard. While her back was turned, Walter took a crumpled ball of paper from his desk and stood up. He turned in Jared's direction, and pretended to wipe his ass.

Wiping himself with my story? Something erupted in the centre of Jared's chest that flashed in an instant to every part of his body. Miss Vickers turned from the board just in time to see Jared bolt from his seat. In seconds he was trying to snatch the story from Walter.

"Jared! *Sit down.*" Her instruction was simply a blur to Jared. Walter held tight to the paper and it ripped. At this outrage, Jared seized Walter around his neck and began to pummel his face. The speed and ferocity of the attack caught Walter off guard and also he was trapped in his desk. He tried shoving Jared away, but Jared gripped tighter and twisted him into a better position to land punches. The action caused then both, along with the desk, to tumble sideways to the floor.

"*Jared!* Stop this right now." Miss Vickers tried to physically restrain him.

Jared barely noticed her. Rage from this, and prior insults, sprang forth with each blow and Walter's nose gushed blood. When Jared let up to avoid the blood, Walter swung his free hand and knocked Jared's glasses onto the floor. Jared bent down to retrieve the glasses and Walter scrambled from the upturned desk.

"Get him Jared!" Alice and Robby yelled.

"Wal*TER* Wal*TER*," The room filled with the cacophony of shouts and cheers.

Miss Vickers tried to seize Jared's arm, but with her crippled fingers she couldn't hold on. Her bad leg threatened to collapse if she moved suddenly and her arthritis meant that holding onto anything proved difficult, let alone boys on a tear.

Jared pursued Walter up an aisle, scooped a math text and threw it. Walter turned to look just in time and managed to deflect the projectile at an oblique angle. It struck a little girl sitting with her hands over her head.

"I'm going to kill you, Walter." Jared spat.

Miss Vickers attempted to keep up with the action, but with her game leg, it was hopeless. One of the straps on Walter's coveralls came loose. Jared grabbed hold of it, then gave it a yank, causing Walter to turn, then careen into the back of a freestanding bookcase. The impact knocked the case, and its considerable contents, crashing forward onto the floor. Walter landed askew amid the mess.

Silence suddenly chilled the room. When Jared looked, he saw Mrs. Trimble, the school principal. Her angry stare reviewed the classroom carnage.

"You two come with *me*!" She pointed a finger at Jared and Walter.

Miss Vickers stood helpless to one side. No one, adult or child, argued with Mrs. Trimble when she was this furious.

Jared wanted to do exactly as he was told, but suddenly he found himself tearing out of the classroom to lock himself in the boy's washroom stall.

Generations of boys had carved the ancient wooden door of the stall. The headline carving read, "Welcome to Hell." Jared sat rocking back and forth, with his hands on the side of his head as his rage dissolved to fear. He sobbed and began smacking his head against the brick wall. Soon, the door of the stall was shaking with such force that the entire cubicle rattled.

"Young man!" Mrs. Trimble demanded. "You come out of there at once."

Do what she says. Tell her you're sorry. Maybe she won't call home. You've really done it this time.

Arthur, a waif in grade one, wiggled through the space at the bottom of the door. Despite his tiny frame, the kid barely fit and when he got stuck for a moment he looked up at Jared with apprehension. Mrs. Trimble continued banging and shouting.

"Open this door."

Arthur finally squeezed under the door and stood up.

"Boy, are you in big trouble."

No kidding.

As soon as Arthur slid the rusty bolt, the door swung open and Mrs. Trimble thrust her face into the cubicle. That trembling wrinkled face reflected her thirty-odd years in the classroom. A hint of drool oozed from the corner of her clenched mouth as if trying to make its escape. She reached out a wrinkled, sinewy arm and dug her long fingernails into Jared's shoulder.

"Come with me, young man. How dare you run from me."

She half-dragged him into the hallway, then held him hostage against her enormous bosom that rose and fell as she walked, like the frill on some nasty Jurassic reptile. Her pumps snapped against the concrete. She thumped up the basement stairs to the main floor and shoved Jared onto a chair in the corner of her tiny office.

"Don't you dare move an inch."

Her threat was not needed. Jared's fight was gone, replaced by panic. He wasn't worried about getting the strap from the principal; indeed he was used to that and would have preferred it to what was going to happen next.

Mrs. Trimble glared as she held the phone against her ear and waited to speak to his mother.

Chapter Twenty-two

"Mrs. Clarkson, it's Mrs. Trimble. Sorry to have to trouble you. Yes it's Jared. I'm afraid so. He attacked Walter Thomkins in class. Walter's nose was bloodied, and his clothes look as if he's been shot. Yes, well I'd rather not discuss this on the telephone Mrs. Clarkson. I must insist that you come immediately and take Jared home. He is suspended indefinitely. "

Mrs. Trimble greeted Elizabeth Clarkson when she arrived. Elizabeth nodded a perfunctory response then looked at Jared. He couldn't face her.

"Why is it that only *my* son is being punished?"

"Your *son*! Come now, Mrs. Clarkson we both know Jared's not *really* your son."

"Jared, please wait for me in the car." After Jared scrambled out the door Elizabeth narrowed her eyes and leaned across the desk. "How dare you say such a thing. Jared is as much our child as if my husband and I bore him ourselves. He has his problems but we love him as our own and you'd better remember that!" She straightened up and started to leave.

"Excuse me Mrs. Clarkson but I'm not finished," Mrs. Trimble said. "I must insist upon a meeting with you and the Children's Aid before Jared sets foot again in this school. We simply cannot, and will not, tolerate any further disturbances of this nature. In any case, those people have no business bringing Toronto's problems into our school. I've already discussed the issue with the school board and I know they will support me one hundred percent on this. Jared is suspended until such time as his behaviour can be guaranteed."

"What about Walter, is he suspended as well?"

"I've spoken with Walter, and I realize that boy is no angel, but the fact remains he was attacked in class and was defending himself. I will be speaking with him again, but have no grounds at this time for any other disciplinary action."

When Elizabeth arrived at the car the look on her face shocked Jared. He'd seen her upset many times before, but not quite like this. Her face was ashen with fury. He tried to muster a feeble greeting.

The ride home was silent except for the Rambler's engine noise. At home she slammed the shift lever into park and gave Jared a look that left him trembling. Tasting her bitterness, Jared cowered against the car door.

"Get to your room and get ready for bed."

Shivering, he fumbled with the door handle, lurched out and stumbled into the house. He ran to his room where he changed into his pyjamas, then sat on his bed. He worried what Mom would do. He knew this time he'd gone too far and figured she was sending him back to the Aid. He began crying. As bad as things might be living here, Jared knew it could be much worse elsewhere. Besides, this was his home now. Help me God, he prayed. I promise I'll try to be a lot better from now on. When he opened his eyes from his silent prayer, Mom stood at the end of his bed. In her hand she held a long stick from the woodpile.

"Tell me what happened?" He could only look at the stick.

"Walter and Roy . . ." He could hardly speak. His mouth was as dry as his eyes were wet. He kept a wary fix on the stick and tried to explain.

"Walter was pushing me around at recess. Miss Vickers read my story and I wanted to show you guys the story but Walter took it from my desk and, and —"

"And what?"

"He took my story and when the teacher wasn't looking he stood up and did a rude thing with it."

"What did he do?" Jared made a half-hearted effort to replicate the insult.

"Alright, then what did you do?"

"I went to his desk to get my story back but he wouldn't give it to me. It ripped and then." Jared's chin dropped to his chest. "And then I got mad."

"And?"

"And I hit him."

Mom sighed, and for a moment her face softened, and Jared thought that perhaps she understood how it happened, and that everything would be alright, but then her face resumed its prior dead seriousness.

"Jared, you're a very smart boy. You know Walter is always doing things to upset you. That doesn't change the fact you've got a terrible temper and you refuse to control it. You've been suspended from school indefinitely because of your behaviour. Do you understand what that means?" She waited but Jared said nothing. "Your behaviour is a serious disgrace to you and our entire family."

"I . . . I . . . can't go back to school?" He knew the answer, but couldn't think what else to say.

"Yes that's what it means, and it also means you must be punished. You understand this, don't you?"

Jared remained silent trying to prepare himself.

"I'm going to punish you in love, the way the Bible exhorts parents to discipline their children."

With that she reached out and grabbed his pyjama top and tried to press him face down onto the bed. Jared twisted away from her and his eyes grew large. He held up his hands in anticipation of the first blow.

"Don't hit me. *Please.*" He curled into a foetal position.

She put the stick aside and forced him face down on the bed. She yanked down his pyjama bottoms, held him in place, and began striking blows across his backside. Before each blow the stick wavered in the air as if she were wrestling with some invisible force. One of her blows struck him square across the back of his hand when he tried to block it. Jared screamed. He wanted to kick her away, but he knew he couldn't. He had to take all of this, but he didn't want any of it.

She moved his hand out of the way and held it to one side, then resumed whacking his backside. With each blow, she puffed. After a few minutes the beating was over and she threw the stick to the floor. She stepped back, shaking and crying then took the stick and without a word, left the room.

Jared felt warm blood trickling on his flaming rear. He buried his face in his pillow to scream,

"You bitch!"

In a futile attempt to quell the pain he rubbed his rear and found that tiny slivers from the disintegration of the cedar were embedded in his skin.

A few minutes later Mom stormed back into the room. She carried a handful of brown paper bags and began grabbing everything in the room – toys, books, models, puzzles, pens, pencil crayons, and his writing notebook. She marched over to the far wall and tore down his posters of airplanes and spacecraft.

Jared watched in stunned silence.

"You will remain in this room until further notice except to go to the washroom," Mom said. "That means you will eat your meals here by yourself. You will have no visitors." She dragged the bags out into the hallway and pulled the door shut behind her leaving Jared alone with only his bed and a table lamp.

His sanctuary had become his prison.

Reflections From Shadow

Chapter Twenty-three

After the disastrous events of the day Jared found it impossible to sleep. He knelt on the floor and stared out the window at Mars in the night sky wondering if there were other inhabited planets in the galaxy. There had to be at least one, like the planet he came from. He sure didn't belong on this one.

If only he could be grown up. Then none of this stuff would be happening; he just wouldn't allow it. Recalling his pain and humiliation he imagined himself with a baseball bat, smacking the shit out of the lot of them – Ed the pervert, Walter, and Roy. He tried to imagine hitting Mom, but couldn't.

A short time later someone tapped on his bedroom door.

"Come in."

His Dad stepped in. He carried a glass of juice and two cookies.

This was the first he had seen of Dad all day.

"Thought you might be thirsty." Dad smiled.

"Hmm." Jared continued to stare out the window.

Dad joined him.

"Nice night, eh?"

"Hmm." Whaddya want? Jared continued staring out the window.

"That's Mars there."

"Yeah." So *what*?

"Mom told me what happened. Made a mess of Walter, eh."

No, made a mess of everything. Dad waited, but Jared refused to speak.

"Look Jared," Dad said. "Your Mom feels bad about what's happened. She's hurting as much as you."

Wanna *bet*?

"Mom talked to Karen Cryderman today," Dad said. At the mention of his Social Worker, Jared winced, his hands started to sweat, and felt as if he might start crying again. Don't even *think* about being sent back. Another kid he knew from the Aid once told him it was bad luck to think about going back.

"Mom told Karen what happened." Dad placed his hand on Jared's shoulder then crouched down to look into Jared's face. "Jared, I want you to know you're never leaving here. I hope you know that. We'll figure things out somehow." Dad slipped his arm around the boy and tried to draw him close.

For a second, Jared felt a little safer, and that maybe things could work out. Part of him wanted to tell Dad he felt sorry for what he had done, but it was too hard to speak. Besides, he wasn't sure what he *had* done that he was supposed to be sorry about.

He was just sticking up for himself.

Chapter Twenty-four

Jared lay on the floor flipping his spoon into the empty porridge bowl. He had only done this a few times when Mom showed up and silently removed the tray. Any form of plaything was apparently forbidden.

For a time Jared rolled about on his bed thinking. He thought about guys in jail. He'd seen lots of T.V. shows, and read books about life in prison. For some unknown reason, the fact and fate of prisoners fascinated him.

He considered that adult prisoners knew the length of their sentence. He had no idea how long he'd have to stay in his room. Prisoners were allowed outside to exercise for an hour a day; he wasn't permitted to leave the room at all. Well, he *could* leave to go to the bathroom, but since the bathroom was right beside his bedroom, this hardly constituted an outing. Guys in jail might get time off for good behaviour, he didn't expect this because Mom's motto was, "I say what I mean, and I mean what I say."

Jared struggled with what he should do next. Part of him wanted to open the door and scream that he would not stay in here, but he felt too afraid. Despite what Dad had told him, such behaviour might be the last straw. Each mealtime when Mom entered the room with his tray, the look on her face reminded him of the sign town workman placed by the millpond every spring. The sign read *Thin Ice. Stay Off.*

Glancing at the window he noticed that the sun illuminated a tiny shadow in the curtain. He pulled back the material and discovered a soldier from his WWII play set; a gray German officer with tall boots, and a riding crop. After looking at it for a time, he hid it inside his pillowcase.

He fell asleep for a long time, and the sunshine crept around the window frame, and moved across the bedroom wall. He dreamt of an older boy playing pinball. Jared watched him for a time.

"Where are we?" Jared asked the boy.

"Up down, north south, east and west. Inside outside, upside down. Today, tomorrow, yesterday. Where we are is really all the same." The boy responded without looking up from his game.

Weird answer, strange guy. The pinball machine continued to ring, chime and flash as the kid racked up points. The boy paused and stared over at Jared.

"And here and there. Not much difference at all."

"Whaddya mean by that?" Jared asked.

The kid resumed playing.

"I mean everything's connected. Darn, missed." He smacked the side of the machine with his hand. "You're puttin' me off the game. Ah, so what, I've been at the darn thing all decade. Hey, you wanna try?"

Nice of him to offer me a turn, Jared thought, but before he could respond, everything in the dreamscape changed as if he had switched to a different channel.

Now he saw men and women dressed in filthy striped clothing wandering around a big area surrounded with barbed wire. Few of the people wore shoes. This place seemed familiar, but why?

The faces of the people were deathly blank as they dragged themselves about. All of them looked much the same except for one man standing to the side. That man was dressed in a neat gray uniform and wore polished boots. Jared recognized him – it was the soldier from his play set. When the soldier looked over in Jared's direction, something about the man so startled Jared that he awoke sweating and disoriented. He tried to recall what was so disturbing about the soldier. And who *were* those prisoners? He wondered.

Forget it. Forget it. It was just a stupid dream, stupid dream. He didn't wake up again until late afternoon. The sunshine had retreated from his room. His pillow soaked with sweat, Jared was relieved to be awake.

Chapter Twenty-five

Each day in solitary seemed longer than the previous, but although he had little else to do except keep track of time, Jared found it strange that he lost track of how long he'd been in there. Only the arrival of food trays broke the monotony.

Each day went from light to dark and then to light again as one day merged with the next.

Jared's bedroom window looked out onto a brick patio where he, Derek and Robby often played. He expected to see the guys there. He was sure that Robby at least would sneak around to see him, but it never happened. Even when he opened the window and listened he couldn't hear the guys playing. Apparently she'd fixed everything.

One morning Derek arrived with the breakfast tray. Later, he came in with a supper tray, but he didn't speak a word. He didn't need to; his face carried sadness and compassion. Jared considered asking him to sneak him some comics, but decided against it. He knew that Derek was not devious, and he didn't want to get the little fellow in trouble.

One afternoon Jared received a small break. He lay on the floor and watched dust bunnies jump away in the breeze as he tried to grab them. When bored with that, he pulled the soldier from his pillow. The warm sunshine made him drowsy. Next thing, he heard a voice, a foreign voice.

"Under der bed. Under der bed, kinder."

"Who's there?" Jared leaped to his feet. He spun about, but saw no one.

Although he knew it was stupid, he had to look in the closet; nothing. He remembered hearing things once in awhile, but that was usually in the basement. He hadn't heard the monster under the stairs for a long time, although he suspected it might still be there.

This voice was different, it had an accent, a German accent? He wondered what 'kinder' meant.

After checking the room Jared felt satisfied that he was alone, but he couldn't relax. Did he imagine that voice? Was he asleep? He sat down on the floor to stare at the toy soldier. A moment later he rubbed his eyes. The soldier seemed to get larger; and its lips seemed to move.

"Look under der bed, kinder," it said.

Now under other circumstances, Jared might have bolted from the room except that he was too stunned. Instead, he obeyed the voice. When he checked under the bed he found, among the dusty shadows flat against the wall, something else Mom had overlooked. Not much mind you, but something. Five wooden alphabet blocks. When he glanced back at the toy soldier, it now appeared the same as usual.

Jared gathered each block, and carefully dusted each one off with his shirt. He sat on the bed and as he turned each of the blocks over and over he thought about what had happened. He kept his eyes fixed on the blocks as if like leprechauns, they might vanish if he looked away. He determined to maintain the blocks in secrecy along with his soldier and spent hours making up games with them to amuse himself.

Using his pointer finger, he tried to stack the blocks, then flick them out one at a time without upsetting them. He soon discarded this game because the blocks made a lot of noise when they fell on the wooden floor.

Next he invented a game he called, *Kreskin*, after that amazing guy on TV. The idea was to use his mind to make a particular letter or number turn up when he rolled one of the blocks. To prevent any cheating, he told the soldier what number or letter would come up next. He had some runs of good luck that caused him to wonder if maybe he did have some kind of power to influence the result.

Jared guessed he was supposed to think about the misbehaviour that had resulted in his exile. Sometimes he did, but most of the time he didn't bother. All of that seemed so far away now; part of a whole other world he no longer belonged to. His world contained no school, no teachers, no people. Only himself, his cell, one soldier, five blocks, dust bunnies, and dark following light.

Jared remarked later that the strangest thing about the whole episode was that once it was over, nobody in the family ever mentioned it again. It was as if nothing even happened. There was no visit from Karen his social worker, and no stupid adult questions about what he had learned. The ordeal simply ended one morning when Derek arrived with his breakfast and the news. For a change, Derek smiled.

"Hey, Mom says you can come out after breakfast, but you're

grounded to the house today. I'll stay in and play with you."

And that was it. It was as if everyone wanted to forget what had happened; and perhaps everyone did. Except Jared.

He remembers.

Chapter Twenty-six

A few weeks later, Jared stood in the stream of sunlight coming in the basement window, a multitude of thoughts cascading in his mind. The monster under the stairs might only be a few feet away but Jared didn't care. Monsters hated sunlight, or maybe like other fears, monsters only popped into existence when noticed by someone.

He bristled at thoughts of his recent confinement, and pined for his natural mother. Maybe she would come for him soon. A lot of people would be sorry when she found out what had been happening to him here. At the same time, he suspected he wouldn't get away from this situation until he grew up.

Grown up. Jared had little idea of what that would be like, but one thing he knew for sure – when he was grown up nobody would ever call him names, beat him up, or do anything like Ed the pervert did. He'll kill them if they try. And there would be no more church.

No church? What was he thinking? Maybe such evil thoughts

about God meant he was damned to hell. Maybe evil thoughts about God constituted the "unforgivable sin?" He could ask Pastor Ronson about it, but he was afraid to ask in case he found out he had already committed it. On the other hand, what had he done really that was bad enough that he should go to hell? Well, maybe he hadn't really meant it when he had walked down the aisle and asked God to save his soul. He *thought* he meant it.

Of course God knew. God knew everything, and maybe God was angry with him. Was that why all those bad things had happened to him? Perhaps the worst was yet to come. Jared imagined himself small and terrified on judgment day with a vengeful God reading out a list of his many sins and blasphemies from a big black book. In his mind's eye he saw God close the book, point at him and thunder,

"Depart from me Jared, I never knew you."

Hell. Death. The words themselves made Jared sick with fear. It wasn't fair that people had to die. Thinking about dying made Jared's heart beat fast and his head dizzy. He'd scoured his mind a thousand times for a way to avoid death, but realized there was no way to avoid it. Everybody had to die someday, and it might happen soon for everyone because the U.S. and Russia had those new bombs now, big rockets with lots of little atomic bombs inside so they couldn't miss their target.

Jared wanted to tell others how scared all this made him feel, but he couldn't. They'd only say he was being silly. He wished he'd stop reading the paper and watching news on TV, but he couldn't.

Somehow he had to know what was going on, and his parents didn't question it. When he took out library books about prisons, and World War II, Mom only shook her head, but she never inquired into his interest in these subjects.

The fragrance of fresh cookies wafted through the house accentuating his empty feeling. He rushed upstairs and snatched several warm cookies off the baking sheet.

"Don't spoil your supper, Jared," Mom said.

He stuffed his shirt pocket, then hurried to his room where he crammed the cookies into his mouth two at a time.

The cookies were peanut butter, his favourite. He hardly noticed.

Chapter Twenty-seven

Robby pointed then said, "Look here Jar' – rabbit tracks."

In wintertime, they saw rabbit tracks everywhere, but seldom in summertime; yet the trail showed a multitude of rabbit prints in the damp soil. Jared noticed that the trail went around a big log, then between two cedars providing a convenient path through the bramble.

"Hey," Robby said. "Bet we could catch one."

Maybe, maybe we could, Jared thought. Probably wouldn't work, but it might be fun to try. They decided to give it a whirl. That evening they sat in Robby's back yard and made plans.

"Geez, Robby, what do we hafta do?"

"Whaddaya think?"

"How about one of those things like on Tarzan where a coil of rope is laid under some leaves and grabs the tiger by the leg?"

"Nah, that won't work. Snares have to be different."

"How?"

"Well, you want to catch the animal on the run so the thing to do is to dangle a wire loop in its path."

"Sneaky. How 'ja figure that out, Robby?"

"Didn't. I saw the Webber brothers do it once."

Jared gave him a playful push. " If you know, why you asking me?"

"To see if *you* knew." Robby laughed.

They rooted about in Robby's basement gathering the things they needed – a length of fine wire, a rusty pair of wire cutters, and some needle-nose pliers.

The basement workshop was a boy's paradise. Robby's dad had filled it with all kinds of wondrous odds and ends, mechanical, electrical, and many other gadgets that defied childish understanding. Sometimes the guys took something "apart" just to see how it "ticked". Robby's dad had given him a few lickings when he found out they were messing with something important, but that seldom deterred the guys. Robby always said there was so much junk that his dad wouldn't miss whatever it was, and usually he was right. Whatever they needed, they could generally find it as long as they were willing to take the time to ransack the heaps of junk piled on workbenches, or lying in boxes all over the basement floor. The garage was much the same; everything in there as well, except the family car.

Robby's dad was calling him for the second time to come in.

"See you tomorrow, Jar'. I better get in before Dad has to come after me," Robby said.

That night in bed Jared went over the scheme and worried that it sounded a little *too* good. While part of him felt excited by the prospect of catching a rabbit, another part of him felt concerned. He didn't really want to hurt anything, but he also didn't want Robby to think him 'chicken.'

Don't worry, he reassured himself; the snare probably wouldn't work. Heck, most stuff the kids made didn't work, or at least didn't work properly. Like that steering system he and Robby had once tried to construct for his soapbox racer.

Next morning, as the boys broke a path into the woods, sunshine glistened through raindrops tottering on the tops of grass stems.

At the site of the rabbit tracks, Robby made a large loop at one end of the wire, then fashioned a tiny loop at the other end so the main loop could slide easily. Jared busied himself stripping bark from the branch they planned to bend over the trail. Jared took the snare wire from Robby and fixed it in place around the branch, using pliers to secure the wire.

"Make sure it's wired good," Robby said. "Don't want the rabbit to yank it off and get away."

Robby bent the branch over and slipped it under the nub of a broken branch on a nearby tree. He considered using an additional piece of wire to fasten the arched branch in place, but decided that it would hold and release without it.

Robby opened the loop, arranged it in the centre of the runway, then covered the bottom of the wire with dirt to fix it in position.

The closer they came to actually completing the snare, the more reservations Jared felt. Killing things to eat was one thing; killing something for the heck of it was an entirely different matter. He thought about that story he'd read once about a rotten kid who liked to torment spiders and flies by pulling their parts off. The story appalled him, but most of all, he figured God mightn't look kindly on boys who hurt one of his creatures for no good reason.

Don't worry, he told himself, a couple of dumb kids weren't catching anything.

He was wrong.

The following day, when Jared finally escaped the house after finishing his chores, he spied Robby shouting from the edge of the woods.

"We got one. We got one."

"You lie like a rug," Jared yelled back. He *hoped* Robby lied. Or did he?

"Really, come see for yourself." Robby said.

Jared experienced both exhilaration, and dread as he ran to see.

When he arrived, and pushed aside the branches to look, a feeling of excited disgust filled him. Their snare had functioned precisely as they had designed it, and now a large brown bunny lay dead on its side in the runway, its eyes staring down the pathway toward some destination it would never reach. During the animal's death struggle, the snare-wire had buried itself deep in the animal's fur.

The boys stared in shock at the animal, and then at one another. Jared would have cried, except that he didn't want Robby to see that. Robby was also mute and looked pale. Jared knelt down and gingerly touched the bunny as if to offer apologetic succour; the rabbit's soft fur was a contrast to the stiffening flesh beneath.

"What should we do with it?" Jared whispered.

"I . . . I dunno." Robby shrugged. "Bury it, I guess."

Neither of them had given a moment's thought to what they would do if the trap actually worked, and now Jared was doubly ashamed that the only thing they could think to do was to bury it.

After the clandestine burial in the woods, Jared spent the rest of the day brooding. He couldn't stop thinking about what they'd done. Petrified of death himself, he struggled to understand what could have possessed him to engineer the death of another creature.

Maybe I *am* evil, he thought. Was this what Pastor Ronson meant when he said that people were born evil, did sinful things, and had to be cleansed and forgiven?

Chapter Twenty-eight

Jared and Derek had been watching the workmen prepare to widen Brandywine, the street in front of the Clarkson house. Surveyors using transits and miles of orange tape staked out the expansion path.

Everyone in the Clarkson family had an opinion about the project. Dad was pleased because finally they'd be rid of the ditch in front of the house. The boys looked forward to the arrival of the big trucks, graders and bulldozers. Mom grumbled about the construction dust she knew would soon descend upon her generally spotless home.

The day after the final stakes and tapes were in place, Derek noticed something.

"Do you think they are going to cut down our big tree?"

Jared sat up from where he'd been lying on the grass nearby and looked at his brother.

"Whaddya mean?"

"Well, look here." Derek pointed to stakes aligned about a third of the way through the tree.

Jared examined the alignment of the stakes and realized his brother was right! Derek was pretty smart for a six-year-old. Jared became tearful and hoped there was some mistake.

"Let's ask Dad," he said to Derek.

Dad was busy nearby in the garage, but despite the short distance, Jared already felt as if he were choking. The memory of the dead bunny, a secret to all but Robby, himself and God, still loomed in his mind, and this situation only added to his distress.

"What's wrong, guys?" Dad asked.

"The big Maple . . ." Jared whispered. He couldn't continue. Derek explained,

"Jared means are the road guys going to cut down our big tree out front?"

Dad put away a gas can he was holding, then sat down on a bucket to talk. " 'fraid so, guys."

Jared began sniffling and wiping his eyes with his sleeve. Seeing his brother upset caused Derek to cry also.

"What's wrong?" Mom's voice boomed from the screen door.

"Under control, Beth," James yelled back. Then, in a gentler voice, he said. "C'mere you guys." He put an arm around each of the boys' shoulders.

The three of them walked out of the garage. Unfortunately, the first thing the boys saw was the Maple tree.

"Why do they have to cut down our tree?" Jared asked. "Why can't they just move the road a little?"

"Yeah, move the road a little." Derek concurred, nodding.

Dad shook his head. "Sorry guys; no can do. That tree's on town property. We've been lucky to have it to enjoy all these years, but it doesn't belong to us. Because it's in the way of the road widening, it's got to be cut down."

Jared broke away and ran to be alone in the backyard. He squatted down on the ground against the house to think. What right did people have to cut down trees that had been around so long? The Maple was big and beautiful and kept them cool in the summer. Cutting down a tree like that just to widen a road was just stupid, he thought. He rested his head in his hands and tried to figure out what to do.

He heard the rustle of shrubbery and looked over at Robby jumping across the boundary of the two properties.

"What are you doing Jared?"

"Those road guys; they're going to cut down the big Maple out front of our house." Jared protested.

"You still have that tree," Robby shrugged, and pointed to the large Beech.

"I don't care! They're not cutting my tree."

"Oh yeah? And how d'ya think you're going to stop them?"

"I dunno, but I'm gonna think of something." Jared looked determined.

It seemed Jared was awake most of that night racking his brain with the tree problem. One thing he knew for certain, he had precious little time to decide what to do. He needed a good idea, and fast. The survey crews had finished and he knew that cutting would begin any day. But what was he, what was anybody, to do about this? Maybe Robby was correct and there was nothing to be done. Finally Jared climbed out of bed and stared out the window waiting for the dawn, and inspiration. Both arrived with stealth, the former turning the sky from black to purple and then pink, as the idea of sending a letter to the local paper jelled in his mind. Jared smiled to himself.

"Bet they never had a letter from a tree before," he said aloud, as if addressing the semi-circular sun on the eastern horizon.

People might actually pay attention. He decided that his plan was solid, but he had to keep it quiet in case Mom or Dad put the kibosh on it. What if they got upset? Well, in that case he'd just pretend he didn't think he needed permission. Besides, every week the newspaper said that readers were welcome to send letters. He was a reader, even if he was only a kid.

Now that Jared knew what to do, he struggled with what to say, and how to say it. The letter had to be good, if it sounded stupid or boring, the newspaper might not even print it.

After breakfast he took his scribbler and fishing rod down to the creek. He left the rod lying beside him unused while he thought. Each time he began he couldn't get the right words and would crumple the sheet. Finally, after three false starts he hit on something promising. The letter read:

Dear Mr. Newspaper Editor,

My name is Max. I'm an old Maple tree and I have lived on Brandywine Road long before any of you people were around. Maybe a hundred years or more. I am in good shape and I planned to be around for a lot more years but now they're planning to cut me down to make the road wider.

My friend, Jared, is helping me write this letter. Now, I don't think it's right that you'd treat an old member of the town this way. I don't think it's asking too much for you to move your roadway a little so that I'll still be around for a long time.

Yours sincerely.

Max the Maple Tree

He read the letter over twice. He liked it. He dashed home to stow his fishing rod, and fetched his bike. He paused to yank open the screen door.

"Mom, I'm going for a ride on my bike. Back in half an hour." The door slammed shut.

"Well, young fellow," the smiling man with the grey moustache and smouldering pipe said as he took the envelope from Jared, "We don't receive many letters from readers your age."

"Actually, I'm delivering it for a friend of mine."

"Oh! And why didn't your friend bring it in himself?" The man's eyes narrowed, and he stared down his nose at the boy.

"Well sir, my friend can't come in because, well…he's a *tree.*"

Jared knew that sounded stupid.

The man's face relaxed. "I see." He placed a hand over his mouth.

The man sat down at his desk and opened the envelope with a fancy knife.

"A note from a tree is it?" As the man perused the letter, he raised his eyebrows a couple of times. When he finished reading, he placed the letter in a bin on the desk. Jared noticed the sign on the bin – Cleared for typesetting.

"Max the tree is lucky to have a friend like you, Jared. I think we can put your letter in the paper; maybe even a picture of you and Max as well."

Jared smiled so wide he thought his face would hurt.

"WOW. Thanks Mister!"

As Jared pedaled home, his mind spun. What should he tell Mom and Dad? He didn't have much time to decide. The man said the photographer would come out later today. Although he was bursting to tell someone, he decided to keep quiet. If Mom found out too early, she might cancel the whole thing. He didn't even tell Derek, although Derek would have "crossed his heart." Glancing at his watch, he saw the hands already showed 2 o'clock. Everyone would know soon enough. He satisfied himself by going outside to whisper to the Maple.

"Don't worry, Max; I've got a plan." He returned to the recreation room and tried to read his Hardy Boys book. A short time later, the front doorbell rang. He dropped the book and tiptoed up the stairs, then held on to the banister and listened through the door to the kitchen to Mom's words filtering from the front door.

"Yes, Jared is at home. May I inquire who you are?"

Jared stepped into the kitchen and poked his head around the corner into the living room. He could see the back of his mother at the door and part of a figure facing her.

"S'cuse me, ma'am. Name's Clancy Jacobs, photographer for the Beacon *Post*." He flashed his press pass.

"I've come to take a picture of your son."

"What on earth for?"

"Well, they tell me your son wrote a fine letter to the editor about a tree in the way of construction at the front of your house."

"Oh, the *tree*." Mom stood back. "Please come in, Mr. Jacobs. *Jared*, come up here please."

"Right here Mom." Jared stepped into the room and looked at the photographer who grasped a large camera by the handle of its enormous flash unit. "Oh, hi. Are you the guy from the paper?"

"Yes, I'm Clancy Jacobs. Nice to meet you, Jared." The man removed the thumb of his free hand from the camera strap crisscrossing his chest and reached out to shake Jared's hand.

"Jared," Mom asked. "Did you write a letter to the paper about the Maple tree?"

Mom was asking one of those questions where the answer seems obvious but adults asked them anyway.

"Had to, Mom. They can't chop down Max."

"Max?"

"Ah, well, I kind of made up a name for the tree."

"Oh I *see*." Elizabeth tried to restrain her giggle. "Alright then, I guess Mr. Jacobs may take your picture, but we may need to discuss this matter further when your dad gets home."

"O.K." Talks were nothin'. He could handle them.

"Stand a little to the left, son – you've got a hydro pole coming out of your head." The photographer chuckled.

Derek, Robby and Don watched from the sideline with Mom Clarkson as Jared posed by Max. Jared had an idea.

"Hey Mister. Can my brother and my friends get in the picture, too?"

"Why not? I need a few shots anyway."

"C'mere you guys." Jared waved them in. "How 'bout my Mom, too?"

"No thank *you*, Jared." Mom said. "I don't need my picture in the paper. My hair is a mess, and everybody will be surprised enough seeing you guys."

The kids crowded in around the Maple with Don and Robby crouching down in front. Derek and Jared hugged opposite sides of the tree.

Later that week when the *Post* hit the streets, Jared was pleased by the positive reaction to the story. Mrs. Vickers praised him for his creativity. Alice was excited for him. Only Walter snickered. Most everyone's reaction was "Hey I saw you guys in the paper." They were featured on the front page, along with Jared's letter. An editorial on page two appealed to the town fathers to enact by-laws to identify and protect the town's large trees and heritage buildings and it praised Jared's initiative.

"Either we act now to protect our heritage, or we are certain to lose it by degrees. We should be grateful for this young man's interest in preservation," the editor wrote.

Jared was so excited that he collected copies of the paper from the neighbours and glued the front and second pages into his scrapbook, along with his hockey cards and the information about President Kennedy's funeral.

Now for sure, the Clarkson's couldn't quite decide whether to be proud of Jared or upset. James gravitated more towards the latter after a television news crew showed up from Toronto to interview Jared. James, a low-key fellow, loathed 'fuss' of any kind.

For Jared, there wasn't much choice.

It seemed that 'fuss' of some sort or other found him at every turn.

Chapter Twenty-nine

Three years hence, Jared had evolved from childhood into that netherworld of adolescence. His voice and body were changing, and while in some ways he felt more certain about some things (even confident about certain things such as his writing), in other ways he felt more confused than ever. Just when it seems you have things figured out in life, everything changes.

Robby's dad lost his job, and his new position relocated the family to Windsor. Jared felt sad about this and knew he'd probably never see Robby and Don again.

Jared also knew he would never see his real mother again, and although sometimes this made him feel sad and curious, he kept this sadness, as he did most everything else, private. He had little knowledge, and no memory, of his mother and the first fitful period of his life. He wondered if she thought of him the way he speculated about her, especially when his birthday came around.

Maybe he had more brothers or sisters, maybe they had walked right past one another in Toronto without even knowing it?

At least the world hadn't blown up, and he was grateful for that.

Derek kept getting on his nerves, always wanting to hang around, or asking him to do kid stuff. Jared's teenaged interests were different. Now he spent hours listening to top thirty songs on CHUM and CKEY radio with his transistor radio, or playing 45 rpm records from his own collection.

One Christmas he received a record player that he promptly deconstructed and reused the parts to design his own 'hi-fi' inside a round wooden cheese box. He ran speaker wire out to the corner of his room and pretended it was stereo. Dad was annoyed, but Mom thought his invention quite clever.

Rock music became just about everything to Jared. Every Saturday he'd walk or ride his bike to the music shop on Beacon's main street to pick up the latest CHUM chart and drool over LPs and 45s he wanted, but knew he could never afford. LPs cost five dollars, but they might as well cost fifty. There was just so much music available. He'd just manage to obtain one or two singles he really liked, then some new song would be released and he'd be frustrated all over again.

After reviewing the status of his favourite song's position on the CHUM chart, he remained downtown with friends at the pool hall, or perhaps the café if he had money for a cherry-coke and fries, or even a quarter for the jukebox.

The best thing in Jared's mind about being fourteen was that finally he was in high school.

In the first few weeks of high school, Jared noticed that a lot had changed since last spring – especially the girls. Or was it that he just noticed how the girls were looking differently at the guys. He came across groups of girls talking in the hallway sneaking peeks at some good-looking guy, then talking and giggling. The guys in the locker room weren't much different. They discussed the girls whose breasts wouldn't stop growing, or those unfortunate ones whose bloom had stalled shortly after it began.

One thing Jared appreciated was that for some reason, kids in high school tended not to notice the mark on his face. Still, if other kids seemed less attentive to that, Jared himself felt even more self-conscious. He worried no girl would ever want to go out with him. Sometimes he wished he was a girl; then at least he might cover the damn thing with makeup.

He missed Alice and hadn't talked to her for nearly a year since she'd gone away to a boarding school. If she were at his school he could ask her to the school dances and needn't worry that she might refuse, or laugh at him for asking.

He volunteered in the school library, checking out and re-shelving books since he spent a lot of time there anyway. He loved books, and working in the library gave him something to do. He had first choice of any new titles that came in, and naturally he didn't collect fines when he returned his own books late. He also worked one night a week after school, helping one of the teachers, Mr. Zabowi, in the science Lab. This gave him access to the supplies, and when Mr. Zabowi wasn't around, Jared conducted his own 'experiments' such as tossing elemental sodium into the sink, turning on the tap and watching the chemical dance. Jared liked Mr. Zabowi because he was an easy-going kind man, quite unlike the jerk who was Jared's own science teacher. That jerk went to the same Church as the Clarkson's, and seemed to think this fact gave him license to discipline Jared as he pleased. He yelled a lot, and once he kicked Jared's ass up the aisle to the garbage can for chewing gum. To be fair, he had warned Jared, but Jared had a bad memory for stuff like that. Besides, science period was right after lunch.

Overall, Jared enjoyed being in high school, especially because he met older guys who had an encyclopedic knowledge of rock music. Some of these guys had failed, or left school and returned. Several wore beards and had long hair; Jared thought them cool. These guys took a liking to Jared and watched out for him.

One guy, Mike, was a musician who played acoustic guitar. He introduced Jared to Dylan, Phil Ochs, and Joni Mitchell. Mike's bedroom at home was a teenager's dream because his parents let him do mostly what he liked with it. Mike had turned the walls and ceiling into a canvas for his artwork and graffiti. He even had drawn an eye on the ceiling with the inscription, *No I won't stop looking down.* In the rest of the room, Mike hung psychedelic posters and sketches of rock stars. A black light provided a psychedelic ambiance at night.

Another older guy, Barlow, was in Grade Eleven. He wore black leathers and rode a chopper he had built himself. The guy looked like he could break you in half if he wanted to, but in fact he was a gentle soul who eventually became a kindergarten teacher. That's not to say Barlow was a pushover. He could be tough as nails when he had to be such as the time he went to bat for Jared. A guy in gym class, fed up with Jared's silliness and endless punning, decided to punch him out. Barlow found Jared crying under a stairwell.

"What happened?" After hearing the story he promptly located the bully in the locker room and took a sizeable round out of him. The guy never bothered Jared again.

Jared felt grateful to Barlow and others who looked out for him, but he regretted being such a weakling. He decided then and there that if he ever had kids of his own, he'd make damn sure they could handle themselves in a fight.

Chapter Thirty

Besides listening to music and reading much of the time, Jared continued to write. He joined the school paper and by Grade Ten was already the editor. He found himself in hot water when he editorialized regarding how school was run. He hated the fact that many of the teachers insisted that students move single file down the hallways between classes, and wouldn't allow kids to stop for a drink of water, or to stop by their lockers to switch books. When he suggested that based on the way they ran the school, the principal and vice principal must have trained in Hitler's army, they were far from amused.

Mr. Duvall, the English teacher who was supposed to supervise the paper, shared the hot water over that one. In his second year of teaching, rumour was that he had graduated from U.C.L.A., had burned his Vietnam draft card, then fled to Canada. Mr. Duvall liked Jared and commiserated with what he called his "antiestablishmentarianism," but after this incident he suggested Jared "choose his issues more carefully, and save his ammunition for really important things." Jared liked him.

One afternoon Mr. Duvall called to Jared from down the hallway.

"Can you come and see me after school, Jared?"

Jared wondered all day what was up.

"Trouble with the paper?" Jared inquired. He hoped not.

"No, no. Nothing like that." Mr. Duvall reassured him. "I want to let you know I'm really enjoying reading your essays and stories. You write well for a guy in Grade 10. Some of your stuff is better than the Grade 13s."

Jared could feel his face flush. "Ah, well thanks, Mr. Duvall."

"You know that the new high school is nearly finished; it's opening next term."

"Uh huh."

"Well, the board has approved special funding for some special arts classes in the new school. I was wondering if you might be interested?"

"But I can't draw or paint."

Mr. Duvall laughed. "Neither can I, but there's more to the arts than those things. Like writing, for instance, and you know I think you're a very good writer. You'd be able to spend more time with writing and things you really enjoy and get marks for it. Interested?"

Jared was hesitant. "I don't know about going to a different school."

"I know the thought of changing schools can be hard, but I'd like you to think about it. Talk it over with your parents. I think you'd like being with other talented kids like yourself."

"Alright, I'll think about it. Are we done now? I have to get to the science room."

"Sure. Oh, just one other thing. This last story you wrote. It's good, but kind of dark. Bad stuff doesn't have to happen every time, you know."

"Yeah, my Mom and dad always are bugging me to write something 'nice.' I guess I just write what comes out."

Chapter Thirty-one

The end of Jared's 15th year, and the start of his 16th, was an exceptionally cool time. Jared did apply to the new arts school, was accepted and he started right after Christmas break. He felt awkward his first day standing alone beside his locker. A tall guy with long blonde hair approached the locker beside him.

"Didn't see a red notebook lying around here did you?"

Jared pulled it from his binder. "You mean this one? It was on the floor. I was going to take it to the office."

"Yeah that's it. Whew, thanks a lot. I'm Clarence."

"I know, I saw your name on the book. I'm Jared. "

Clarence noted Jared's writing folder with pages bulging with papers hanging out the edges.

"You a writer?"

"Sort of. How 'bout you?"

"I'm an artist. You know Jared, just tell people you *are* a writer. If you don't believe it, nobody else will either. I'd like to read some of your stuff sometime."

"Yeah sure, if you let me see some of your art. "

From that moment on they were friends.

Jared thought Clarence was an amazing artist, even if his themes tended towards a style one might call "adolescent morbid." Lots of skulls, blood and gore.

"All of it well *executed*," Jared punned. Clarence groaned.

The other neat thing was that Clarence's dad worked in the entertainment booking industry and had taught Clarence the business. Clarence was already making money hiring Ontario groups such as Grant Smith and the Power for dances in the local town hall. He let a few kids in free in exchange for their help running the events. One day, when somebody bowed out at the last minute, Clarence asked Jared if he'd like to help.

"Sure, of course!"

Now, Jared knew he would have to sweet talk his parents. He knew they considered dances as tools of Satan, although to be fair, his parents had lightened up somewhat. Indeed, to Jared's surprise Mom and Dad agreed to let him participate. Jared decided it was because of Clarence's special knack with people. Everyone liked him.

"God knows what is in people's hearts," Mom often said, and although she'd never admit it, Jared thought she understood that all the good people in the world didn't necessarily attend Church.

Anyway, it was Clarence who laid first toke on Jared.

That particular milestone happened one warm spring evening. Clarence pulled his red VW bug up the Clarkson's drive as Jared whipped a Superball off the sidewalk and bounced it over the roof of the house to Derek waiting in the back yard.

"Hey Clarence, what's happening?"

Clarence grinned. "Want to go for a spin?"

"Sure! Lemme ask."

They went into the house where Mom busied herself rolling out pastry dough on a breadboard. She smiled at them.

"Hello Mrs. Clarkson." Clarence said

"Hello Clarence."

"Another great pie in the works?"

"Yes. Are you saying that because you'd like some?" Mom teased.

"Well, I wouldn't refuse a piece," he confessed. Jared interrupted their banter.

"Can I go out with Clarence awhile? "

"And where might you gentlemen be going?"

"Just out for a coke."

"Homework done?"

"Yes." It was a lie, but a little one. Although his homework wasn't *actually* done, Jared planned to get up early tomorrow to get it done. Knowing when he'd get it done was almost the same thing to Jared as having it done.

"Alright, but be home by ten; it's a school night."

"No problem. Bye Mom."

Shortly Clarence and Jared bombed down Mill Street, with *White Rabbit* blasting from the car radio. Clarence glanced at Jared.

"Wanna get high?"

"Ah, sure." They were heading out of town.

"Where we goin' Clarence?"

Clarence pulled a tiny foil package out of his shirt and showed it to him. "To get high."

"Ah. Whaddya mean?" Well, Jared sort of knew what Clarence meant, but not really. His knowledge of such things, up to that point, was strictly theoretical.

"It's hash. Take a look, but don't drop it. It's Indian black."

Hmm, O.K., hash. Jared had heard of it, but had never actually seen it before. "What is 'hash' Clarence?

"Incense of the Gods." Jared looked puzzled.

"Hashish is concentrated marijuana. You smoke a tiny bit of it off a cigarette or in a pipe." Clarence pulled a Du Maurier from the orange package on the VW's dash, then began singing along with the Airplane,

"...Re*mem*ber, what the dormouse said – Feed your head." He used the fag as a pointer in the air to punctuate the song's beat.

When the song ended he popped the cigarette into the corner of his mouth and offered the pack to Jared.

"Smoke?"

"Uh . . . Sure. Thanks." Jared took the cigarette and pushed in the lighter.

"I'm going to find a quiet side road where we can get stoned without interruption." Clarence looked over at Jared sitting in silence beside him.

"You *do* want to get stoned, don't ya, Clark'?"

"Why not?" Jared replied. To be truthful, he wasn't sure at all, but he figured that if Clarence had tried this stuff, it must be alright. Besides, he might never get another chance.

The punchbuggy slid about on the gravel as Clarence

accelerated down a farming sideroad. The breeze carried the smell of fresh manure through the open car windows. Jared puffed like crazy on his cigarette but tried not to inhale too much. He smoked once in awhile, but still wasn't used to it. He tried not to cough.

Clarence suddenly geared down, and brought the car lurching to a stop at the side of the road.

"Ever try this stuff before?"

Jared shook his head.

"Well, first time for everything, eh?"

Clarence carefully placed the small foil package onto a *Hot Rod* magazine he had spread on his lap, then opened the smallest blade in his pocket knife to shave off a flake of the sticky substance. Jared watched the process with amazement. He'd never seen hashish before, or even marijuana for that matter. From its appearance, he could see why people sometimes referred to it as "shit."

Clarence pressed in the cigarette lighter and gave him instructions.

"Get ready to inhale as soon as it starts to burn."

When the cigarette lighter popped, Clarence yanked it from its place and held it vertically. He dropped the flake of hash directly onto the red hot element and almost immediately the substance glowed, then exploded in a puff of smoke. The smell was potent, exotic, and instantly permeated the car. It was one of those odours you tasted as much as smelled.

"Just breathe it in, then hold it in your lungs as long as you can. You're really gonna' like this, Jared."

Jared did as instructed, but wondered how long he had to hold his breath. He held it for what seemed a long time, but except for his lungs feeling as if they might soon explode, he didn't notice anything much. He exhaled and Clarence reloaded.

"Are you going to have some now?" Jared asked. He didn't

know if they were supposed to take turns or what.

"I'll have some in a minute; this next one's for you. I already had a few tokes earlier. Ready now?"

Clarence already stoned? Maybe that explained why he seemed kind of strange, like singing along in the car. Jared hadn't seen him do that before. Clarence held the lighter close to Jared's face just as the smoke rose in a burst.

"Now."

Jared tried to suck in as much of the smoke as possible, but he took in too much, and the resulting irritation in his throat and lungs caused him to cough.

"Don't cough; you'll blow your toke." Clarence barked. "Hold it as long as you can. Cough *later*."

Easy for you to say, Jared thought. He was turning purple trying to stifle himself.

"O.K. O.K. You can breathe now." Clarence howled with laughter when Jared exhaled like a bursting balloon.

"Hey, don't spit on my car." Clarence pretended to make a big deal of wiping off the dash with his sleeve. "How ya feel?"

Jared looked over and saw a grin across Clarence's face that almost connected his ears. Jared felt a little dizzy, but that was about it. Maybe this stuff wouldn't work for him. Just his luck!

"Well, how is it?"

"Nothing much, really."

Clarence appeared untroubled, "Just wait a few minutes... the stuff creeps." He fired a toke for himself, then cranked the bug's starter.

"Let's head over to the store by the lake and get a pop."

"Whatever you say." The cigarette and the tokes had left

172

Jared's throat raw.

The store by the lake was one of those clapboard ones like those in cottage country. A rusty metal *Coke* sign, with general store written below, was nailed on a post by the front door and appeared near the end of it's useful life after years of exposure to the elements. The store's large front window, comprised of many small panes of glass, was filthy.

Clarence parked, then Jared opened his car door. He felt as if he floated from the car, then he burst out laughing at the sight of an ancient Sky Chief gas pump. It reminded him of that silly joke about aliens making first contact at a gas station. The alien steps up to the gas pump and says, "Don't just stand there with your finger in your ear; take me to your leader." Well, it was damn funny at the time.

Inside the store Jared took what seemed ages to select a beverage; and finally elected for something totally weird, ginger beer. Clarence laughed at the choice, then took it and Jared's money to pay while Jared wandered around the store. He looked at the dusty beach toys and other stuff that had obviously languished on the shelves for years. He examined a plastic model kit of Ratfink on a skateboard and considered buying it, but put it back on the shelf. Buying stuff in this headspace might not be the wisest idea.

Jared felt as if they had been in the store for a long time, although later Clarence insisted it was only a few minutes. Anyway, next thing he knew, Jared heard the VW's horn blasting. He barely recalled leaving the store, but shortly was sitting in the front seat of the VW; or so he thought. Clarence was there beside him, but strangely seemed rather far away.

Clarence looked at him and nodded,

"All set Jared?"

"Yeah, lets go."

Clarence put the car in gear, let out the clutch and the car bolted backwards, disappearing from Jared's sight and leaving him sitting there. A moment later, Clarence roared back into the parking spot; laughing like hell.

It was one of those weird things that only happened when you were stoned.

While they were in the store, an *identical* VW had pulled up beside their car. Not noticing, Jared had climbed into the wrong one.

Realizing his error, Jared leapt in embarrassed panic from the car. As soon as he emerged, and understood how damn funny the whole situation was, he began to belly laugh. He was sure he hadn't laughed like this in a long time; perhaps never. He laughed so hard he had to hold onto the car to support himself as he made his way round to join Clarence.

"Good shit, eh?" Clarence smiled.

"I guess so, I guess so."

"You *guess* so. What the hell does *that* mean?"

But Jared didn't reply. He slammed the car door, settled back in his seat and closed his eyes. In his mind he watched a million coloured lights flashing, then a multitude of brilliant blue cubes rotating in harmony with the music on the car's radio.

"Waddya really think, Clark'?" Clarence shouted over the engine noise.

"Fuckin' A, Clarence." Jared opened his eyes and gave two thumbs up. "This stuff is cool." The words seemed to echo in his head before they emerged.

As they rode back to town, some of Jared's favourite songs played on the car radio.

"It's three in a row on Ten-Five-O." Bob MacAdorey, the CHUM radio jock crooned. The songs included *Turn Turn Turn*, *Light My Fire*, and *Opportunity*, a track laid down by Toronto's premier band, Mandela Crusade.

"We still have an hour before you have to be home, Jared. Let's check out the Focus and see who's there."

"Whatever you say Clare'."

The Focus was a restaurant in Beacon where teenagers liked to sit around in groups, sharing large plates of fries and gravy, or blowing smoke from their cigarettes through drinking straws into cherry cokes to make 'Devil's brew.' Going there was definitely a good idea; Jared was having too much fun, and felt too strange to go home. One thing seemed rather odd though; despite Mom's usual fantastic dinner, Jared was suddenly famished.

Chapter Thirty-two

Regardless of any initial apprehensions about getting stoned, smoking dope soon became a preoccupation for Jared, and an expensive one at that. Some mornings he smoked up on the way to school as he took the short cut across the farm fields.

He had the idea that being stoned might add to his endurance in Phys Ed class; it didn't. It proved more useful igniting his imagination during English class. He hated stupid questions by teachers, and sometimes he'd inject stupid answers. An example was the day Mr. Litsiver, his English teacher, read aloud from an English novel.

"The sailor admired the buttresses." The teacher stopped reading to ask, "What's a buttress?"

Annoyed by the "stupid Socratic," Jared fixed a serious expression onto his face, and raised his arm.

"Jared. What's a buttress?"

"A lady butler."

The class erupted in laughter, but his serious demeanour had taken in the class. People thought he *was* serious.

Other times, he would amaze the class, and the teacher with his interpretations of certain literary passages. Usually, however, he hoped nobody would ask him to repeat it.

One thing was for certain, being stoned did absolutely nothing for his performance in Math class. The requisite care and concentration of numerical logic posed a problem to Jared at the best of times. Under the influence, well, mathematical logic seemed to elude him altogether. He'd struggled every year in Math, each year falling further behind in comprehension and basics. By high school it seemed that if he passed at all, it was only fifty percent. Indeed, if he received a passing grade at all, Jared suspected it was primarily because the Math teacher had considered the dire consequence of Jared failing and being in his class again next year.

Often Jared simply gave up trying to understand Math and spent class time rocking back in his chair, talking to friends, or seizing opportunities for one-liners and puns that brought him warnings, or ejections into the hall.

He came up with inventive means to wreak havoc in Math class. His favourite was his birdcall routine. Clarence had taught him several birdcalls, and at this Jared was a quick study. While the teacher's back was turned, he'd make birdcalls that became louder each time. Finally, the teacher would stare outside with exasperation and walk over and slam the window shut. Naturally, the class would erupt in laughter.

That prank worked well in Math, but didn't fly, so to speak, in Geography. It turned out the Geography teacher's hobby was Ornithology. He caught on immediately and arranged for a certain 'bird brain' to report for the next week to his 'cage' after school.

Despite his distaste for Math, Jared became obsessed with a particular numbers problem of consuming interest, that being the shortage of coin to buy 'smoke'. Lids didn't last very long when you smoked every day, and his job in the lab only earned pocket change.

One Sunday morning in Church he contemplated this problem while fidgeting during one of Pastor Ronson's more annoying sermons.

"Yea brethren, the scientists would have you believe that Evolution is a fact. The truth is that Evolution is not a fact at all, but the musings of Godless men who would remove the creator from his place . . ." And blah blah blah. Ronson was hot. Jared bristled and fought the desire to raise his hand and challenge his stupidity. It disgusted him that people could believe that everything in the Bible was literally true. He thought it was too bad the world *wasn't* flat. If it were, he'd put people like Ronson on a raft and hope they sailed off the edge.

Anyway, that Sunday morning Jared decided that from now on the Church would be taxed, and he appointed himself the tax collector. The scam worked like this.

Unlike his foster son, James Clarkson had a great facility for numbers. At some point the Church had decided that James's 'ministry' would be to serve as the Church treasurer and bookkeeper. Every Sunday James lugged a beat-up brown leather case with straps and buckles to Church. For some reason, that case spooked Jared. Maybe it was because of its resemblance to the ones Nazi officers carried around in the movies. Anyway, Dad being the Church treasurer gave Jared the means and the opportunity. He already had the motive.

The main reason he got away with it was that although most people put their donations in sealed envelopes to obtain a tax receipts at the end of the year, a surprising number of people simply dropped cash and coins in the offering. Dad grumbled about having to roll those coins by hand, so Jared simply offered to help with this and *voila*; the fox was in the hen house.

The plan worked great. Indeed, like a fine motorcycle the thing was perfect - until the collision.

Chapter Thirty-three

"Jared, would you help me with this?" Miss Merkley struggled with a piece of balky stage scenery. Only a week remained until the annual school variety show.

"Sure." Jared held the gangly palm tree while she secured it in place.

"There. That's got it. Thanks Jared, you've been a great help."

"Yer welcome."

Mrs. Merkley paused from fixing the scenery.

"How's your skit coming along?" She wiped her hands together. "Mr. Litsiver says that you have a great idea in the works."

"I haven't quite finished writing it, but it's almost done."

"What's it about? Something to do with Vietnam?"

"Yeah. It's an anti-war thing."

The teacher turned to a girl standing nearby who was in Jared's class.

"Have you heard Jared's skit, Susan?"

"No, but I bet it's going to be great."

Jared blushed, "Don't know about great, but thanks. I still have a few things to work out."

"You'll figure it out; you always do." She smiled, then glanced at her watch. "Oops gotta go. My bus will be here in a few minutes. See you tomorrow."

"Bye, Susan."

Jared watched her walk out of the gymnasium, her dark straight hair gleaming down her back. Her graceful movement, outlined by her pink cotton dress was appealing. Susan was in several of his classes and Jared sometimes talked with her. He knew she liked him; actually lots of the girls liked him, but he always wondered if any of them could ever like him in that *other* sense of the word. Terribly self-conscious, he never found out.

In the game of love, Jared remained in the dugout. He never got up to bat let alone first base. For some reason, any time he tried to get up his nerve to ask one of them out, all he could think of was how stupid he might feel if she laughed at him, or told him to get lost. And what if she told other people?

Privately, he struggled with the reality that he wouldn't want to go out with a girl who was marked like himself. This realization made him uncomfortable and angry. He couldn't help it if he liked the pretty girls the same as anyone else, and part of him assumed that the girls must feel likewise. At school dances he stood around and listened to the music. Sometimes he helped organize the dances and tried to avoid paying too much attention to Clarence who always was out on the dance floor with some cute babe. Clarence made the whole thing seem so easy, or maybe the girls made it easy for him. Yeah, that was it. Clarence had it *made*! Pretty girls would hang 'round him, flashing their eyes, and asking him to dance. Watching him, Jared sometimes felt envy, even jealousy, and then guilt. Why shouldn't Clare' have fun with the girls? Jared hated feeling jealous, but sometimes he just couldn't help it.

Jared turned away from his feelings of angst, and continued lettering the sign he would carry on stage during his skit. The large sign had a different message on each side. Because he believed in the importance of the anti-war message, he needed to make sure that the words were visible from the back of the gym. Sign making, with its endless stenciling and colouring was tedious. It had to be done on time, and it had to be done right.

"If you want things done properly, do them yourself," Dad often said. Working as the school's newspaper editor had taught Jared this truth, the hard way. Sometimes he'd assign stories to people who didn't really care that much about them. Then either the job didn't get done at all, or it was done badly. He was particular about the papers quality and often did much of the work himself.

It took him two days to finish the sign for his skit. It was plain, but readable from a distance and that was the main thing. If he wanted fancy, he'd have to ask Clarence, or one of the other art students, but they were busy painting sets and building props.

One afternoon, while walking to his next class, Jared heard the chime that preceded overhead announcements. "Would Jared Clarkson please report to the office."

Jared changed direction and wondered why he was being summoned. Maybe he'd missed too many classes getting ready for the variety show?

The high school office was a large open space where two harassed secretaries scrambled to answer phones, type, mimeograph papers, and handle walk-in inquiries. As he entered the office, one of the secretaries, struggling with a balky duplicating job, gave a look as if to say, "What do *you* want?"

"I'm Jared Clarkson. They paged me to come down here." "Yes, come in. Mr. Jollico is waiting." She flipped up the countertop to admit him behind the desk, and pointed to the principal's office. Jared didn't need direction.

"Ah, Mr. Clarkson, come in, come in," the principal said. Jared's English teacher Mr. Litsiver was there as well. "We have been discussing your skit for the variety show." The sign Jared had made for his skit leaned against the wall.

"Clarkson, I understand you have written a political skit for the variety show; is that true?" The principal said.

"Yeah, something wrong with that?" You fat slob, Jared thought. The principal took a breath.

"Well, yes and no, Clarkson. Now understand I'm pleased to see our students interested in what's going on the world, but the purpose of this variety show is to entertain."

"Oh, my skit's very entertaining . . ."

"Look Clarkson, I haven't seen your script, but I've heard about you from your previous school, and we've discussed things you've written in the school paper from time to time." The principal took another deep breath. "Within the school itself, I'm inclined to be lenient, but when it comes to something for the public such as the variety show, well, I cannot permit the show to become a platform for political views. I am afraid I must insist that you think of something else to do for the show."

Jared tried to remain cool.

"I just spent two days working on this sign. Can't you at least read my script?"

"No. Mr. Litsiver has told me enough. I'm afraid the subject is closed."

"Like your mind?" Jared blurted. Shit, did I *really* say that?

The principal leaned forward in his chair, placed his elbows on his desk and clasped his hands together.

"I am going to pretend I didn't hear that, Mr. Clarkson. I don't expect you to like my decision, but I do expect you to abide by it. Now, I'd suggest you leave before you say something that I won't overlook."

As he left, Jared snatched the sign and tore it in half. He threw it on the floor and banged the principal's door behind him. He ignored the two secretaries who followed him with their eyes as he stormed past.

At the supper table that night, Jared stared down at his plate. He moved chunks of meat and potatoes around but didn't open his mouth to either eat or say anything.

"All set for the variety show?" Dad asked.

Jared looked up.

"No, I'm not going,"

"How come?" Derek asked. "I thought you were working on a neat skit."

"Not any more. Jollico put the kibosh on it."

"And why was that?" Mom asked.

"He says my skit is too political."

"Political? What does he mean by that?"

"It's an anti-war thing." Dad made a disapproving 'tsk' sound, and shook his head.

"Why can't you do a funny skit like the other students?" Mom asked. Jared looked disgusted.

"Forget it!" An awkward silence pervaded the rest of the meal. After wolfing a piece of apple pie he pushed back his chair, and went to his room where he worked up a front page for a special edition of the school paper. The headline read, '1984 arrives early.'

In his editorial Jared discussed the illusion of free speech for young people and predicted that not only would his comments be unwelcome, he doubted the principal would allow the paper to circulate. He decided also to say his good-bye as editor. He figured that the paper, at least in its current form, was finished.

Next day Mr. Litsiver appeared uneasy as he reviewed the copy.

"I think you know I can't print this."

Jared only scowled, accepted the copy, then walked away without comment.

After some thought, he deleted specific references to school, then stapled copies to the hydro poles just clear of school property.

Chapter Thirty-four

"*What* are you doing?"

Jared's neck cracked audibly as he looked up at mom. *Shit, this is it.* He hadn't heard Mom coming, now she'd caught him sitting on her bedroom floor.

Church money was in his hands, and beside him the collection bag lay open. Panic flashed through his body. He jumped to his feet and he shook as he tried to think of something to say. He had to think fast. Nothing much that he could say would change anything and it occurred to him that for once he hadn't prepared any lies should he be apprehended.

For as long as possible, he avoided Mom's face.

"Nothing. Well not *nothing.*"

"Well *what* then?"

Tell her that this was the first time. No, he wasn't saying that. The hurt in his Mom's face made Jared feel sick, sick of his lies and deceit, sick of himself.

"Stealing from the Church . . . from the Lord? How could you even *think* of such a thing?" She removed the money from his hand, put it back in the deposit bag, then carefully placed the deposit bag into James's briefcase.

Jared stood in silence. His face was hot and his stomach churned.

"What's the matter with you, Jared? You don't need for anything; why would you do something like this?"

When he failed to respond, she began to tremble, then weep. Watching her pain caused Jared to think of that verse in the Bible about the sins of the father being visited upon the children, except this time it was the reverse. After a few moments, she regained her composure.

"How long have you been doing this?" she demanded.

"A long time. Dunno, a few months."

"*Months?*" She held her hands to her ears as if she couldn't believe what she heard.

Jared moved away from her.

"How much money have you taken? What have you done with it?" She snapped.

Jared said nothing. Anything he said would be equally futile or disastrous.

"I'm *waiting*, mister. *Look* at me." She demanded.

He remained silent and continued staring down. On impulse, she gripped his chin and jerked his face towards her. At this, he grabbed her wrist and shoved her away. *Nobody* was *ever* putting their hands on him again.

"You get to your room, mister, and don't come out until you have some answers. Your Dad, the pastor, and I will be waiting for an explanation."

188

At the mention of the pastor, Jared exploded.

"To hell with the pastor. I'm *glad* I took the money."

Mom landed a ringing slap on his cheek.

"How dare you swear in this house, and about our pastor. *Who* do you think you are?"

Derek entered the room, glowered at Jared, then put his arm around Mom. Jared clenched his jaw and ran to his room.

He lay on his bed and punched the pillow. What a fuck-up I am. He kept repeating this in his mind. He seized the Gemini rocket model he had just completed building and dashed it to pieces on the floor.

Now he'd really done it. What was he to do now? Tell them he used the money to buy dope? They didn't even know he smoked cigarettes. Should have thought of that before, stupid. If he had thought of it before, he hadn't paid it much attention.

Only one course of action appeared open to him now. He had to leave, and he resolved to be gone before Dad got home.

He snatched his knapsack from the closet and began throwing things into it. Socks, underwear, some t-shirts, a sweatshirt. He took what little money he had in his top drawer. The knowledge of where he had gotten the money stung, but he had little choice. He wouldn't get far without money.

When finished packing, he tore a page from his notebook and wrote:

Dear Mom and Dad,

There isn't much point saying I'm sorry for what I've done. It won't fix anything and besides if I were truly sorry, I wouldn't have waited to be caught. I know I've always been a disappointment to you guys. I'm a disappointment to myself. I'm going away from here. I'm not sure where, or what I'll do, but I know it's the best thing for everyone. I can't stay here any longer.

Jared.

He unclipped the window screen and dropped his pack to the ground. He climbed out the window, jumped from the ledge to the patio, then after ensuring no one was around to see him, hurried through the neighbour's backyard, then started across the farmers field nearby.

An hour later, he arrived at the service centre on Highway 400.

Gotta call Clarence. He searched in his pocket to find a dime. The phone rang and rang until finally Clarence picked it up.

"Clare'."

"Hey there, Clark', glad you called. Want to go to the drive-in tonight?"

"No, I can't. Listen, I'm in a lot of trouble. Mom caught me stealing Church money. I'm taking off."

A diesel truck starting up nearby obliterated Clarence's reply. Jared was forced to set down his backpack and hold his hand over his ear.

"What did you say Clare'?"

"I said Church money? Are you *nuts*, Clark'? They can put you in jail for that." Jared hadn't considered that. It was another good reason he had to clear out.

"Where you going?"

"Not sure...I'll figure something out."

"You better figure fast, man. Listen, come on over here with me. The fossils are away for another two weeks."

"Thanks Clare', but I don't think so. That's the first place my parents or the cops would look for me."

"Well, whereabouts you headed? You must have some idea."

"I dunno…maybe Calgary. The paper says there are jobs in the oil industry." What he would actually do when he got there was a complete mystery; he'd have to figure it out as he went.

"How are you getting there?"

"Thumbing, I guess.' Jared's voice wavered as he continued in a loud whisper. 'I'm damn scared, Clarence. I've never been anywhere by myself."

"Got money?"

"A little."

"Jeezus, you can't take off without dough. Look, meet me at the Focus. I'll let you have what I can."

"No, I can't. I'm already at the service centre on the highway. They might be looking for me in town already."

"Alright. Let me think.' After a moment he continued. 'Stay there. I'll see you soon."

Jared hung up the phone. It was great that Clare" wanted to help, but this was Jared's own mess.

Some forty-five minutes later, Clarence finally showed up and the relief on Jared's face was palpable. He noticed that the back seat of the VW contained boxes of food and camping gear. Clarence stuck his head out the window and grinned.

"Hop in Clark'; I'm coming with you."

Astonishment filled Jared's expression.

"Why would you do that?"

"Why do ya think? 'Cause you can't go by yourself. Anyway, I've always wanted to go out west. I left my parents a note saying I'll be away until school. It'll be O.K. Dad said he didn't like the idea of me staying in the house by myself anyway. I brought the rest of the money they left for me to buy groceries and stuff. Whaddya say?"

Jared managed his first smile of the day.

"O.K. then, hop in." Clarence shoved the passenger door open and Jared climbed in.

Chapter Thirty-five

Until now, Jared had never been north of Bracebridge. The winding roads, granite outcrops, endless miles of forest and lakes were amazing. They'd been driving for several hours, and twilight's golden hues jiggling on the lake waters lent a certain calm to what he would recall forever as one of the worst days of his life.

"We better start thinking about stopping for the night,"Clarence said. "How 'bout we stop at the next cheap campground?"

"Sure." Jared didn't care where they stopped, or even *if* they stopped for that matter, because each mile carried him further from his troubles. Being with Clarence lent a sense of adventure that diluted his self-loathing.

Jared had thought many times about running away and now it had happened, although to be sure he hadn't much alternative. Still, when Jared thought about Mom and Dad and Derek wondering where he was, he felt guilty and sad, but that couldn't be his main concern now. He had to move forward. I'll send them a postcard in a few days to let them know I'm alright, he decided. Clarence turned off the road and into the driveway of a small campground.

"This place good? Whaddya think?" Jared read the words *Beaver Campground*. The words, made of white birch letters nailed and wired together, dangled precariously overhead across the driveway. Clarence pulled up to the small cottage with a sign on the door reading *Office*, where a tall man with a potbelly and a beer pulled himself out of a dilapidated Muskoka chair, and wandered over.

"Help you guys?"

"We need a campsite, any left?"

"Yeah, we have a couple left. It's four bucks a night – in advance." A look of suspicion swept across the man's face as if he had second thoughts. "You boys ain't planning to stay up all night makin' noise and causing trouble, I hope? If y'ar, I'm telling you right now. I'll boot your asses out of here whatever the time is, and they's no refunds."

"No problem," Clarence said. "We'll be quiet."

"How long you plannin' to stay?"

"Just tonight. We're driving out west."

"To Calgary." Jared added.

At the last part, the man reviewed the two of them, and the battered VW, then snorted as if that were the most ridiculous thing he'd heard all day. Clarence handed the man three dollar bills and a handful of silver.

"Four bucks exactly," Clarence said.

The guy stuffed the money in his pocket, then pointed to the campsite area. "Pull in over there, number twenty-three. And remember; no trouble, or yer outahere."

As soon as they were out of earshot, Clarence gave Jared a poke.

"Real asshole, eh?"

"Yeah, but we better do as he says." He'd had enough confrontation for one day.

It took them only a short time to set up the orange pup tent, and throw their sleeping bags inside.

"Ouch." Jared slapped his face. With the sun down, mosquitoes clacked their knives and forks in anticipation.

"Damn. Forgot the repellent," Clarence moaned. "Have to get some tomorrow. Let's get a fire going; smoke'll chase those suckers off."

The campground had an ample supply of firewood, and they found kindling and brush nearby in the woods. Soon they squatted beside a small, yet energetic campfire and Jared spooned pork and beans from the cook pot onto paper plates.

"Man this is great. I'm starving." They snatched pieces of bread out of the bag and dipped it into their beans.

After they'd stuffed themselves, Clarence rolled a joint.

"Are you sure it's a good idea to smoke here, Clarence?" Jared still felt nervous about the guy at the gate.

"It's fine. We'll stay downwind behind the car and the smoke will blow away. Nobody's gonna notice." He lit the joint with a burning twig from the fire.

Jared's anxiety evaporated with the enormous spliff and they spent the next few hours beside the fire, giggling, and checking out the roadmap to see how far they'd traveled. The night grew chilly and damp with a north breeze, and Jared pulled his jacket tighter around him. Finally he nodded off.

"Ready to call it a day?" Clarence asked.

"Yeah." They drifted into the darkness to pee in the woods, doused the fire, and shortly they were scrunched side by side in the pup tent.

"Clarence, do you think we'll really get to Calgary?"

"Sure we will. Anyway, I intend to have one hell of a good time trying."

Jared had been awake for a while, but didn't want to leave the comfort of his sleeping bag until nature's call absolutely demanded it. When Jared finally moved to extricate himself, Clarence woke up as well.

Jared tasted jungle mouth. Damn, he'd forgotten to brush his teeth last night. For his part, Clarence looked terrible. His long hair was sprawled all over the place, and he sounded grumpy.

"Had a bloody stone jabbing into my back all night." Clarence began massaging his neck after shoving his hair out of the way.

Jared decided to keep his distance, and busied himself building a fire and fetching water to boil. After setting the pot on the fire, he washed his face, then brushed his teeth camp style, swishing his toothbrush in a cup of water, then spitting the mess onto the grass.

Once cleaned up, he felt better. Now the water was boiling.

They made instant coffee and toasted slices of bread over the fire. Their lack of patience meant that one half of the bread was burnt, but no matter; they slathered enough jam and peanut butter to cover the taste. With each bite, they had to hold the sandwich away from themselves to avoid the mess oozing out the sides. Watching each other eat, and trying not to wear the glop, provided their first laugh of the day.

"Any milk for the coffee?" Jared asked.

"No," Clarence snapped, "Couldn't think of *everything* in twenty minutes."

Jared remained silent until Clarence gave him a poke.

"Don't be so serious Clark'. It's no big deal."

Jared smiled weakly. Although they've been on the road for less than twenty-four hours, it seemed much longer, and Jared worried that Clarence was already tired of him.

Chapter Thirty-six

It was 1967, the summer of love, and young people were out on the road to celebrate Canada's hundredth birthday. As they drove north, Jared and Clarence passed several sets of these hitchhikers. They waved hello and flashed peace signs back at them. They skipped paired hitchhikers but offered rides to loners.

One radio station after another faded out, keeping Jared busy fiddling to find a rock station. The endless forest landscape slipped past them like some great herbivorous dream, and Jared nodded off. He awoke sometime later to the sound of gravel crunching beneath the wheels. Clarence was pulling over to pick up a young woman hitching alone at the side of the road.

Long blonde hair flowed underneath her large floppy black felt hat and a perfect smile shone from her clear tanned complexion. She toted a backpack, and a guitar with a daisy painted on its front.

"Hello dere you guy, tanks for stop-hing." She smiled as she seized her hat before a gust of wind blew it away. "How far you are going?"

As far as you'll let me, Jared thought with a smirk.

"Calgary," Clarence replied. "But we're flexible. Where you headed to?"

Jared heard Clarence and thought, whaddya mean *flexible*?

"I ham on my way to visit some friend I have met in Toronto. Dey are living on a little farm near to Fort Frances."

"Oh yeah, Fort Frances," Clarence said. 'I've seen that place on the map. Near the Manitoba border. It'll be crowded, but we'll give you a lift. Any extra coin you can spare for gas would be appreciated?"

"Well, dere is some money, but not much, or I would have taken ha bus."

"No sweat; we'll make do. Ah, I'm Clarence, and this is my buddy, Jared."

"Howdy." Jared waved at her.

"It's nice to meet you guy – I ham Melissa. Bin travellin' from Drummondville, Quebec since May."

Jared couldn't look at her or detect her scent on the breeze, without blushing. Some babes in this world ought to be cloned and Melissa was one of those. Clarence poked him in the ribs, and out of his daydream.

"How 'bout you give me a hand making some room here?"

The guys jammed as much of their own gear into the trunk of the VW as possible, then Clarence squeezed Melissa's stuff to one side in the back seat.

"You don't mind hopping in the back, do ya?" He whispered to Jared.

Jared did mind, but said nothing.

By late suppertime, they'd covered another hundred miles and had almost reached Thunder Bay. They decided to stop for the night and camp near a side road. Melissa prepared a mean stew with fresh stuff they'd picked up along the way. Afterwards, they sat around a campfire while Melissa sang songs and talked about her travels.

"Hexpo '67 was really neat. I was dere for a week. Hey, why you guy don't come and stay dere at the farm, too. My friend, I know dey won't mind. Dey don't get much visitor."

"Sounds good to me. Whaddya think Clark'?"

What could he say? Jared wasn't enthusiastic, but he wasn't surprised. Clarence and Melissa obviously were hitting it off.

"Well . . . I guess so."

Jared slept in the car that night so the giddy couple could share the tent. Jared wanted to feel happy for Clare's good luck with Melissa. However, after sitting alone in the car trying to sleep, and listening to giggles and laughing from the tent, Jared felt only envy. He'd never have a babe like that. Chicks like Melissa went for tall cool guys like Clarence, or jocks, not short guys with glasses, pimples, and large birthmarks on the side of their face.

He thought of successful guys on TV, guys like Dr. Kildare or The Saint. They all looked good. The only TV guy he looked like was Gilligan. When you are young, ugly is the worst thing.

Next morning after breakfast the three of them set off. When Clarence suggested they discuss travel plans, Jared was surprised, he'd figured the stopover at Rainbow Farm was a done deal.

"What do you know about this place where your friends live?" Clarence asked Melissa above the engine and wind noise.

"Just ha little farm in da country. I never been dere. I meet

Patsy and her brother, Byron, selling stuff they have make hon Yonge Street in Toronto. Dey make leather stuff, and candles – very nice. They make this belt I ham wearing. I was talking with them and they tell me dey have sold near all der stuff so I invite dem to stay at my friend's place. Den they invite me to visit dem sometime. I told them I ham coming soon out west and dey were so happy."

"Whaddya say Clark'? Shall we check out the farm?" Clarence asked.

"Guess." Jared's response was drawn and sullen.

Melissa turned around to look at him. Clarence glanced in the rear-view mirror.

"You *guess*. What the hell's *that* mean, Clark'?" Clarence asked. "How 'bout some positive waves here? It sounds cool; we don't have to stay if the place is a bummer." When Jared stayed silent, Clarence prompted. "Well?"

"Maybe you guys should just go alone." Jared gritted his teeth. "I'll hitch the rest of the way to Calgary."

Clarence pulled over to the side of the road and turned around.

"What the *hell* are you talking about Clark'? What's with you?"

"Nuthin'."

"Don't give me that nuthin' shit. Think about it. On your own without money. The cops will scoop you in a week and send you home. Is that what you want?"

"No, no, course not." Jared's mind spun. What the hell was going on? What *did* he want? Among all the piss and vinegar brewing, it was hard to tell.

"Well, what's it going to be?" Clarence asked. "Get it *together* Clark' or get *out* right here."

"Fuck off, Clarence!"

Melissa, quiet until now, intervened.

"Knock hit off. What's wrong wit you guy? I tot you har best friend. Make love not war, heh?"

Both guys looked at her, then each other, then started to laugh.

"That's right, make love, Jared," Clarence said. "And be sure to wear some flowers in your hair."

"Fuck off, Clarence." Jared repeated, this time with good humour.

"Look," Clarence said after a few minutes of silence. "We'll check out the farm for a couple of days and see how it is, then we'll get on our way, O.K.?"

Jared still felt skeptical and worried that somehow they wouldn't make it to Calgary. Still, if Clarence had made up his mind to stop, well he *was* in the driver's seat after all.

Some hours later, they knew they neared their destination, but they kept getting lost with Melissa's navigation. Jared had relinquished the job because reading the map with the car moving made him sick.

"I'll tell you one thing Melissa," Clarence said. "You are the coolest gal I've ever met, but you can't read a map to save your life."

Fortunately, Clarence had a sixth sense for direction, and late in the afternoon they finally arrived at the farm.

Rainbow Farm sat on the edge of a small creek that ran along the road for a bit, then meandered across the farm. Somehow the place looked more promising to Jared than he'd expected.

"Place looks cool," Clarence said.

Hope so, Jared thought. Cool or not, Jared wanted to get out of the car right away. He had a headache and his stomach had been upset all afternoon. At one point they stopped while he heaved at the side of the road.

Clarence drove up the lane and parked beside the little farmhouse nestled amid several large trees.

"Dere she is!" Melissa leapt from the car, leaving the door open, and began waving her hat and shouting, " Patsy."

The woman working in the garden with a hoe, looked up and shielded her eyes against the sun to see who was yelling.

"Melissa." The woman dropped her garden tool and the two women started running towards one another. When they met they held hands and spun each other about and hugged.

The guys walked over to join them.

"Melis'," the woman said. "I never thought you would actually come. I'm soooo glad to see you!"

"Told you I would come to visit. Oh, Patsy, dese guy are my friend, Clarence and Jared." She pointed to each of them in turn.

Jared tried to be polite but with his stomach churning, could only muster a faint smile and a wave.

"Hi there." First Patsy shook Clarence's hand, then turned to Jared and took his hand. "Hello, Jared. Nice ta meet cha."

She had a way that Jared found pleasant and warm. He felt embarrassed when he realized he still held her hand after what seemed a long time. As he went to pull his hand away, she gave it a squeeze. Clarence stood with his arm around Melissa's shoulder.

Patsy gave them a quick tour of the farm buildings.

"Byron will be so surprised to see you, Melissa. We still have a little work to finish up, and then we'll make supper. Why don't you guys relax for a bit; there's beer in the fridge if you like." Patsy began clapping gently. "It's so *great* you came, Melissa," and threw her arms around her again.

While the two women headed back to the garden, Jared and Clarence retrieved beers from the kitchen, then busied themselves unpacking their gear. Shortly, a very tall young man with a beard, and wearing a leather work-apron, emerged from the barn.

"Hi. I'm Byron. Can I give you guys a hand?" He offered an enormous hand to each of them to shake in turn.

Jared was fascinated with Byron's appearance. Guys with beards always seemed so much older, but Jared guessed from the beaded choker around his neck that the guy couldn't be that much older, maybe twenty-one. Byron admired Clare"s car.

"How's your Beetle run? I had one once. It ran great until we put the torch to it and made it into a dune buggy. My friend totaled it in the woods the first time out."

"That was pretty stupid," Jared blurted. God, what did I say that for? He could see Byron and Clarence looking at him as if he were crazy.

"I *doubt* the guy cracked it on purpose." Clarence commented, then resumed his conversation with Byron.

Embarrassed, as well as sick, Jared was happy to disappear. He wandered off to an old hand pump and worked up some cold water to soak his head, and take some ASA.. Drinking that beer was definitely a bad idea. He lay down on a swing hung between two Maples and closed his eyes to give the pills time to work.

After a late dinner, Jared returned to the backyard and sat on the swing. He still felt uncomfortable about what he'd said earlier to Byron; the two of them had sidestepped one another at supper.

Nevertheless, Jared liked the farm's tranquility. For maybe the first time in his life he noticed silence, broken only by the swish of branches and leaves rustling with the breeze. A guy might actually be able to do some serious thinking in a place like this, and Jared's thoughts turned homeward.

He missed home, but he'd have to get used to it; he was on his own now. Busy in his thoughts, Jared didn't hear Patsy approach from behind him.

"Hi Jared. Nice evening isn't it?" she asked.

"Oh, hi, Patsy. I really dig the quiet out here."

"Me too. I like the action when we visit Toronto or Van' to sell the stuff we make, but I love it here. Guess I'm the kind of person that needs lots of room."

"Well, you've certainly got lots of room here. It's a really neat place. Love your workshop in the barn."

"Thanks Jared, you're so nice. Byron and I spend a lot of time in there making stuff. I mostly make candles. I'll show you how to make a sand candle if you like."

"Sure, I'd like that." They spent the next few moments in comfortable silence, then Jared sensed Patsy looking at him with a concerned look.

"Something on your mind?" she asked.

"Ah, no, not really. Well maybe . . .but it's nothing I want to talk about right now . . . if that's alright."

"Sure, it's alright. Just let me know if you want to talk. I'm a good listener. Do you think you guys are going to stay here for awhile?"

"I really don't know what to say, Patsy. I mean I'm really enjoying it here and everything, but Clarence and I are headed to Calgary. We didn't plan to stop anywhere." But, even as he spoke, Jared found that the idea of spending more time with Patsy was becoming more attractive by the moment. She had a way of making him feel good, but at the same time kind of uncomfortable.

"We don't get many visitors at Rainbow Farm. It would be great if you and Clarence stayed for a little while." She leaned forward. "At least until Byron puts you to work."

They both laughed.

Jared liked Patsy. Despite her plain features, she had a great smile, brilliant green eyes and curly brown hair to her shoulders.

"Byron's making a campfire and Melissa's going to sing some songs. Shall we go along?" She asked.

'Yeah, sure, I'd like that."

They headed off together, Patsy's arm looped inside his.

Next morning, Jared was startled awake by one of the house cats walking across his chest. He groped for his glasses and then gave the offending feline a pat on the rump. He thought roosters were supposed to be the first ones up on the farm. He lay there remembering the fun they had last night singing songs around the campfire with Melissa and Byron on guitar, Patsy on flute, and Clarence rolling joints. Jared had rattled a tambourine. The last thing he recalled, he and Patsy were cuddling together on the chesterfield, listening to Joni Mitchell.

As he wiggled to pull on his jeans inside his sleeping bag, he could smell wonderful things coming from the kitchen. He was only half dressed when Patsy poked her face into the room.

"Oh, finally you're awake! I thought you were going to sleep all morning," she said, smiling. "It's already 7:30." She spied the cat beside him. " Prometheus wake you up? He hates anyone else to be asleep if he's up."

"I was getting up anyway. Hey, what smells so good?"

"Apple pancakes and Maple syrup. Hope you're hungry?

207

"I'm famished. Can I use the bathroom for a bit?"

" 'Natch, make yourself at home."

As he brushed his teeth, it occurred to Jared that he was eating only about a third of what he'd normally consume at home. No wonder he felt hungry. He heard Patsy calling from the kitchen.

"Breakfast in five minutes."

He wondered where Clarence and Melissa were. They'd vanished after the campfire and he supposed they must be in one of the rooms upstairs.

Chapter Thirty-seven

Jared was nervous because he'd never tried psychedelics, but Melissa had assured them she had used this microdot before, and it was fine stuff. So several days after his arrival at the farm, Jared and Patsy lay on the grass under a big chestnut tree with interlocked fingers as they waited for the LSD to take effect.

"Days like this just don't come any better," Jared murmured as they basked in the warmth of this early July day and stared up at the sky through the branches.

Some forty minutes after they'd dropped the acid, music from Patsy's tape deck began to sound unusually alive to Jared; the lyrics to the Beatles *Sergeant Pepper's Lonely Hearts Club Band* exuding hidden meaning. Jared closed his eyes and felt himself floating, his body shimmering. He looked at Patsy and noticed that a blue glow surrounded her body. It reminded him of a picture he'd seen of an East Indian yogi sitting in a lotus position with a multi-coloured aura around him.

Patsy sensed his gaze and turned towards him. Her movement seemed to occur in slow motion. For an instant Jared thought he could see several Patsies, and he blinked in astonishment. She brushed away an errant curl falling into her eye and began to giggle. Jared joined in. Their laughter seemed wholesome and joyous. He couldn't remember laughing like this in a long time, or maybe he never laughed like this. All cares flew from his mind and he felt intensely connected to Patsy and everything around them.

The sensation between them turned electric when Patsy moved closer and he slid his arms around her. Energy from their kiss radiated throughout his body, then settled inside him like some marvelous gemstone. Patsy stood up, pulled him to his feet, and began to spin him around. He absorbed her smile, her warmth and her love, and wanted to tell her how wonderful he felt, but no words seemed adequate. The closest description might be that verse from the Bible about peace that passed all understanding. Yeah, that was it; they swam in an ocean of universal love, maybe this was God's love. In that moment as he experienced this love, Jared realized it had existed always, and would continue long after they were gone from this life. He felt that his insight was more than an illusion created by the LSD; the drug was merely one key unlocking the portal of understanding. Later he would find it difficult to describe this experience; only those who have been through it can relate. He knew that others, especially cynical adults, would deny the reality and importance of such experiences and dismiss it as biochemical illusion. Maybe so, but wasn't all human perception, in the final analysis, an interaction of chemistry and electricity, light and sound? It didn't matter.

All that really mattered to Jared right now was the moment, and he meant to make the most of it. For the first time in his life he feasted on consciousness, one exhilarating millisecond at a time, and time itself was inconsequential. As he and Patsy danced, his feet seemed to barely touch the ground any longer. Had they taken flight? They moved together in absolute harmony, neither of them leading nor following.

During the hours that passed, Jared felt that he had evolved somehow into a much different person. He'd felt the pulse of life energy that flowed from the planet into each of them, then back into the world with everything resonating in a perfect balance.

Now the two of them sat quietly on the grass. Jared had grown used to the sharp flavour of the drug seeping into his mouth with his saliva, then draining down his throat to be reabsorbed in his mind. He wondered if that astringent taste gave the drug the name "acid."

He touched Patsy's chin.

"I loooove you." He had to speak in a loud voice. Although he felt close enough to be a part of her, in another way it seemed as if he beckoned from across some great chasm.

"And I loooove you," Patsy echoed back.

They stood up, then she moved closer to receive his kiss. His arms floated out to gather her in slow motion and they connected as if they were two astronauts tethered in space, accomplishing the first cosmic coupling, while the universe looked on.

Sgt. Pepper's Lonely Hearts Club Band continued to play quietly, as Jared and Patsy clung to one another, and kissed to the mantra of the sitar; their hands in free-form ramble upon one another, the sense of touch at once non-sexual and soothing, and then unbearably erotic an instant later.

"I've never really felt like I belonged anywhere, not the way I

211

feel I do with you right now, Patsy."

"What do you mean Jared? Of course you belong. Don't forget, you're majorly stoned. Just relax and stay with the moment." She squeezed his hand, and tilted her head against his shoulder as they ambled alongside the creek.

"No, *really* Patsy, it's more than that. All my life I've thought that I belonged somewhere else, but for the first time I think I know who I am and *why* I am."

"*Why* you are? That's profound, Jared. Better write that one down for later on in case you forget."

At the teasing he gave her a playful swat on the arm.

"I'm *kidding*," she said.

"Sorry, it's just that this whole thing is so, so much farther out . . . This whole thing, I mean . . . I had absolutely no idea . . ."

Patsy had to giggle.

"Sorry, Jared. I have no idea what you are talking about. We'll be back to planet earth in a couple of hours; just relax and enjoy what is happening." She broke away from him and ran in circles by herself, arms outstretched, and her eyes closed. Jared mused aloud.

"All I knew about these kind of drugs was from stories in the paper about people trying to fly out the windows at Rochdale College."

"Yes, well, I can understand how that might happen. That's why it's important to make sure you get your stuff from someone you trust, someone who has already tried it themselves, and most important, the environment needs to be safe and peaceful. That's why I love it out here in the country – no worries."

"Except for bears?" Jared asked.

"There are no bears here, just a few deer mostly . . ." Patsy suddenly let loose a punishing shriek.

Jared spun around to look as Patsy fell to the ground, shaking and chortling.

"I *knew* there was no bear." Jared defended himself.

"Sure ya did. C'mere you big chicken." She pulled him down to the ground and gently placed his hand onto her breast.

It was nearly dark, and Jared felt ten feet tall as they strolled back to the house. The feeling had nothing to do with the drug; the acid had mellowed out into a body stone some time ago. Jared simply felt great. If sex was always were always this good, no wonder adults kept it all to themselves.

The tape deck pulled on his shoulder, so he changed sides and took Patsy's other hand. The batteries had died two hours ago, but they hardly noticed given twilight's melody of frogs croaking, crickets calling to their mates, and birds hurrying to gather a final mouthful before dark. Some distance away, they heard what seemed a symphony of wings. Looking up, they observed a cloud of bats emerging from the forest canopy into the open sky for a night of feeding on insects.

Jared's day of beginnings was coming to an end, and like all pleasant dreams, he worried that it might slip away and he'd forget, or perhaps he'd wonder if it had happened at all.

Chapter Thirty-eight

Patsy stared at him with one hand fixed on her hip. "You did *what?*"

Jared was sorry he'd told her anything.

"Look, forget it. I thought you'd understand. What was it you were saying the other day about being such a great listener?" He looked away to think. What was to understand? He was a thief who stole from his family and his Church? Logic wasn't particularly the point and he defended himself.

"Why should you care what I did anyway?"

"Sorry. I can't help it. What you did was majorly creepy, stealing money from your parents and the Church to buy dope."

Another chilly silence descended.

"I don't know what to say, Jared. I mean, I like to get high as much as anyone, but stealing from God . . . well that takes a lot of...well I don't know what it takes, but it's pretty weird."

Jared's eyes flashed and he fumed as he listened.

"And when you got caught, instead of facing up, you took off from the people who looked after you your whole life?" Patsy looking at him as if he had kidnapped the Lindberg baby caused Jared to explode.

"What makes you such a fucking expert on my family and life?" Indignation churned his guts, although he knew it wasn't the righteous kind. He clenched his teeth. "It wasn't exactly a picnic in my family, you know."

"What the hell are you talking about? Nobody's family is a picnic. At least you *have* parents. Byron and I don't. Our parents weren't perfect, but they were great in lots of ways and we loved them. One Saturday night five years ago some drunken asshole crossed the centre line with his pickup . . . and . . . well . . . now it's only Byron and me." She began weeping.

Jared paced around, trying to think of comforting words.

"I'm sorry about your parents, but I don't know what any of that has to do with *me?*"

With that, Patsy turned and stormed off to the house. Jared watched her until she reached the door of the house.

Women! He wanted to scream.

What should he do now? He knew one thing for certain; he couldn't stay in this place any longer. He went to find Clarence, hoping he'd agree to leave. Whatever Clarence decided, Jared knew that his welcome at Rainbow Farm had expired.

He found Clarence and Melissa under the tree by the river. Clarence lay on his back with his hands behind his head listening to Melissa strum her guitar and sing *Mr. Bojangles*. At Jared's approach, she stopped playing.

"Clare'," Jared puffed. "I gotta leave here right now. Patsy and

I just had a terrible fight."

"C'mon Clark'. You don't have to split just because you have your first lovers spat." Clarence continued looking in the other direction chewing a long piece of grass.

"It *wasn't* a lovers spat. She's not my lover!"

Well, she was, but she wasn't...was she? Jared's temper rose to a boil when Clarence continued to ignore him. More than anything, Jared hated being ignored, especially when it was in a flagrant manner that said people just couldn't be bothered with you.

"Fuck *off* Clarence."

That got his attention. Clarence sat up and stared him in the eye.

"*You* fuck off Clark'; you're really getting to be a pain in the ass."

"Fine."

Jared took off, seething as he ran to the farmhouse. He collected his gear and soon he was trudging alone down the country road.

He'd been walking for at least two hours, and the clear sky had given way to cloud. His neck and face were sunburned and he appreciated the cooling raindrops that began to fall for a time as he stood beside the Trans-Canada highway. After a time the rain stopped and the clouds broke up. Exhausted and thirsty, Jared sat on his backpack. He tried to look friendly and make contact with the drivers' eyes as he stuck out his thumb, but after another hour and no ride, he pulled his backpack over his shoulder and resumed walking.

As he walked, he tried to make sense out of how he really felt about Patsy now, and how he'd felt during the last few days. He watched spectacular shades of red and purple appear among the clouds in the twilight sky, and noticed the sun appearing to accelerate in its path as it approached the horizon, as if in a hurry to get somewhere. An interesting illusion that, he thought. It occurred to him that many things in this world were illusions.

Clarence had come looking for him. Part of Jared wanted more than anything to get in the car, but he just couldn't do it.

"Don't screw with me, Clark'.' Clarence warned. "Get in now, or I'm outta here."

"Good riddance!" Had he *really* say that? Yes he had, and that was it. He'd watched the Beetle disappear in the dusty distance.

When night arrived, the new moon left the world in total darkness, except for the brilliant display of the cosmos. Jared stared in awe at the stars; he'd never seen the constellations in such grandeur. The light pollution of Beacon and the entire area near Toronto obscured the view of the heavens to a degree he'd never realized before. He figured his Dad would love the view and he wished Dad were there with him right then. Underneath that immense night sky he felt particularly small and alone.

After another half mile, the lights of a truck stop emerged in the distance and he sighed with relief.

Inside the café, Jared stood out as the only young person among a small group of farmers, truckers, and roadhouse staff. As he peered at the menu, he could feel his waitress sizing him up.

"Try the spaghetti and salad special; it'll stick to your ribs longer than French fries and gravy."

How'd she know he was thinking of fries and gravy? Anyway, she was probably right, and since this might be his last meal for awhile, he agreed.

"That sounds good."

When she returned, his plate looked suspiciously as if someone had topped it up with enough food for two guys.

"Uh, thanks . . . thanks a lot." Jared smiled at her.

She gave him a wink then turned to fill the cups of two men sitting across from him. They'd been eyeing Jared since he sat down. Eventually, one of the men gulped the rest of his coffee, said, "so long," and headed outside to his rig. The other man continuing to sip his second cup of coffee caught Jared's eye.

"Where you heading, son?"

Jared wondered if he should be talking to this giant of a man with a bald head and a luxurious beard that seemed to contain all the hair that used to be on his head. He wondered why guys didn't go bald on their chins as well. The guy seemed friendly enough and Jared, well he was more than ready for conversation.

"I was heading to Calgary but now I'm not really sure." Except for no money real quick, he thought. The two dollars for his meal would take a third of what he had left in his pocket.

"Where ya from there good buddy?"

"A place in Southern Ontario called Beacon."

"Hell, I know that place; used to short-haul supplies and finished caskets in and out of there. What's that company's name-real funny one?"

"You mean Renders?"

"That's it." The man snapped his fingers. "Strange name for a casket place, don't ya think?"

"I . . . I don't understand."

"That word, render, it means slaughtering animals."

"Oh, I never knew that before."

Jared had to agree it was funny, in a twisted sort of way. He smiled as he recalled the day that he, Robby, and Derek were scared out of their wits in that factory. The man noticed his smile.

"What is it?"

"Oh, just remembering a funny thing that happened to me and my brother and my friend a few years ago in that place." Jared didn't continue. Thinking about Derek and Robby made him feel sad, so he changed the subject.

"Where you headed?"

"Toronto. I do a run between Van' and T.O. every week."

"That's a long ride, don't you ever get sick of driving?"

"No, I love driving, although the winter driving in the mountains can be hairy sometimes. I'm Frank, Frank Heppell." The fellow reached out his hand for Jared to shake.

"Jared. Jared Clarkson."

"Pleasure."

After a short time the man took a look in his coffee cup, and finding it almost empty he replaced it on the saucer without making the slightest sound. Jared was amazed that a guy who looked so rough could have such finesse.

"How come you aren't sure where yer headed?" Frank asked.

It was a good question, and Jared didn't know how to answer.

"It's kind of a long story, but I am in a tight situation right now."

"You mean you got no money."

This guy had the knack of getting to the meat of things.

"Well, yeah, that's about the gist of it."

"Well my company has a rule about not taking hitchhikers, but then again you weren't hitchin' when I met you. If you like, you could ride along with me to your town, or straight into Toronto. I might even front you a few bucks till you git yerself sorted out. What do you think?"

"Why would you want to do that?"

"Well, truth is I could use some company for the rest of the ride. That's about it. Well that, and I got no family. And maybe I just have a few more bucks to burn than most guys, although Lord knows there's lots of times in my life I didn't."

Jared didn't know what to do. He wanted to go to Calgary, but he was broke, and what would he do when he got there? He'd depended on having Clarence with him, at least for a little while.

"I'll be back in a minute; you let me know," the trucker said, He walked towards the washroom in the back.

When he returned he placed a black Stetson on his head and prepared to leave. With the hat perched on top of his six-foot plus height, his jeans, vest and cowboy boots, the guy reminded Jared of 'Hoss' on *Bonanza*.

"Well, made up your mind?" The trucker inquired.

Jared still didn't know what to do, but maybe meeting this guy was a sign.

"Yeah. I'd like to come along, if that's O.K."

"Yep, sure it's O.K."

At the till, Jared began digging in his pocket to pay his bill. The man waved him off.   "Jean, this is for our suppers," Frank said to the waitress. "And give me a double-double for the road." He tossed six dollars on the counter. "Keep the change."

"Ah, thanks, thanks a lot." Jared felt pleased, but embarrassed at the trucker's generosity.

"No trouble, son. How 'bout a coffee or a pop to drink in the truck?"

"No thanks. I'm fine." He would like one, but he already felt he owed this guy, and after a ride to Toronto he'd owe him big time.

"Sure you do. Don't be shy to speak up for what you want in this world, son. It's going to be a long while before we stop again."

"O.K. I'll have a Coke."

"Jean, give me two Cokes." He tossed her another dollar.

As they pulled onto the highway, and he watched Frank working the two gearshifts on the rig, Jared decided that maybe it was true that if one door closed, another one opened. He was glad he'd stuck his foot in before that door slammed shut, too.

Chapter Thirty-nine

Jared's boss, Wolf was shouting from the front of the store, "we're getting low on chips."

Jared was only ahead by one pail of French fries, hardly an adequate amount for Good Friday, the busiest day of the year in the fish and chip shop. Fridays were always busy, but Good Friday was the absolute worst. After six hours of working he could barely manage the demand, let alone work ahead for tomorrow.

He sighed, looked around to make sure that nobody watched him, then reached up for a sack of potatoes from the top of the pile. He pulled it loose and let it crash to the floor. This was a no-no, but he felt too tired to care. One time Wolf caught him doing that and barked,

"They come here for fries, not mashed."

Right now Jared couldn't give a frog's fuck *what* they came for. His muscles ached and he'd gladly quit except his employment prospects elsewhere looked worse. Besides, Wolf had just given him a raise, and he always got his meals free. Good thing he loved greasy seafood. And Wolf rented him a room upstairs above the shop. It had a hotplate and fridge and only cost forty bucks a month. From there Jared could get to work in seconds.

One other roomer, an alcoholic, lived across the hall. Sometimes they'd meet in the hallway but neither of them had introduced himself. Jared felt sorry for the guy whose self-destruction seemed an invisible type, a kind of fading away that other people hardly notice or care about.

Jared figured he'd earned every cent and more of his wages today. He'd lost count of how many bags of potatoes he'd gone through, but it had to be a record because one mountain of potatoes had vanished and he'd started on the second. On days like this, he figured Wolf owed him a bonus.

Wolf came to the back and removed a thawing tray of halibut from the fridge. Jared took five for a smoke and watched the boss work while the chipper digested a load of peeled spuds and spewed fries out the other end.

No one except Wolf himself was allowed to filet the fish; he was downright amazing with a knife. He shaved each fillet perfectly, one after another, shorting neither the customers, nor himself.

"Fish is expensive," he said. "And der customers work hard for their money."

Judging from the wads of money that were taken from the till every hour on busy nights, Jared figured Wolf didn't need to cheat the customers anyway to make lots of dough.

He admired Wolf, and his wife, Gerda. Wolf was one of those people who likely had the brains to do anything he wanted; somehow he'd landed in this little goldmine and it had worked out very well for them.

"A few more years," Wolf would say sometimes. "Then Gerda and I retire in comfort."

Retire to what or where was anyone's guess. Sometimes the two of them talked about returning home to Hamburg, Germany.

Germany. The guy sure talked enough about the place. It was always Hamburg this, or Germany that.

The two of them had been born and grown up in Hamburg, but didn't know one another in those days. Each of them had been fortunate enough to be elsewhere when Allied bombers destroyed the city. At eighteen, Wolf was drafted into the German infantry. He finished the war manning an artillery battery near Munich, after a shell misfire during the early days of Operation Barbarossa blew away the bottom half of his right leg. Since then he'd used an artificial leg. He didn't seem to mind the loss. Given the eventual outcome of the Russian campaign, Wolf said he considered the sacrifice of his leg 'a million dollar injury,' for it meant he was shipped home to Germany before he could freeze, starve, be killed, or captured with the rest of the sixth army at Stalingrad. The leg didn't slow him down much.

"Chips to the front," Gerda called.

Jared stubbed out his cigarette and then placed the drain lid on the final pail of chips. He let the water and chemical mixture pour down the drain in the floor. As he watched the flow, he thought about the many places that water had traveled since the beginning of time, and where it might go in the future.

Without the water, the pail was much lighter. He carried it to the front and dumped the chips into one of the large plastic tubs under the counter.

He returned to spud patrol and dumped more potatoes into the peeler, then added the hose, and flipped a switch to initiate the machine's terrible whine. He'd overloaded it and he knew it. Overloading wore out the machine and made it much noisier, but it did the job quicker. As the potatoes bounced and rolled on the spinning granite stone, Jared lit another smoke. He thought about what had transpired since his arrival in Toronto.

Had it really been two years since he left home? Yes it had, and he still hadn't called or written the family. He missed them but as time passed he hadn't a clue what to say. He guessed that's how people lost touch. That part of his life seemed far away, almost a part of someone else's life.

Now Toronto was his home. As for family, well he didn't know who that was any more.

On summer nights he wandered the Yonge Street strip chatting up the hookers, talking to street people, or scoring lids to get blitzed.

During the winter he remained alone in his room reading classic novels and science books. He'd become accustomed to the endless drone of Dundas Street traffic, punctuated by the rolling steel of trolley cars every few minutes, and distant sirens. When he felt cooped up, he went to Grossman's, a bar on Spadina.

Grossman's was a traditional watering hole where a guy could sip draft from old-fashioned curved glasses and listen to free live rock music provided by local bands playing for exposure and free draft. The atmosphere of slum chic attracted University of Toronto students looking to unwind from Nietzsche or pre-med biology. In those days everyone smoked, and by the early evening the place was so murky the band didn't need any dry ice for the stage show. Purple haze summed it up quite nicely, and nobody cared about joints being smoked so long as you were discreet.

Grossman's clientele consisted of an interesting menagerie of the cream and the scum of the city. The main difference between the two groups was that the cream would eventually rise. They'd graduate, cut their hair, go to work for IBM and five years later they'd be selecting table crystal. The scum, on the other hand, would be grayer and still at Grossman's swilling money they'd panhandled earlier in the day.

Jared knew some of the staff – Randall, one of the bartenders, Azar, the Pakistani bouncer, and some of the students. In particular he liked one couple, a Jewish guy named Mensch, and his girlfriend, Dix. His real name was Simon but everyone called him Mensch because he was a left-leaning social work student known as a soft touch when people needed anything. He had an eye for lost souls and a warped sense of humour. He took an interest in Jared.

"Otta get a practicum credit for the time I spend down here with you guys." Mensch joked.

Jared wondered what he meant by 'practicum' but didn't ask. It sounded like a Latin word for masturbation but Jared kept that weird thought to himself. Anyway, the point was Mensch really knew how to listen. Having someone really listen was a shocker when Jared first experienced it. Most people, including himself, didn't really listen, they were busy crunching a response and waiting to hijack the conversation. Mensch was different. He had a way of letting you know, without saying a word, that what you had to say was important. When he did say something, it usually confirmed what Jared thought, or even he wanted to say, but couldn't express. The guy could be downright spooky that way. But most of all, Jared liked Mensch because he wasn't a stuffed shirt; he and Dix could party on with the best of them, and they always made Jared feel welcome.

Finally, Jared had chipped the last pail of potatoes for the night.

"Good work," Wolf said. "It's finally starting to die down. Let's clean up and call it a day."

Jared nodded and picked up his pace. Quitting time was the best part of any workday, but especially this one.

Chapter Forty

Two years of endless routine in the fish and chip shop, as well as life in general, had worn Jared down. He started taking sick days off to recover from bouts of drinking, or simply get high and read. Sometimes he wandered around the University of Toronto slipping into one of the lecture halls to listen to whatever. Some of the stuff was interesting, but much of it was arcane and foreign. English lectures left him feeling maudlin because he hadn't written anything himself for a long time.

One day as Jared browsed through one of several used bookshops near the campus on Harbord St. he kept taking the same book, leafing through it, then putting it back only to return twice to repeat the process.

"Can't make up your mind on that one?"

A scholarly-looking woman with red hair tied in a ponytail, and black demi-glasses perched on the end of a pointy nose spoke to him.

"Well, actually, I'd like to get this one but I don't have any money."

"May I?" She took the book from him and opened it to examine the price. "Ten dollars. I've seen you in here before. If you like, you could move some boxes of books and do some sweeping up for me in exchange for it."

"Ah thanks, but I'm not feeling very well today. Think maybe I'll just come back when I have some money."

"As you wish. Shall I hold it for you?"

"Yeah. Sure, I'd like that."

The book concerned depression. Recently he'd been reading books about the mind because recently it had occurred to Jared that he might be losing his. The Black Dog, as Churchill referred to depression, was nipping at his heels. The dark mood had crept upon Jared with such stealth that it had him in its grasp before he knew it. Oh sure, he'd noticed the problems he had either getting to sleep, or wanting to sleep all day, or waking up in the night and staying awake. His appetite had dropped off; he was losing weight, and he made excuses to stay off work.

In some ways, the insomnia seemed the worst of the lot because he'd lie unwillingly wide-awake for hours, pondering some idea from a book, wrestling with his fears, guilt and self-doubts, or trying to reconstitute fragments of dreams from nights past. By morning he was in no shape to go to work, and one thing was certain – he was fast running out of excuses for missing work. Soon he'd be like the guy who ran out of sick time and have to call in dead.

"And why you can't work today?" Gerda asked in despair. As understanding as she and Wolf had been to this point about his growing absences, she gave him that look that told him he had almost used up whatever goodwill remained in the bank.

"I just feel punky, sick to my stomach, and I haven't been sleeping."

"Well take off today Jared, but I want you to go see a doctor," Gerda said.

"Alright."

He didn't go. For one thing he had no idea if he had health coverage, and even if he did, he didn't know his health care number. He headed back upstairs and returned to bed. Later when he woke up bored and nervous, he smoked hash until he was numb. Needing more air and less monotony, he headed over to Grossman's.

Mensch spied him standing at the bar and waved him over.

"Sit down buddy. Where ya been for two weeks?"

Jared forced a half-smile on his face and nodded hello from oblivion. He was almost too stoned to talk. What a stupid waste of money. The hash had only deepened his murk and added paranoia to the mix. The other people sitting at the table seemed a distant blur to Jared, but he sensed their thoughts, as they looked straight at him. He fidgeted in his chair and twirled his draft glass. He felt them staring at his mark and moved his hand to cover it. He wished he could cover his entire face, or better yet vanish altogether. Flushed, hot, and agitated he suddenly stood up, jarring the table and knocking over his own beer and two others. Two glasses fell against one another, shattered, then spilled. Beer and shards of glass flowed across the table while people swore and jumped up to avoid the tsunami of suds. Jared stood shaking, and Mensch placed a hand upon his shoulder and spoke in a low soothing voice.

"Jared, it's O.K. Take it easy, everything's alright, pal. It's just an accident."

One of the other guys arrived and pushed Jared.

"You owe me a beer, asshole."

" Fuck off." Jared spat. Mensch grabbed the guy and said,

"Go sit down, Steve. I'll get you a beer." Mensch shoved a buck into the guy's shirt pocket and guided him away from Jared.

Someone had fetched a cloth and proceeded to mop up the mess. Jared began to leave. Attracted by the disturbance, Azar the bouncer arrived and appeared concerned.

"Gotta go outside. Fresh air. . . I'll be fine."

Mensch looked unconvinced, but let him go.

"Can I come round to check on you tomorrow?" he asked.

Jared nodded absently, then headed to the door. Once outside he hurried along the street and felt people looking at him, the hippies selling jewellery, and the bent Chinese man shuffling towards him. Jared tried to avoid their eyes, as if somehow that would make him inconspicuous.

Next he heard someone talking. He looked around, but couldn't locate the source. The voice seemed to come from everywhere, and nowhere, it was neither entirely his head, nor outside it. The voice's message was clear.

You're a screw-up Jared, a total flake. You have always been a screw-up and a flake and you always will be. Why don't you kill yourself and get it over with.

Who . . . what the hell was going on? Jared was smart enough, even in the midst of panic and confusion, to recognize that this scenario wasn't normal. He couldn't be *that* stoned, or was he? Frightened, he started running to try to get away from the voice. Lost in thoughts of imminent madness, he collided with a bag lady carting her possessions in a bundle buggy. She swore at the intruder like an animal protecting its patch.

She had several missing teeth. The few black and yellow teeth remaining, combined with a dirty grey cloth wrapped around her head, gave her the appearance of an old crone. Suddenly a most bizarre, hysterical thought occurred to Jared – he might be staring at his *real* mother, and he began to giggle. The giggle erupted into laughter. His *mother*. The idea seemed at once so preposterous, yet possible.

At his sudden levity, the crone's stare morphed into a scowl. She extracted an umbrella from the buggy and brandished it. Her shouting and poking seemed hilarious and Jared's laughter consumed him. The more he laughed, the louder she yelled. People stopped to look at the pair of them. Jared pulled himself away and was still laughing as he disappeared up the street. Behind him, he heard the old woman's outrage subside.

His laughter evaporated as quickly as it had set upon him, and like a riptide, his depression came pouring back, more intense than before.

Arriving home, Jared stopped to look in the front window of the fish and chip shop. The sailfish in the window, accompanied by a lobster trap, seemed another creature out of its element and Jared felt a certain affinity with it. He made his way up the steps and into his room where he fell onto his cot, then rolled back and forth trying to find a comfortable position. Unable to resolve it, he picked up a dusty audiocassette from the floor and wiped it off on his shirt to read the title – *The Sounds of Silence*.

He hadn't seen that tape for weeks. He shoved it into the tiny player from the pawnshop on Jarvis, then leaned against the wall and listened to the monotonous squeak as it rewound. When the machine snapped at the end of the rewind, he pressed play.

He stared at the plastic milk crates full of books and other junk stacked against the opposite wall, and thought about the old crone. Maybe the two of them weren't so different. Everyone had

233

baggage; hers was simply more obvious, portable. This room was his bundle buggy.

He dozed off, only rousing later when his favourite track on the tape began to play. Simon and Garfunkel's singing, "I am a Rock" resonated, except for one thing.

This rock did feel pain.

Chapter Forty-one

It was just as well, Jared thought. He was sick of peeling spuds. Wolf seemed apologetic, and said he could stay in the room for a month, but what was he supposed to do now? Fired was fired, and Jared had very little money.

He wandered up and down Yonge Street, his hands plunged deep in the large square pockets of his paratrooper jacket from the surplus store. At one point, he stopped for a smoke.

Perhaps it was the forlorn look on his face as he leaned against a wall, but a well-dressed man in a suit noticed him and stopped.

"Wanna make twenty five bucks?" he asked.

Jared looked up.

"Doin' what?" Jared had an idea what, but he asked anyway.

"Come on a date with me."

Jared moved away, then addressed the man with venom.

"Go fuck yourself."

"Might have to," the man replied, then turned on his patent leather heel and walked away.

The brief interaction left Jared even more depressed. Now people were trying to hire his ass for twenty-five dollar blowjobs. Twenty-five fucking dollars. He wouldn't do that for a thousand, or would he? He started to wonder how much someone would have to pay him before he would do something like that? Not that he wanted to, but it was said every man had his price. He wondered what his might be.

Quit thinking such bullshit. He wouldn't do stuff like that for any price, even if that price were offered.

He had to figure a way to get some dough, but the sex trade wasn't it. His financial dilemma only served to deepen his general malaise. He resumed ambling down the sidewalk, glancing at store windows for job signs.

Dishwasher needed. Nah. Hey, maybe he could get a job in one of the record shops. That sounded good, even fun, but when he checked with Sam's, then A&A, and finally Sunrise, he found that none of them were hiring. He continued walking up one side of Yonge to Bloor, then down the other side to Queen Street. He passed two panhandlers working the corner of Yonge and Dundas and glanced into the baseball cap on the sidewalk. Unless they had taken money out, it only looked like three bucks for an hour's work. He concluded that panhandling likely wasn't worth the trouble. Something more lucrative had to exist, but by the end of the day he hadn't found it. He felt tired and discouraged and headed into the Elephant & Castle pub to buy some pizza and beer. He knew he couldn't afford it, but he didn't care. He planned to get drunk, then go home.

He sat at the bar watching the Ti-Cats hammer the Argos.

After his fourth beer, the Boatmen were losing 28 -7. *Argos are gone*, he thought. On the spur of the moment, he re-evaluated his situation and made an executive decision. He'd use the rest of his money to buy himself a lid, then try to get out of Toronto. He'd call Jet, his dealer. Jet seldom disappointed and usually had connections for quality stuff even when other people were dry. If this was to be Jared's last lid for awhile, it had to be good.

He dragged himself off the barstool and headed for the pay phone. The Beatles *Get Back* blasting from the sound system forced Jared to plug his ear after dialing. Several rings later, Jet answered.

"Yah." Jet always talked as if his mouth was full of marbles.

"Jet."

"Yah. Who's askin'?"

"It's Clark'. Listen, I need some of the Colonel's Herbs. Got any?"

"Yah. Come round in an hour; I'm kinda busy right now."

"O.K., see you."

Each step creaked as Jared ascended to the second floor apartment that Jet called home. At the top of the stairs Jared rapped on the door. No answer. He rapped harder, still no response. Where was Jet? Jared hoped he hadn't walked ten blocks for nothing. Maybe Jet was asleep. Jared tried the door and when he found it unlocked, he gave it a careful push and looked in.

"Hey Jet. You here?"

Nothing.

Strange, Jared thought. He was expecting me. Well, maybe he stepped out to get some smokes or something and left the door open. Jared decided to let himself in to wait. He sat down on the couch and looked around at the hundreds of posters that covered every inch of the walls, ceiling, and doors. Jared liked the effect it gave of being inside an immense 3-D collage. He started leafing through a *Rolling Stone* that featured Jimi Hendrix on the cover.

The air in the apartment reeked with the odour of pot. Smoking paraphernalia such as roach clips, a hash pipe and a bong lay scattered about on the wooden hydro spool that served as a coffee table.

Jared felt the beer catching up with him after his long walk and set aside the Rolling Stone to find the bathroom. First he opened a closet door, so he moved on to the next one. A large poster of James Dean on his bike covered it.

He pulled open the door and stood there stunned. Jet was sprawled on the floor with a tourniquet loosed around his left arm and a syringe still stuck in a vein. Beside him lay a blackened spoon, an open baggie of white powder, and a Bunsen burner still flaming.

"Shit."

Jared rushed to feel Jet's wrist and neck, then placed his ear against the guy's chest. There was no pulse, his eyes were bloodshot, and his tongue drooped from his open mouth. Jared ran to the phone and dialed zero. He shook so much he could barely speak. He had to call for help, even though he knew that Jet was toast.

"Send an Ambulance quick! 225 Bonista Street, Apartment 1. Street drug overdose." He hung up before the operator could ask for his name.

Better get the hell out of there before the cops arrive. He thought of something, ran back to the bathroom and knelt down to examine Jet's pockets. In one pocket of Jet's coveralls he found a wad of cash. He struggled to extract the money and was astounded to discover a hefty stash of fifties and hundreds. He stuffed the money into his own pocket, then hurried to the living room. He scooped a lid of dope he found inside a box on the

238

bookshelf, then dashed out the door. At the bottom of the stairwell he met the ambulance crew.

"In there." He pointed up the stairs, then hurried out.

He heard a siren approaching from the other direction and hoped the cops wouldn't notice him leaving.

Don't look back. Walk slowly. Don't draw attention. Shaking, Jared fought to remain cool but the image of Jet lying dead remained a shock. Everyone called the guy "Jet" because he was always high, but Jared didn't know Jet was a needle freak.

As he hurried, Jared wondered about the right and wrong of stealing from a dead junkie. What did it matter? Jet didn't need the dough any more. Besides, he figured the cops would likely just scoop the dough themselves if he didn't.

Now several blocks distant from Jet's building, Jared began to breathe easier, but he continued sweating until the Queen streetcar arrived, and the cops didn't. He paid his fare, sat down, patted his wad of dough, and managed a wan smile.

Finally, things were looking up.

Chapter Forty-two

The garish illumination of Amsterdam's red light district reflecting in the water caught Jared's eye and he paused to lean against the iron railing to peer at the people on the other side of the canal. Nearby a group of street buskers plied their talents, miming and juggling for change. A prostitute across the water sitting in the front window of a building held sale. She rested an index finger suggestively upon her cleavage, and softly wagged her black stocking-clad leg up and down as she fixed eye contact with males passing by. Jared filed her image for later and returned his gaze to the lights dancing on the water while his mind wandered to memories of his recent days in Amsterdam.

He'd arrived here from England in a dark mood after days of drizzle and cloud. He felt hounded by that sense that he was supposed to go somewhere special but while he had no idea where that was, somehow he knew that destination wasn't England. Almost daily he wrestled with nightmares that were like curtains opening a crack, giving him a glimpse of something, then slamming shut before he'd seen enough to grasp onto. Dying to get high and forget about the dreams, he decided to go to Holland.

Jared hadn't intended to remain in Amsterdam so long, and seemed to know that what he sought wasn't there, but he was having such a good time that he couldn't drag himself away from this theme park for libertines. Still, he had to be careful; Jet's dough wouldn't last forever.

He made an effort to economize by staying mostly in the youth hostels and buying bread, cheese and sliced meats from deli's rather than eating in restaurants. This preserved his cash for priorities like smoke, psychedelics and beer. He didn't mind staying in the youth hostels; they were economical and he met lots of cool people. With hostels, the standard rule was that people had to move on every few days. The crush of young people in the city constantly seeking new digs made housing a challenge, but eventually he found a few places to stay and would rotate from one place to another.

He thought about that unusually warm fall night a week ago he spent the night tripping on magic mushroom with two guys from Wisconsin. By the next morning he'd been up for nearly twenty-four hours and his skin felt like crinkly plastic. Although his body was exhausted and needed sleep, his mind continued to race. His friends packed it in to crash around 4 a.m., but Jared stayed up to wander the canal streets while fingers of light tickled the horizon, the world seeming to return from the dead in the waxing daylight.

He'd come upon a street market receiving a delivery of cut

flowers for the day. The deliveryman unloaded buckets of flora, then chatted with the merchant. Jared admired the blooms and found himself tasting and hearing, as much as seeing the vibrant colours. The fragrance tasted like white and dark chocolate, and the crisp morning breeze caused the flowers to waver. As the blooms shimmered, Jared thought they produced a faint hurdy-gurdy sound.

"Ah, you like my flowers."

Jared looked up to find the deliveryman speaking to him. The man gestured charitably with his hand.

"Enjoy. Free are their smells!" Both the deliveryman and the merchant laughed and Jared joined in. For a second he thought a bucket of Fresia giggled as well.

"From Nord America?" The deliveryman asked.

Jared nodded.

"States or Canada?"

"Canadian."

Both men smiled.

"Very good. And what is the Canada's part you are from?" Jared found the man's Dutch accent warm and soothing.

"Ontario, a town called Beacon."

"Sounds a place to be calling one back. How long you are staying here?"

"I've been here for a few weeks. Hadn't really intended to stay so long, but I like it here a lot. Love your art galleries, especially the Rijksmuseum. I'm sure learning about art in a hurry."

And he was too. Prior to this trip, the only impressionist he knew of was Rich Little. He'd get stoned and spend mornings wandering the galleries of the great museums. One day a Rembrandt self-portrait winked at him. No one standing nearby could understand what the young man found so damn funny.

"Have not been going to Rijksmuseum myself for long time, shince was I a schoolboy." The deliveryman's gentle grey eyes peered from the weathered brown face etched by years working in the sun. A shock of white hair peeked out from beneath an old black leather sailor's cap.

Jared liked these men.

"It's great how neat and tidy, green and beautiful everything is in your country."

"Holland being a very tiny country, ve have to make of all space good use." The deliveryman's face grew reverent. "You know it is thanks been to Canada soldiers our country is free again. I am remembering the soldiers of Canada being so kind giving to us hungry children food and chocolate."

Jared felt proud of Canada's troops as he listened, and understood in that instant how it might be honourable to die fighting for a good cause. At least then one's life and death would count for something. In general, Jared was anti-war, at least as far as the Vietnam War was concerned, but he realized that World War II was a different situation altogether. As he mused about the sacrifices of the young Canadians so long ago, Jared's own life seemed suddenly facile and vacuous.

The deliveryman offering his hand brought Jared from his thoughts.

"I am Adrian Van Nostrand. Please excuse my English speaking."

Jared shook the man's rough tanned hand. His dark stubby fingers reminded Jared of partially smoked cigars.

"Ah, pardon my Dutch. I'm Jared."

"And vere it is you are staying?"

"A room near the Vondelpark."

"Good, good. Vell, I must be gone now. Good-bye."

The deliveryman doffed his cap, tugged at his trousers, then set off to his next stop. Jared took another sniff of the flowers. They were quiet now. With morning also in full bloom, he'd headed back to his room to sleep.

Jared noticed the prostitute was getting out of her chair and drawing a curtain across the window. Must have landed a John, he figured. He wondered if prostitutes enjoyed the sex sometimes? He hoped they did. He sensed someone stepping up beside him.

"G'day mate, nice woman, eh?" It was an Aussie traveler he'd met a few times.

"That she is."

"Going to give her a go mate?"

"Yeah, right."

Even if he had the money, Jared doubted he'd ever feel comfortable paying someone for sex. He felt uncomfortable about people making their living that way. He decided to respond with a joke.

"With my luck, I'd pick the black widow of the lot and she'd eat me right afterwards."

The Aussie howled and slapped him on the back.

"I know a few birds in Melbourne like that mate."

Reflections From Shadow

Chapter Forty-three

Jared had run into people unexpectedly before, but never so far from home and that was why, at first glance, Jared concluded he must be mistaken. After all, the fellow was a long way off, and anyway, tall long-haired blonde guys were common in Holland. Jared almost decided to move on, when the fellow tied his hair back into a ponytail with a familiar gesture, and when the fellow turned around, the Canadian flag on his pack nailed it. Jared became so excited he had to pee. The guy standing at the corner of the Leidestraake and Mint Square was Clarence. Jared tried to make his way towards him.

Given their close proximity to the train station, Jared worried that Clarence might be leaving the city.

Jared manoeuvred through the crowd but with so many visitors, he it was difficult to continue his diagonal shortcut and track Clarence at the same time. As Clarence moved towards the

Paleis Dam and the train station, the crush of tourists increased. Jared shoved past a man who blasted him in a drunken Brooklyn accent.

"What's the rush asshole?"

Jared ignored him and continued shouting.

"Clarence. Clarence."

He tried jumping up and down and waving his arms for attention, but he received only a negative response from the people nearby justifiably annoyed at somebody yelling in their ear. It was futile anyway; the crowd noise only swallowed his voice. His only chance was to catch up to Clarence, and that possibility dimmed as Clarence melted away in the distance.

Jared struggled to find small breaks in the crowd while trying to keep Clarence in view and failed to notice the water hose strung across the paving stones to water an island of flora. Jared tripped on the hose and fell forward. A man grabbed his arm, which tore his shirt, but partially broke his fall. He still gashed his knee badly on the cobbles and blood began flowing down his shin. Damn, he had no time for this. He grabbed a tissue from his pocket and tried to blot the wound on the run.

A crowd of tourists now blocked his view and when he finally negotiated a position of view, Clarence was gone. Jared smacked his hand to the side of his head.

"Damn."

He set off towards the train station, holding the tissue to his knee. If he removed it for more than a few seconds, blood ran into his sock, but that was the least of his concerns.

When Jared arrived at the Leidestraake, he couldn't see

Clarence near either the Paleis Dan or outside the train station. He hurried on into the station and ran about checking the various ticket and waiting areas, but saw no one resembling Clarence.

Actually, not finding Clarence at the station consoled Jared because this probably meant that Clarence wasn't headed to the station after all. This realization provided some relief, but not so much as the relief when Jared found the men's room. He had to pee so badly by then he was dancing. After relieving himself, he wet a paper towel and cleaned the blood from his leg. Another traveler noticing him said,

"I'm a medical student can I help you?" The fellow washed his hands at the next sink, retrieved some antiseptic and a bandage from his kit, and proceeded to clean and dress the wound.

"Thanks. Thanks a lot." Jared smiled. He splashed water on his face to cool himself.

He limped back from the station because now his knee ached. He wondered if the ache had just started, or maybe it had been aching since the fall but he hadn't noticed.

He popped some ASA, then spent the rest of that day hobbling from one hostel to another. At each, he left a prominent note on the message board telling Clarence he'd be at the northwest corner of the Vondelpark every day at noon for the next week. He also left a message at the American Express office. The woman at the office grumbled because he didn't have one of their cards, but reluctantly accepted the message.

As he walked about the city, Jared kept a sharp lookout.

He knew what Clarence was up to – smoking his brains out somewhere. This knowledge didn't help him much because Amsterdam had dozens of "coffee houses" where cannabis, although technically illegal, was openly smoked and sold.

At noon the following October day, summer had returned for one last blast. The sun reflecting from the stone made the temperature of seventy degrees Fahrenheit feel more like eighty. A breeze provided some relief.

Jared stood in a shady spot under a tree in the Vondlepark sharing his first joint of the day with two German travelers. After acquiring that special glow, he sat with his back against a tree and rested. He hoped that unusual stuff, good stuff, might happen. Good stuff happened sometimes when he was stoned such as when he'd experience 'Zen Pool' and make four or five difficult shots in a turn.

"Good stuff," he asserted.

The Germans agreed.

The one German wore a colourful vest that could have come from Tibet. Things like that weren't unusual; some of the young people in Amsterdam had traveled to amazing places, but eventually they all seemed to pass through this city that had become a Mecca for young people to meet, argue, make love, smoke pot, and laugh.

Jared watched a young couple making out noisily on a patch of grass nearby.

"Otta call this place the *fondle* park," he quipped.

"Bitte?" One of the Germans had a puzzled expression on his face as he tried to cipher Jared's words. Jared dismissed it with a wave.

"Too hard to explain."

Then from behind the tree, Jared heard a familiar voice.

"Well Clark', I see your jokes are just as bad as ever."

"Clarence!" Jared leapt up, forgetting his sore knee. "Far Fucking Out."

The two of them laughed like hell, hugged and slapped each other on the back. People nearby stared at the crazy Canucks.

"Jeez, Clare', so great to see you." Jared began spitting questions faster than a machine gun at Vimy ridge.

"How long ya been here? Where ya stayin'? How are ya?"

"You too. Three days in a hostel. I'm great. What else do you need to know?"

"Funny guy, Clarence, funny guy. Oh, man, this is so cool." Clarence put his arm around Jared's shoulder.

"Great to see you too, Jared. I kind of worried you'd vanished off the planet after that day up north."

Jared twitched at the reminder of a day he'd much rather forget and changed the subject.

"Let's head over to the Amstel Brewery. Free beer and snacks with their tour."

"Sure, I'm easy. We can catch up on the past couple of years." Jared waved goodbye to the Germans, and they set off down the Hofftstraat.

"What have you been doin' Clarence?"

"I went to the Ontario College of Art for a year after finishing high school. It was O.K. but I'm kind of sick of school so I'm taking the year off and may not go back. Somebody my dad knows is the creative director in an advertising agency. Dad showed him some of my stuff and he likes it. The guy said I can call him when I get back."

Jared became quiet.

"That's great Clare'." He felt happy for Clare', but suddenly ashamed that he himself hadn't even finished high school.

When they arrived at the Amstel Brewery, the line-up for tours was several blocks long.

"Forget it," Jared said. "I'll buy you a beer."

"Yer on."

They turned around and headed back to the café and bar district. As they walked together Jared couldn't help smiling. Meeting Clarence seemed an omen. He sensed things would soon start happening. He hoped that they would be good things.

Chapter Forty-four

A week later, the two of them lay in a tiny dark room located on the fringe of the tourist district. Jared struggled to sleep but despite his tired body, dark thoughts stimulated his mind and kept him awake.

"Hey Clare', what do you think happens to you when we..?" He stopped mid-thought.

"When we *what?*" Clarence replied. "I was nearly asleep."

"Sorry. I meant when we die."

"Why you asking?"

"I dunno. I was just thinking about it and wondered what you thought."

"Well, I dunno. Probably nothing...probably just like going to sleep or the lights goin' out. Why you asking?"

"Been on my mind."

Clarence rolled over on his cot, sat up and switched on the table lamp.

"Whaddya mean on your mind? You O.K?"

"Yeah, yeah. Just thinking, that's all. I mean dying can't be all that bad . . . it happens to everybody and everything doesn't it?"

"I think what you mean is that being *dead* isn't so bad. The *dying* part, that's a whole other thing."

"Good point...It's just that, well all that stuff they brainwashed us with when we were kids in Church...I *know* it's bullshit, but sometimes I worry that maybe it's true."

"Well, so what if it *is* true? You're not an evil person. You didn't murder Kennedy or anything did you?"

"Guess not." Jared giggled.

"You *guess* not? What's the hell is it with you, Clark'? You're not the same guy I used to know back home."

"How's that?" Jared's tone sounded hesitant.

"For one thing your long face, and you're hardly ever pestering me with your stupid puns. Matter of fact, you haven't talked much at all the last couple of days."

Jared propped his face with his hand,

"Well, I *am* different than the guy you knew," he said. "I was in T.O. for two years and some shit went down there big time. I was nervous and bummed out a lot." Jared paused. "I just feel like I've screwed up my whole life."

"Whaddya mean 'screwed up'?"

Jared was quiet for a moment, then barked,

"Why you staring at me?"

"Why you getting riled Clark'? *You* started this conversation, not me. Are you trying to piss me off?" If he was, Jared didn't know why.

254

"Look, don't just spit out stuff about death, and feeling like a screw up then get pissed when I ask what you mean."

"O.K. O.K. It's just that I've been thinking about home and things."

"What things?"

"Forget it. Like you said, I'm just in a mood."

"Look Clark', if you don't want to talk about something, don't bring the goddamn thing up."

"I'm not bringing anything up, just thinking out loud. O.K... Well, maybe I am. Partly it's these dreams I've been having."

"Nightmares?"

"Not exactly nightmares, but they're spooky. I wake up and can't seem to shake this feeling of dread and it poisons my whole day. Maybe I've just been getting cracked too much. I think I need a break from Amsterdam."

"To do what?"

"I dunno; go someplace where I won't be getting wrecked every day."

"That's doable. What are these dreams about?"

"There's a few of them, they're similar but not the same. Some nights they have something to do with my birthmark. Like one night, I was standing in the bathroom trying to sand the fucking thing off my face with a file."

"So, you wish you didn't have a birthmark. What's so surprising about that?"

"Nuthin' except it relates to dreams I had years ago where I saw half-dead prisoners carrying stones, and German soldiers. One soldier in the dream, an officer, used to scare the hell out of me. He seemed really familiar somehow. Anyway, what I started to tell you was I woke up yesterday with a strong feeling that I'm supposed to go someplace."

"Yeah, where?"

"Germany."

"Yeah, Germany. So what's the big deal?"

Jared shook his head. "No, you don't understand."

"Understand *what*? Do you want to go there or not?"

"Yes, I do, but for some reason, maybe because of these dreams, I'm afraid of going to Germany."

Clarence made a spooky sound.

"Doo, doo, doo, doo. Next stop - the Twilight Zone." Clarence started to laugh.

"Funny Clare', very funny. Listen, it would be great if you'd come with me. I know you've only been over here two weeks."

"No problem. I've got the drift of what happens in the Dam. If I want, I'll spend some time here later. I have to come back here to get my flight anyway."

"Good point. Well, can we leave tomorrow then?"

"Whatever." Clarence gathered his sleeping bag around himself and turned off the light. "Now can we *please* get some sleep?"

Thirty minutes later Jared was still awake. He sat up.

"Clarence," he whispered,

"Umm?"

"Thanks for being a pal."

The only response was a snore.

Chapter Forty-five

The guys stared furtively about the Munich S-baun. They rode without a properly cancelled ticket and risked a stiff fine. The day prior, a conductor had fined a man on the spot for the same offence. Today they wanted to see if they could get away with it. Jared listened to a German couple speaking, and leaned over to Clarence as the vehicle began to move.

"Hard to believe that the English language is closely related to German, they sound so different."

"Yeah." Clarence nodded. He raised his voice. "Especially in those old black and white newsreels with Hitler yelling and shaking his fist."

At the mention of Hitler, two people sitting nearby stared at them. One of them, an old man with wrinkled pale flesh, round black metal glasses, and a stern bearing apparently touched

Clarence's funny bone. Clare' began laughing.

"What's so damn funny?" Jared felt his face flush with embarrassment. Clarence covered the smirk with his hand.

"What *is* it?" Jared asked again. Clarence motioned him closer.

"Suppose that guy over there were Dr. Mengele?"

"Oh sure. And what would Mengele be doing here on the S-baun in Munich? Hiding in plain sight?" He looked over at the man again, and the idea that Clarence might be even remotely correct gave him the creeps. As a matter of fact, during the past two weeks, this whole country had given him the creeps.

When the S-baun arrived at the Marienplatz, Munich's central square, the guys disembarked and headed up the Am Platz to get a beer at the Hofbrau Haus. When they stepped off the baun, Jared felt relieved to see the last of the old man.

The very size of the Hofbrau Haus astounded Jared. Although it was the middle of the week, the Hofbrau held hundreds of people. Waitresses garbed in white blouses and long colourful skirts with Black Forest embroidery hurried about carrying full 1.5 litre clay mugs in each hand. Industrious bussers rushed back and forth collecting the empty tankards. A small band of three men garbed with lederhosen, bright green shirts and matching hats with feathers provided traditional German polka music. Two of the men were tall and thin. The third, a short slight tuba player, appeared he might topple over in a breeze.

Clarence found an unoccupied table and they sat down.

"Guten Tag." A young waitress addressed them, her head at a tilt. She held an empty round tray against her hip.

Clarence held up two fingers.

"Beer-zwie."

She smiled and wiped the table clean before leaving. As she worked, her breast grazed Jared's arm and he felt a pleasant stir. His daydream was interrupted when Clarence began reading from his travel guide.

"It says that Hitler and his cronies used to meet in this place."

"Get out."

"No seriously; it's right here in *Let's Go*. They might have even planned the putsch here."

"Planned what?"

"A putsch, a coup. You know...when people overthrow the government by force."

"Well they didn't plan very well did they? Didn't he go to prison after that?"

"Yeah that's right, and while he was in prison that's when he wrote *Mein Kampf*."

All this war-talk made Jared edgy. Considering that the most devastating conflict in history had begun and ended in Germany, it seemed incredible that almost everything they had seen in the country, even buildings that looked old, now stood in good condition. The guidebook said that only three percent of Munich had remained intact after the Allied bombing in 1944, but you'd never guess to see it today. Hamburg appeared much the same, except for a bombed-out Church that hadn't been rebuilt. It seemed as if the entire country had been whitewashed to erase the Nazi period. But appearances were deceiving. What Jared found most ominous was an eerie feeling that he recognized some of the buildings and streets, although he had never visited Germany before. At first he figured it was only because he'd watched too many war movies, but somehow he knew it was more than that. It was so troubling that part of him wanted to leave the country, but he couldn't. Not until he discovered why he'd had to come here.

A German man sitting alone at an adjacent table raised his tankard in salute to the young travelers. The fit man had curly hair, a brushy moustache, and a pleasant smile. He seemed one of those people who preserve themselves well and appear much younger than their actual years.

"American?" The man asked.

"Canadian," Jared replied.

"Ah, Ca...na...da. Prosit." The man raised his beer once again.

The waitress arrived with the guys' beers just in time for them to join the toast. Clarence waved the man over to join them and the three clicked their tankards a second time.

"No more Hitler, no more Churchill," the man proposed.

The comment unsettled Jared. Why did the guy mention WWII right away? Did he *know* Jared had been thinking about the war? Or perhaps the waves of that war continued washing ashore in the present for all of us.

Clarence continued his discourse with the man. Despite the language gap, their tones were cordial. Jared let Clarence keep the conversation going while he slurped his second beer and continued thinking. When he had consumed well over his usual limit, and the room started to spin, Jared felt panic rising. He pushed back his chair and stood up.

"Hafta go." He held onto the table to steady himself. "I feel sick."

It wasn't only the alcohol affecting him. It seemed as if he suddenly were filled with a kind of sickness he'd never experienced before. Like some kind of bile he wished he could just throw up and be rid of the feeling, but he couldn't.

Clarence sounded disappointed. "How come we have to go? Not having a good time?" His eyes were fixed on a pretty fraulein nearby.

"I dunno what it is Clare', just gotta go, that's all."

"Fine." Clarence chugged the rest of his beer and signaled the waitress for their bill.

"Danke," she replied and smiled.

Clarence stayed back to shake hands with the German, but Jared hurried to the exit.

Outside Jared noticed gray cloud now blanketed the sky to the horizon; the gray melding with the colour of the stone buildings as if both heaven and earth were draped in the same gloomy tarpaulin. Periodic gusts of wind driving a sprinkle of rain served to further dampen Jared's mood as they made their way down the platz.

Chapter Forty-six

Once again, Jared had slept little during the night before and the monotonous clatter of the S-baun train wheels lulled him into drowsiness. Beside him Clarence tapped his foot as he read *Let's Go*. Jared opened his eyes and glanced over at his friend.

"Stop that tapping, Clare'. It's bugging me." Looking beyond Clarence, through the train window, Jared saw that the cityscape of Munich had changed to countryside.

"Finally you speak. Why ya so quiet?" Clarence asked.

"Tired. Didn't sleep well again last night."

"More dreams?"

"Yeah. I'm someplace, no place in particular, but I don't know who I am. When I look around there are some people. I don't think they know each other, but in some strange way they do."

"Who are the people?"

"Can't remember really, but I do recall seeing that German soldier guy dressed in an officers uniform. Think I've told you about him before."

"Yeah, so what happened this time?"

"Nothing really, I'm just looking around at the other people and suddenly it's as if I'm looking at *myself.* I know that sounds crazy."

"Dreams *are* crazy. That's what makes them so damn interesting. Maybe you were thinking about where we were going today."

"Maybe. Anyway, it went on and on, and I wished I could wake up. When I did wake up I felt as if I'd hardly slept."

"Stay tuned, maybe part two is tonight." Clarence laughed, then slapped him on the back.

"Yer a real comfort to me, Clare'."

The S-baun slowed, then rolled gently to a stop at the train station. A small wooden sign on the station read *Dachau.* Clarence and Jared gathered their daypacks and moved toward the exit.

The day was clear and mild, and Jared wished he had remembered to bring his clip-on shades. They stood for a minute on the train platform while Clarence checked the guidebook for directions to the camp museum. Jared waved off an approaching taxi driver.

"Guide book says there are two buses. We can take whatever one gets here first."

"Sure." Jared nodded.

At that Moment, a bus pulled around the bend and came to a stop nearby.

"Here's one, 724 Krautgarten," Clarence said.

The word 'Kraut' leapt out at Jared, and his previous day's panic at the Hofbrau Haus flooded back. His heart pounded and suddenly he wanted to get right back on the train. If he were alone he might well have done so. Instead, he followed Clarence onto the bus and paid the ferryman.

The bus meandered through the pretty town with its ancient stone Church, 16th century castle overlooking from a hilltop, and the Bavarian Alps in the distance. From the guidebook, Clarence read that the town was once known as a centre for artists and writers. However, to Jared the town seemed a façade, more deception in a country of smoke and mirrors, and his stomach churned.

The bus halted near the edge of town beside a signpost reading *Dachau Museum*. The visitors become silent and huddled together as they approached the visitors entrance. Jared was the exception, he lagged behind because he began to hear a faint buzzing and rubbed his ears. Clarence touched him on the back.

"You O.K.?"

"Yeah ... fine. I'll be along; here's some dough, get me a ticket."

The group soon reached the walls of the front gate leading into the compound. They followed an arrow sign indicating "tickets this way" in several languages.

Now alone, Jared continued feeling shaky, and the buzzing sound increased. When he stopped walking, the buzzing lessened and he felt a little better. Clarence and the rest of the group were now far ahead. When Jared resumed walking, the sick feeling and the buzzing returned, this time much more intensely. He stopped again, this time closing his eyes to manage the dizziness and found himself transfixed to the spot and the buzzing grew louder.

Now Jared has no idea how he got from the modern day visitor's gate to the original camp gate, the Jourhaus, on the other side of the compound, but when he opened his eyes, there he was. The warm air of a moment ago was chill against his face, and the buzzing had stopped.

Where was everybody? Jared stood alone, except for military capped figures moving about in the tiny windows of the room above the gate. One German soldier, a rifle at his side, stood guard. Strange, Clarence hadn't said anything about people dressed up like soldiers. Stepping forward, he noticed German words welded into the design of the forbidding metal gate.

Arbeit Macht Frei. "Work makes you free." The translation came to him easily, but how? He wheeled about to look for Clarence and the others but saw no one. What the hell? This wasn't the place where he'd just been.

At first he thought he might be having one of those weird states he remembered from his childhood when he would find himself somewhere and not remember how he landed there. No, this seemed different, and besides, those other experiences were only childish imagination.

Maybe everyone had moved ahead without him and he would find them waiting inside. No, that couldn't be it; this was a completely different part of the camp. He decided to approach the guard.

"Sprecht Englisch?" How'd he know to say that?

No response. The guy didn't even seem to notice him. Ah, Jared got it; maybe this was a deal like Buckingham palace where the guards couldn't speak or notice you and visitors make a game of trying to make them laugh.

No, that wasn't it either because Jared recognized other

differences about this place such as the texture, feel and behaviour of the atmosphere, the reality itself. As long as he stood still, his surroundings were mostly unremarkable, however, given the slightest movement, the atmosphere seemed to acquire a semi-liquid, three-dimensional consistency, like the surface of some vast pond reflecting its immediate surroundings. Any movement caused the surface to become animated and he saw vibrations moving away from him in all directions, caressing reality itself in the manner of stones rippling a pond. Jared moved his hand back and forth, amazed at this strange reality that engulfed him. When he resumed walking the buzzing started up again.

He walked under the brick gatehouse, then past the guard. As he moved, he made a pathway in the soup of this reality. He pushed open the iron-gate and went inside. The guard continued to ignore him, so he carried on past the wire fence, and the narrow footbridge spanning a deep dry moat.

The bright blue sky of a few minutes ago had disappeared, replaced by a menacing shade of black and purple. Horizontal lightening flashed between the clouds. Jared was disoriented and wanted to scream. Had the lynchpin of his sanity come loose? Most terrifying was his sense that although he felt like screaming, he somehow understood it was pointless.

Once inside the perimeter wire of the compound, he stood at the edge of a large open space covered with gravel. Somehow he knew this place – the *Appellplatz*, but how?

Even considering the question itself was troubling, as if by doing so he might summon bad luck.

Jared sweated with the realization that not only did he know the name of this place, he also knew its purpose. Images of the prisoners of Dachau attending roll call several times a day flashed into his mind. He felt as if he himself, an officer, had just strolled out from one of the many buildings. Memories of endless roll calls, macabre and sickening, came to mind.

He recalled prisoners shivering in the cold as the guards counted them again and again, because the prisoner total must tally precisely with the figure held by the senior officer sitting at the front table. That tally included the recently dead prisoners, each one laid neatly in rows behind the line of their living barrack-mates, the dead not permitted disposal until a precise reconciliation of the camp census provided official leave to do so.

What the hell *is* all this? Am I *dead*?

"Clarence." He shouted.

The sound of his voice reverberated in his head, before emerging outside of himself to ripple reality as it went, like drapes moving in a breeze. The laws of physics seemed different in this place, if indeed "place" was what this was.

Jared glanced back and noted that the gate sentry remained completely oblivious to his yell. Ah, Clarence was behind this. He must have put acid in my coffee on the train. Any moment Clare' would burst out from somewhere, laughing like hell.

Alright Clare', Jared thought, you can come out now, before I wet my pants - or worse.

But as much as he'd wanted to believe this hypothesis, he knew that such a mundane explanation wouldn't fly. He began running. As he accelerated, the substance of reality folded around his body, then slid past him in the manner of a slipstream of smoke in a wind tunnel moving over an airfoil. and the buzzing grew louder. Reality felt neither solid nor liquid, yet somehow contained qualities of each. Jared was at once a part of this bizarre reality, and yet separate.

When he reached the centre of the Appellplatz he needed to rest. Moving through this soup tired him and his breathing was laboured. As soon as he stopped, the buzzing ceased and the eerie stillness returned.

Where was everybody? Others had to exist here. But with the exception of the guard at the gate and the faces in the guardhouse windows, any others seemed to exist only in his mind's eye. Or maybe there *was* no difference between mindscape and landscape in this place?

Jared stared at the immense red brick building constructed in a large "U" at one end of the Appellplatz. The building's brick exterior contrasted with the stark wooden barracks. Was this brick structure an administration building? Somehow Jared knew it wasn't.

On its roof, for all to see and reflect upon, were painted large white words in German. Again, somehow Jared easily translated.

There is one road to freedom. Its milestones are obedience-diligence-honesty-order-cleanliness-temperance-truth-sacrifice, and love of one's country.

Behind him, Jared heard voices. Spinning about caused a momentary whirlwind in the reality. He observed a large farm wagon entering the other side of the Appellplatz from between two of the wooden buildings. Six men dressed in blue and grey striped garb pulled this wagon heaped with stones. Despite the grim weather, only three of the six men wore shoes. Each prisoner struggled against wooden flanges running crossways at intervals along the wooden tongue that harnessed them to their misery.

On top of the load, sat a German soldier. He held his unbuttoned gray coat closed with one hand, in the other he held a bullwhip. He stood up and snapped the whip above the prisoners' heads, striking one of the prisoners on the back. The prisoner's scream distorted the fabric of the reality, and Jared watched in horrified amazement as the waves generated by the scream pulsated through the soup towards him in slow motion. The shockwave engulfed him with the man's pain and rage and Jared fell to his knees. He wanted to run and seize the whip from the guard, but his disorientation was profound, and he was immobilized in this kneeling position. He could only watch as the wagon continued its tortuous and creaky path across the square. His knees felt the vibrations of the wagon's cartwheels moving over the gravel.

"Tempo. Tempo. Los Los." The soldier on the wagon shouted.

The words sounded as if they were channeled through a synthesizer and they emerged distorted like audio fudge. The soldier followed up with another snap of the whip that caused another prisoner to loose his footing and fall. Some of the others stopped pushing for an instant to permit the unfortunate soul to regain his stance. Expecting punishment, several of the men raised a hand to shield their backs. At this, the soldier commenced to curse loudly in German, the resulting verbal firestorm assaulted Jared through the soup causing him to squirm, retch, then pass out on the ground.

Some time later when Jared returned to consciousness, the wagon had disappeared. He pulled himself upright, and shuddered as if trying to shake off this horror.

Maybe, he thought, I don't exist anymore since nobody else apparently could see or hear him. Maybe I'm dead. If so, was this to be his hell? As he drew closer to the rows of barracks, he could hear above the omnipresent buzzing in the background whenever he moved, a rising cacophony, the groans and wails of a thousand people. The sound reminded Jared of that description of hell in the Bible where there would be, "weeping, wailing, and gnashing of teeth." Although the sound iced his soul, he continued his approach.

He noticed that the size of the barrack building itself appeared to ebb and flow with the human misery within. At one moment the building seemed as if it were but a model in a railway layout; the next it appeared to loom far overhead. Looking up, he felt ill. He related this feeling to when he used to lay on his back at the base of the Toronto Dominion tower and stare straight up the side to the sky, the reverse vertigo making him ill but fascinated.

He looked beyond the barracks to one of the camp's seven guard towers where a soldier stood with his rifle over his shoulder and smoked a cigarette while scanning the enclosure. Jared felt instantly conspicuous, but reminded himself no one could see him. He entered one of the barracks buildings and was stunned.

Constructed to house perhaps two hundred, at least a thousand people were crammed into this Dante's fish tin. Bunks overflowed with people gazing out, lying down, or talking. The narrow walkways between the bunks were jammed and people needing to move about barely squeezed past.

Each man wore ragged and filthy prisoner garb and most were barefoot. Coughing, wheezing and sneezing punctuated the voices of the miserable trying to converse. The odorous stench of urine and feces mixed with cigarette smoke and the sweat of humankind assaulted his senses. Oddly, Jared found it difficult to isolate individuals within the group – all seemed a part of one great tortured organism.

Jared watched prisoners enter the barrack door and try, with futility, to prevent tracking in muck from outside. A guard entering the barrack shouted at one of the prisoners to remove his filthy shoes.

The prisoner's eyes, perhaps at one time a brilliant green, appeared bleached by his ordeal to a hint of their original hue. He made haste to comply with the guard's demand, but not fast enough, so the guard propelled the fellow forward onto the floor with a jackboot to his backside. Next the guard seized the man's pathetic footwear, opened the door of the potbelly stove, and tossed them in. He warmed his hands in the brief flame provided by the meager fuel.

Jared could only look with despair and helplessness upon this outrage, and wondered why he must witness this. At the same time, it occurred to him that if this camp was his hell, he was grateful for one thing; at least *he* was safe from the guards. He worried that might suddenly change, however, because apart from up and down, nothing else about this place seemed predictable.

Jared had no idea how long he'd actually been there. From moment to moment it seemed like an hour, a day, or a week. He tried not to consider the possibility he might never escape this place, for such a conclusion might well precede total madness. He found it odd that he experienced neither hunger nor thirst. Having seen enough in the Barrack, he moved on.

For a time he wandered between the various buildings watching the guards and prisoners. His invisibility continued to amaze him, and under other circumstances it might have been amusing. Instead, he felt like Scrooge visiting the past and terrified of his future. He watched a guard and a leashed Doberman passing and feared the beast might sense him. It continued past him without notice.

Another solider, carrying a box with medical insignia, approached, and Jared decided to follow him to one of the barracks in the middle of the group. On the door a sign read, *Eintritt verboten.* Entry forbidden, but why? The other barracks didn't have this sign. He continued after the soldier through the doorway, and had just cleared it when the door slammed through him. The soldier stepped on Jared's foot, but neither of them felt anything. Jared wondered if he had, indeed, become a ghost.

Despite external appearances to the contrary, once inside, Jared realized that the function of this particular barrack was different. He stood in a small anteroom filled with spare medical equipment, and shelves with ledger books. A prisoner sat transcribing reports at a small table with a typewriter as if immune to the sounds of groans and coughing from the room beyond. With trepidation, Jared stepped past the prisoner's desk and entered the second room.

The windows of the room were boarded up, its sole illumination a clear bulb on a wire. Four men stood in the room, two wearing black officer uniforms, the others in prisoner garb. All stood around a large shallow rectangular steel tank on the floor. With their backs to him, the men in uniforms obstructed Jared's view into the tank. He moved closer. At his approach, one of the two officers suddenly swiveled in his direction, as if sensing something. The man's face caused Jared to shake. It couldn't be, but it was.

Jared was staring at a double of himself, albeit a somewhat older version, each of their birthmarks identical except for being the mirror image of its counterpart. Jared's mind spun. The officer was that guy he'd glimpsed so often in his dreams.

The doppelganger stepped away from the tank and removed a silver flask from the front pocket of his tunic. He took a swig, then stepped to one side allowing Jared to see into the tank.

The painful groans came from a semi-conscious man dressed in flying gear floating on his back in the water. One of the helpers dumped a bucket of ice into the tank. Two wires ran from the

273

man's body to instruments held by the other technician. One wire led from the flyer's chest area, the other from underneath him. The officer reviewed his pocket watch.

"Temperature check," the officer demanded.

The technician fumbled with the instrument as he attempted to orient its dial in the dim light,

"Schnell!"

"26.4 rectal, 28.0 abdomen, Untersturmfuhrer," the technician replied.

The officer carefully noted the figures in a ledger.

Jared, continuing to be mesmerized by his doppelganger, positioned himself for a better view. Was that officer really him? This and a thousand other questions exploded in his mind, causing his body to tremble, and his head to pound as if two guys with hammers were breaking out.

When Jared crouched down in the dim to look in the flyer's face, he felt the blood suddenly drain from his face and he began to retch.

The flier, close to death in the freezing water, was also a doppelganger.

Clarence.

Chapter Forty-seven

Jared struggled to regain his composure. He wanted to help Clarence. He stepped into the tank, knelt down, and tried to grab him, but Clarence passed through his hands as if he were something between a spectre and a slippery liquid. It seemed as if Clarence was both there, and not there, at the same time. Jared tried to seize him, but each time came up with empty air. Jared wondered again if any of this was real? Maybe it was just some kind of macabre mirage, or a hideous projection of his imagination. Jared knew that his rescue effort was futile. Unable to stare helplessly at his friend, he climbed reluctantly from the tank.

Later Jared said he was amazed at how changes of location seemed to occur without him having any recollection of the transport because after exiting the tank, the next thing he recalled he was tearing blindly down the narrow street that separated the two rows of prisoner barracks. The faster he ran the more resistance he experienced from the atmospheric soup. His breathing grew difficult and he finally had to slow down. Even moving slowly, reality continued folding and distorting about him as he stumbled on in primitive flight. Finally, forced to rest, he saw that he had arrived at what appeared to be the punishment area for those accused of breaking the camp rules.

The primary instrument of torture was a stout tree from which a prisoner dangled. The man was suspended with his hands secured behind his back, causing his upper arm bones, strained beyond their limits, to twist from their sockets. The man hung limp.

The man's predicament distracted Jared from his own terror. He tried to undo the knots binding the man; however, just as with Clarence, the rope simply passed through his fingers leaving Jared painfully impotent to help. Then, in that moment of desperation, he thought to ask God's help for the fellow.

Jared felt guilty asking God for help. He didn't think he had that right any longer. Pastor Ronson said that asking God for help during times of emergency was like using him for "fire insurance." Jared reasoned that he wasn't asking for himself, and began to pray.

"Dear God, please help this man and Clarence. Stop their suffering. Don't let Clarence die because of me. And forgive my sins against you and others."

His eyes closed in prayer, a certain lightness and calm came over him that lessened his own physical discomfort. His mind filled with brilliant images from home.

He saw his parents smiling and welcoming him home. He saw Clarence and himself dressed in tuxedos, standing at the front of the little white Church and staring with expectation down the aisle towards the door where Alice, his childhood friend, beautiful in wedding white, smiled then stepped inside and moved with the rest of the wedding party towards him. Their families, friends, and boundless love filled the Church.

Next a kind of haze obscured his mind and then the pinball guy from his dreams emerged from the murk, still at his game. When he noticed Jared, he stopped playing, and pushed his baseball cap back on his head.

What *is* all of this? Jared asked, without having to say a word aloud.

"It's what I've always told you; everything in the universe is an aspect of everything else. Today, yesterday, tomorrow. Light, dark, man and woman. And all of these parts are facets in the magnificent jewel comprising who and what each of us really are. Balance in everything, and love for yourself and others is the purpose, and these qualities are within your reach. And when we strive for them, we touch the hand of God."

Jared gasped and feared the pinball guy would disappear before he could ask something else.

"But, but what am I supposed to believe in?" He blurted. "What's true?"

The pinball guy looked at him with compassion and said nothing, but Jared felt his soul fill with understanding. Christianity, Islam, Buddhism and most other religions were aspects and glimpses of God-ness, paths to God-ness, none of them exclusive or complete. Human beings could never hope to perceive the entire picture because of the limitations of human perception and intellect, and the complexity of it all. Being their brother's keeper was every soul's mission.

The voices of two prisoners dispatched to cut down the prisoner startled Jared from his epiphany. They laid the prisoner onto a small wooden cart and rubbed his arms gently to assist circulation. They tipped a can of water to his lips. At their ministrations, the man began to stir.

Jared prayed, *thank you God!*

Relieved, Jared's thoughts returned to his own predicament. He reasoned that the most logical way out of this place must be where he'd come in, so he headed back to the Jourhaus gate.

He passed the electric fence and crossed the footbridge traversing the dry ditch. Ahead of him, still at attention, stood the same guard. Jared reached out toward the soldier in curiosity, but although the fellow remained oblivious, Jared noticed the background buzzing grew louder, and the reality itself appeared to move away from his hand, appearing to distort the sentry more with each second as if Jared's palm were possessed of some great repellent force. The background buzzing and the visual distortion escalated until finally the sentry vanished and a strange horizon came into view.

The horizon seemed to contain billions of endless loops twisted together in a pattern that seemed at once utterly chaotic, yet harmonious. As Jared continued to extend his arm, the buzzing increased to an almost painful volume whereupon the stringy loops began to arrange themselves into hundreds of hexagonal cells, each cell abutting others on all five sides. The total effect was that of some vast honeycomb. Looking closer, Jared saw that each cell was a kind of window or portal to a different place or time.

In one cell, he observed primitive ape creatures huddling about a fire; in another humans slept in stasis chambers while androids piloted a star ship to a new home for mankind elsewhere in our galaxy. Other cells displayed wondrous planets and objects of cosmic beauty, their beauty a stark contrast to the evil of the concentration camp. Jared understood that the sum of man's atrocities and profound ignorance of the interconnectedness of everything must have caused reality itself to be distorted, even torn. The weight of mankind's shame filled him with profound grief.

One of the cells nearest the horizon line attracted him. As he got closer, the cell grew larger. Inside he saw the visitors standing at the other camp entrance and as he listened carefully, he heard Clarence shouting through the buzz. He reached toward the sound of Clarences' voice.

"Where *are* you Jared?"

"Here I am," Jared yelled. "But I don't know where 'here' is. It's someplace else."

At that moment Jared observed that his reaching hand began to stretch like Pinocchio's nose, then disappear into the cell.

Chapter Forty-eight

Clarence whirled about at Jared's voice that came from everywhere, yet nowhere. Suddenly, from thin air appeared a disembodied finger, then the hand, and finally the full arm of Jared's army surplus jacket. A buzzing noise grew louder by the second.

"What the *hell?*" Clarence leapt back from the phantom arm continuing its movement towards him. As the arm began to retract, Clarence leaned forward.

"Damn." He grabbed the hand and tugged.

Jared's body materialized partly into view, then Jared tried to pull himself loose, Clarence clasped on with his other arm, braced his feet and yanked. Jared emerged from nowhere with a satisfying pop like that of a cork pulled from a bottle of wine. Behind him, the window in reality closed with an audible snap, and the buzzing suddenly abated.

Each of them initially leapt back at the unexpected appearance of the other, then Jared latched onto his friend like one of those deprived monkeys in Harlow's lab.

"Jared . . . what the hell *was* that?

"No swearing. Thank you, God, thank you, God," Jared whispered.

"Jared it's O.K.; it's O.K."

Jared held on and continued repeating his prayer of thanks.

Now Clarence had seen Jared in weird states before, and vice versa, but never anything like this. He frowned at Jared and rubbed his back.

"You're fine Clark'." He nodded. "Everything's O.K. now . . . Where were you? What was all that?"

"Don't know . . . just get me outta here."

"Maybe I should take you to a doctor." Clarence hardly got the words out before Jared regressed to the Harlow monkey again, and clamped again onto Clarence's arm.

"No, no doctor . . . Just get me *away* from here."

A moment later, Jared's instinct for flight resurfaced and he ran.

"Hold on, where are you going?" Clarence kept a firm grasp on his jacket.

Jared yanked himself free and bolted from the camp down the roadway toward the bus stop. Clarence caught up and ran alongside him..

"Alright, alright, no doctor."

Jared continued to stumble along, his face white with shock, only managing to whisper.

"Have to get away."

"O.K. We'll go back to town and I'll look after you. But what *happened?* I leave you for two minutes, you disappear, and then appear like a ghost out of thin air!"

At this statement, Jared stopped and stared at Clarence in disbelief.

Two minutes? "Don't ask Clare'. Just...don't...ask." He continued to repeat the last part under his breath as if it were a survival mantra.

Waves of fear continued to roar through Jared, mostly because he was obsessed with the idea that at any second he might suddenly be returned to that unspeakable place. He avoided looking back towards the camp, as if doing so might compel bad luck or retribution in the manner of Lot's wife turning to a pillar of salt as she peered back upon the destruction of Sodom and Gomorrah. When he reached the bus stop, Jared entwined his arms about a signpost and continued shaking, sweating, and gasping for breath.

When the bus arrived, he barged to the front of the queue, leapt on board, and slammed a handful of change into the fare-box without bothering to see how much he had deposited. He ignored the driver staring at him in disbelief and stampeded to the back of the bus.

Jared lay down on the back seat, drew his legs and arms up into a foetal position and resumed trembling. Shortly, Clarence squeezed in beside him.

Back in their tiny room in Munich, Jared tried telling himself that he was safe and could relax, but neither his body nor his mind were having it. Adrenalin and exhaustion fuelled his agitation as body and mind reeled in the face of irreconcilable physics, and the phantasmagoria of his experience.

Now Jared had always found it difficult to believe that someone's entire concept of reality or their belief system might change in an instant, but now he understood. Saul's experience on the road to Damascus held resonance and he imagined Saul becoming Paul in an instant. The words Damascus, then Dachau, began to perseverate in his mind. Dachau, Damascus, Dachau, Damascus. He shook his head to make it stop, but it was as futile as trying to terminate those annoying jingles once they start up in your mind.

Jared was unable to speak to Clarence, or even look him in the face. Eventually, fatigue, a handful of ASA, then darkness granted Jared a few hours of merciful sleep.

When he awoke in the dark, he sat up and smoked one cigarette after another trying to comprehend what had occurred. His head had stopped spinning, but now he experienced waves of fear, disgust and confusion, each wave more intense than the last, as if he were caught up in some kind of psychological labour. He grew petrified about what might happen next.

Clarence got up to offer Jared bread and cheese and tried to engage him in conversation.

"Talk to me," Clarence said, rubbing his friend's back, but all efforts at conversation proved fruitless. Exhausted and confounded, Clarence finally gave Jared his space and returned to bed.

Over the next few days Jared remained distant from Clarence, and everything else. He later said that even if he'd wanted to explain what had occurred, it seemed that somehow he didn't speak the same language as other people any longer. He sat at the little table in the room, smoking, or lay on his bed in silence,

284

staring at spots on the filthy ceiling.

Clarence began going out for longer periods by himself. He brought back food for Jared, but gave up trying to talk because for the most part, Jared simply ignored him.

Jared had little appetite for anything and his malaise, black and clinging, deepened. A prickly, mottled beard grew on his face and he ignored all but the most basic demands of nature. He tried to stay awake as much as possible, because when he fell asleep, flashbacks tormented him. In his dreams, he kept seeing Clarence in the freezing tank asking "Why?"

Waking hours were little better because then Jared was filled with recriminations thinking that at this very moment in that other place, Clarence was being tortured, apparently at Jared's very hand. He looked away whenever Clarence returned to the room.

Finally, Clarence stopped reaching out to Jared except to bring him food, much of which ended up in the garbage. The two grew oblivious to one another.

A week passed before Jared started coming around. He began to eat, shave, and wash himself, but still he had no idea what to tell Clarence, or indeed whether he should say anything. To make matters worse, Jet's money was running out. He knew he couldn't remain overseas much longer. One afternoon while Clarence was away, he filled his backpack, left a few marks on the table for his share of the room, then headed for the train station.

Jared enjoyed being outdoors again walking down the Platz but occurred that despite his long-time fascination with magic, he had only ever mastered the disappearing act.

Chapter Forty-nine

No one knows how Alice in Wonderland was following her journey down the rabbit hole, but it is probably safe to say that her life was never the same. Neither was Jared's.

Since childhood Jared felt that he didn't belong in this world. Now that his reality had been jerked 180 degrees, he thought he had evidence of this. Along with the confusion and sense of displacement, feelings of guilt and self-loathing remained. All Jared could think to do was to keep moving, although apart from his impending financial crisis, he had no idea why.

Back in England, Jared made his way on the tube from London's Victoria Station and checked into Holland House, one of two youth hostels in the city. The airline told him it would likely be several days before he could obtain a standby flight. It was early December and Jared guessed the planes were booked solid with businessmen keen to slam the door on one last business deal of the year, families on the move for the holiday, and burnt-out, broke young travelers like himself. Jared didn't mind waiting for a flight because he had little idea of what to do when he arrived home. There at least, if he couldn't find work he'd try welfare.

Hostel rules required him to be out between certain hours, and so each morning after "breakfast" (the Brits flattering a stale bun, jam, and terrible coffee with this handle), Jared purchased day passes on the tube and visited tourist sites. To be truthful, he didn't care if he saw anything, but with the weather dreary and wet, he needed to be indoors anyway. He was grateful for the minimal traffic at tourist sites.

Although London was festooned for the holiday, Jared didn't relate to the gaiety. The dungeon in the tower reflected more his state of mind as he went about in his own private London fog. Sightseeing provided a degree of respite from his self-recrimination, but his dark mood projected onto everything.

Visiting the British Museum, Jared fumed as he stared at the graceful stance and archaic smile of an old kingdom Egyptian granite. The Museum was essentially a warehouse of booty stolen by the Brits' during the colonial era. He concluded that perhaps a hundred years ago the English archaeological establishment might have had a rational for 'protecting' artifacts, but that argument wouldn't fly today.

Jared laughed sarcastically at the display chronicling Dr. Livingston's 'discovery' of Victoria Falls. Apparently, nothing really existed in the world until a European had seen it, given it a proper European name, and placed it on a map.

The third evening in London, on his way back to the hostel,

Jared stopped in at a local pub, the Brass Lion. He sat alone thinking, drinking, and stewing in his own depression. Memories of the doppelgangers, especially his feeling of helplessness where Clarence was concerned, occupied his mind. He continued swilling dark beer until he'd reached the point of comfortable numb. The bartender attempted to make conversation with him.

"You from Canader, Guv?"

"Yeah...howdya know?" Jared's voice was lifeless, his eyes and mind lurking somewhere else. He didn't really want to talk.

"Oi can tell it from yer bloody accent, mate." Jared smiled; he found it peculiar to think of Anglo-Canadians as having an accent, but after traveling, he now appreciated that some things, like accents, were only noticeable against the relief of some other culture or place.

"Been over 'ere long?"

"Yeah, few months. Going home tomorrow or Saturday."

"No place like 'ome eh?"

"Yeah, yeah I guess so."

The bartender's comment evoked pangs of homesickness and dread in Jared and he determined to change the subject. He glanced at his watch; it was well past suppertime. He started to order fish and chips, then thought the better of it. Fish and chips left a bad taste with him now because it reminded him how he'd let down Wolf and Gerda.

"Maybe I'll have the steak and kidney pie and some mushy peas."

"As yer like it, guv."

As yer like it. He wondered if the Brits actually talked like that, or were they just putting it on for the tourists. As he waited for his meal, it occurred to him to check the possibility of a flight the next morning.

In the phone booth he pulled a handful of coins from his jacket pocket. Have get rid of this junk before I leave. He needn't have worried because he lost several coins trying to figure out the phone. He wouldn't miss those bulky English coins. Maybe their weight was the reason the English measured their currency by the pound.

After connecting with Air Canada, he learned that he might land a standby seat the next morning. He decided to arrive at Heathrow early to ensure a seat, and worried that he might not wake in time. Unable to sleep, he lay in the dark wondering why, apart from impending poverty, he was going home. Sure he'd had his fill of Europe, and he missed home, but maybe what he missed didn't exist any longer. He thought about his family and how good his life had really been, and how he hadn't realized or appreciated it. He wished he could be a small child again and start over; this time he'd try to do things properly.

If life was a merry-go-round, Jared figured he fell off long ago. Now he could only stand to one side and watch it go round.

Chapter Fifty

"You've been with us for several weeks now," Simon addressed Jared one morning. "How are you feeling now, compared to when you first arrived?"

It was a fair question, and Jared did feel better, at least insofar as his mood. The anti-depressant medication, now chugging at full throttle, was helpful, but facts were facts. His mood wasn't the primary thing. Medication didn't alter his memories, horrible dreams, or his confused sense of reality and self-loathing. He tried to sound positive.

"I'm better than I *was*. That is, I don't want to kill myself. And I finally read that story."

Simon looked puzzled.

"You know . . . that story you mentioned to me. I stopped by the library the other day while I was on a pass and looked up Plato's *Republic*."

"Yeah, I'm with you, the allegory of the cave." Simon nodded. "What did you think?"

"Those ancient guys had most everything about life figured out, didn't they?" Jared's face became wistful. "Maybe the only thing we've done since then is to rediscover those old truths."

"Any particular truths you have in mind?"

"I dunno, really. Well, maybe one thing." Jared paused, his face downcast.

"That maybe it's better to stay in the dark."

The silence following was one of empathy. Finally, Simon narrowed his eyes, then leaned forward.

"Well, it has been said the truth will set you free, but first it will make you miserable."

Jared had arrived back in Toronto with about enough money left in his pocket to take the airport bus downtown. It was literally a one-way ticket to the street.

After shivering that first night in a stairway, Jared sought out the social safety net. He discovered that welfare couldn't help much without an address, and by the time he found one and sorted out the red tape, the room was rented. This happened twice, so he decided to remain in a men's shelter. One night, as he slept, someone took his wallet and identification. He was fed up with the place, and if it had been summer instead of December he'd have slept outdoors. Although it was nearly Christmas he only felt like the Grinch bothered by the "noise, noise, noise," of people's coughing, and talking. Unlike hostels in Europe, this place was jammed with the down-and-out.

After days wandering endlessly on the streets, he had lost

weight. With little money left from welfare, he figured it was just as well he hadn't much of an appetite. When he got hungry, he made the rounds of the soup kitchens. One of his favourite stops was a place near College and Spadina called the Fred Victor Mission. One day as he sat gobbling his free chili, he thought of a slick, if sarcastic, advertising slogan for the place.

Get on the spot relief with Fred Victor.

Something in the back of his mind told Jared that it was a bad idea to return to Jet's neighbourhood, but he didn't listen. Perhaps it has something to do with thieves compelled to return to the scene of their crimes, or arsonists drawn to their fires. Jared hoped he might find someone he could crash with until he could find a place of his own.

The streets of any city have their own kind of radar system. Jet's old neighbourhood was no different. They were onto him before he saw them coming.

"Well, well, lookie here, it's Jet's old pal, Clark'."

What the...? In an instant they grabbed him by the collar and shoved him down an alley. Jared thought he recognized one guy but he had never seen the other guy.

The familiar guy shoved him against the wall and held a knife to his face.

"Odd thing, isn't it, Clark'? Jet goes to rock and roll heaven, and you're the last guy to see him alive."

"Look. I... I went there to buy some weed and he was in the bathroom dead. I called the ambulance."

"Called the ambulance, eh? Real nice, eh Billy?"

"Really." The second man agreed.

"Funny thing though," the first man said. "Jet's chick says there was no money with him when she went to the morgue to identify him. Now I *know* he had two thousand bucks in his pocket that day."

"How . . .how would you know that?"

"Because I was coming later that day to get it, that's why."

He grabbed Jared's collar, along with a handful of skin in the process, and thrust him against the wall. His knife creased Jared's throat.

Despite the freezing temperature, Jared sweated. "Listen, I'll tell you, but please don't hurt me."

"O.K., talk." The second guy stood lightly on Jared's sneaker, ready to stomp should further persuasion prove necessary.

"Alright, I took it. The whole two thousand."

"And of course, you have none of it left." The thug snarled. He stood close enough that Jared thought he saw his own fear reflecting in his assailant's eyes.

"I figured Jet didn't need it . . . I figured the cops would just scoop it anyway."

To his surprise, the guy took the knife away and let him go.

"Alright, but you owe me."

"But I don't have any..." The thug returned the knife to Jared's neck. "I'll try to get it somehow."

"You'll do more than *try*. You know Clark', some guys might just kill you for this right here and now, but I ain't chancing jail time for a lousy two thousand bucks. But that don't mean you don't owe me. I'm giving you one week, and if I don't get my money back...Well, maybe yer going to wish that I did kill you."

He walked Jared back to the street and pointed to a coffee

shop nearby.

"Next Tuesday at one p.m. Be there. And don't try to bugger-off someplace. If you are anywhere in T.O., I'll find you *eventually.*"

They let him loose, then headed off.

After only ten days back in Toronto, Jared had enough of the turmoil in his mind, and the mess his life had become. He made an important decision.

One afternoon, after panhandling a little money, he entered an out-of-the-way variety store. Waiting until another customer occupied the owner with a purchase, he slipped several bottles of Tylenol into his pocket. The East Indian shopkeeper glancing in the large round surveillance mirror saw him and in a flash was around the counter after him. Jared took off, charging through the front door and down the street.

"I am calling police. I am remembering you." The man shouted.

After a few blocks, Jared slowed his pace to a walk. Just to be safe, he turned down a laneway behind some houses. He didn't know where to go, but continued moving west. As he walked, large snowflakes began falling and wind gusts propelled litter across the street.

Now that Jared had made up his mind to kill himself, a strange calm settled over him. Perhaps killing himself might help Clarence, as well as putting an end to his own misery.

After walking for two hours, he arrived near High Park. He bought a coffee and donut with the last of his money, then wandered around the small zoo in the park and commiserated with the animals. The bison standing in a small pen seemed as miserable as Jared, each of them in a cage. If this weren't Toronto, he'd have set it free. He'd have to settle for letting himself out.

Few people were in the park that December afternoon so no one noticed a young man sitting on a park bench washing down handfuls of pills with gulps of tepid coffee.

Jared hadn't really slept for two days, and when finished taking all of the pills he lay down on the bench and pulled his two dollar Sally-Ann overcoat around himself.

Chapter Fifty-one

Overhead, the hospital page boomed.

"Any available doctor to the delivery room."

Jared could hardly believe what he was seeing - his entire family, waiting in the lounge to see him.

The page distracted Jared and he didn't notice Simon approaching from behind. When he did notice him, Jared's eyes flashed and he snapped.

"You *betrayed* me. I never gave you permission to bring them here."

Simon looked uncomfortable, and for once remained silent.

Jared kept his voice low. "I ought to sue your ass."

"Listen, Clark'. . ." The social worker started to explain.

He was interrupted by movement from the other direction. It was Jared's mother.

Elizabeth hesitated, then stepped forward and put her arms around Jared. He felt her tears dampen his cheek and he put his arms around her. He was too choked to speak.

Her voice shook. "Thank God we've found you. I've prayed every day that we would see you again."

Jared reached out his hand to the man standing behind her.

"Dad."

The two of them remained silent, looking into each other's eyes. Jared realized he'd never seen his Dad crying before.

There are times in life, when the circumstances of a moment change everything, and things come full circle to a resolution neither expected nor anticipated. And even where people have been at polar opposites, suddenly a bridge, albeit a rickety one, can appear over the seemingly impassable gulf that has divided. So it was that day for Jared and his family. Almost.

Jared spied his brother standing alone in the lounge doorway. The two young men sized each other up with unease.

"Let's go sit down," The social worker suggested.

The family followed Derek, but at the last minute Simon elected to give the family privacy. He pulled the door shut and left.

"Derek," Jared reached out tentatively to his brother. He couldn't think of anything else to say.

Derek remained silent but took Jared's hand. Everyone sat down together, except for Derek who perched himself on a window ledge some distance away. No one spoke until Mom initiated a conversation.

"We've been so worried about you. Where have you been all this time?"

"Kinda complicated really . . . I'll tell you everything in good time . . . You already know about Clarence and I going up north."

The hurt look on her face stung him. What a stupid place to start. He looked away.

"It's alright, Jared," Mom said. "We're all nervous right now. We just have to be patient and hear one another."

Mom was right. That's exactly what they had to do.

"Listen, I did some really stupid, wrong things. " He paused.

"Yes you *did*." Dad's voice had an edge. "But go on."

"After being up north, I was in Toronto working in a fish and chip place for about two years and living in a room. Then I went over to Europe and met Clarence again in Amsterdam and we traveled..." Jared's voice trailed off, suddenly worried that certain things might spill out before he was ready.

"Why didn't you call or even write to us?" Dad asked. "We've been worried sick thinking we'd never see you again." Dad's voice carried the numb resignation of someone who has reconciled himself to a loss, and is now in shock learning he has been fortunately mistaken.

While James spoke, Elizabeth began crying again. Jared tried to explain.

"Look. I wanted to write to you, I really did . . ."

"What *crap*," Derek said from across the room. "The only person you ever think about is *yourself*." His tone was caustic.

Mom tried to intervene. "Derek, what a thing to say!"

Jared raised his hand and said,

"It's alright, Mom." He shifted in his chair to look at his brother but remained silent. Finally, Mom began speaking again.

"Jared, I'm sorry for the wrong things I've done like hitting you, and speaking to you when I let my anger get the best of me."

Derek interrupted, "What are you talking about, Mom? You did *nothing*." Anger swept across his face. "Jared's the one that wrecked everything."

Elizabeth looked sternly at Derek.

"I have discussed this with your father, and God, and I have to put right the things I've done wrong. What Jared has done, and whether and how he makes amends is between himself and God, and those he has wronged."

James placed his arm around his wife.

"Your mother's right, Derek, we made mistakes raising you guys but whatever we did, we meant well."

Jared continued to be surprised by what he heard. He had expected something different, and as he sat listening, he decided that being blamed might have been easier to take.

"Look, " Jared continued. "I have wrecked things, especially myself. I missed you guys. Time went by, and some stuff happened when I was in Germany that made me hate myself . . .," he couldn't finish. The room was dead quiet for several minutes while he composed himself.

Mom took a clean handkerchief from her purse and began to blot his tears. Flushing at the gesture, Jared took the linen and crumpled it in his hand.

"So much has happened to me, and most of it is so weird that I still don't know what to do with it. He held his hands over his face.

"What is it, son?" James asked.

"I tried to kill myself with pills. That's why I'm here in this hospital."

At this revelation, James moved his head slowly back and forth, as if he was uncertain about what was hearing. Elizabeth put her arm around James and wept. Jared tried to comfort her and Derek moved closer to place his hand on Mom's shoulder. Jared returned Mom's handkerchief, and after wiping her eyes, she stuffed it in her sleeve.

"We want you come home, Jared," Mom said. "Come home and let us try to help you."

Overwhelmed, Jared had trouble speaking.

"I'd like to, but really, you guys don't even know who I am anymore. I don't believe what you believe, although I think I believe in *something*. I miss you guys."

James spoke next.

"You're a man now, Jared. You must find your own way in this world, and decide on what you are going to believe. But we are your family, and always will be. Please don't ever leave us like that again."

Derek remained on the perimeter, apparently undecided. Jared knew that peace between them would take time.

"I'd like to come back home, more than anything, at least until I can get a place of my own and a job."

"Then it's all settled," Dad said. "Let us know when you can leave the hospital."

Chapter Fifty-two

Jared knew that he was about to be discharged from hospital; his nurse had advised him that a recent influx of new patients in the post-holiday season was pressuring the bed situation. Dr. Miller said he could leave today, but Simon had left a message for Jared to see him before he left. Jared wandered over and rapped on the social worker's door.

"Simon, it's Jared. Are you by yourself? "

"Yeah, come in." Jared entered and flopped into his usual chair. Simon offered Jared a cigarette.

"Smoke?"

"No thanks. Decided to quit smoking, except ones that give a buzz." Both laughed, then Simon lit up.

"Dr. Miller says you can leave anytime now. How are you feeling about things?"

"Well, good and bad. Good, because I've talked to my family. I'm going to stay with them for awhile until I find a job. I think it's great they want to be there for me." He paused.

"And the *not* so good part?"

"I still don't know what to make of the experience at Dachau. I mean, what does it really mean, and what am I supposed to do with it?"

"What piece of it are you referring to?"

"I guess the knowledge of who I might be, and what can be done about Clarence. Don't get me wrong, I don't feel depressed exactly. But I still can't help wondering if I deserve a good life after everything that's happened and what I know."

Simon nodded with understanding. He inhaled another long drag from his cigarette, then exhaled near an air cleaner humming on the table to one side of him.

"You've been through a lot in your life, Jared. You've seen things that most people never imagine, let alone experience, but I have to tell you that I can't help feeling what happened to you wasn't meant to punish you or wreck your life. Maybe you need to consider what else it means."

"I don't know what else it could mean."

"Well, what have you learned about yourself from all of this?"

"That my double is evil, and I've been punished, and will continue to be punished, because of what's happening in that other place."

"Really?" Simon rubbed his chin in thought. "Now if punishment is the only purpose, why do you think you were allowed to go there and then come back again?"

"To live here with that knowledge."

"Maybe. But I can't help feeling there's more to it than this." As if suddenly inspired, he rolled his chair closer. "Listen, I wonder what important things from the experience you have *forgotten*?"

The question puzzled Jared.

"I not sure what you mean. I thought I remembered everything."

"Perhaps, but why do I have the feeling that you're blinded by all the horrible things, and have forgot something - perhaps the most important part of all?"

"Like what?"

"I don't know, but you do. You just don't know that you know." Simon paused to shrug. "And you may not recall it today, but in time you will. It's more a question for you to think about, rather than something to answer right now." He paused to take another drag. "Now I don't necessarily mean there is some easy answer, but I can't help thinking that you've had this experience for some good purpose. To put it another way, the whole thing seems like a lot of trouble if the only purpose is to make you suffer."

Jared sat riveted, trying to understand. Maybe Simon was right, but what was he forgetting? He closed his eyes and tried to remember what important things he might have forgotten or overlooked. He found it hard to focus on anything except the horror. He stood up and paced about the tiny office; at one point he smacked the corkboard on the wall.

"I'm trying, but I just can't remember anything else."

Unperturbed, Simon proceeded with the confidence of the criminal lawyer playing dumb while he proceeds with examination.

"You told me that after you asked God to help the prisoner hanging from the tree, you felt different. What did you mean by that?"

"I can't think."

"O.K., Let's try another route. Some visualization."

Jared agreed.

"Alright, listen to this tape, and close your eyes." Simon selected a tape and placed it into the machine. Shortly the sound of water flowing and birds chirping began to play.

"Feel the chair against your body, pay attention to your breathing…in and out." Simon breathed audibly with him, and spoke in a low monotonous tone. "You are walking slowly down a staircase… down the staircase, one step at a time and with each step you feel more relaxed, deeper into hypnosis… more peaceful."

Jared's chin dropped to his chest as he focused on his breathing and Simon's voice.

"When you are ready, whatever doors that need to open will open. Your mind is very wise and is going to remember what you need to remember . . . and tell us things you have forgotten, things that are important for you to know."

Jared found himself fully absorbed into the hypnotic state of mind that teetered somewhere between wakefulness and sleep. He listened as Simon continued speaking. Finally, Simon grew quiet and waited patiently in the manner of the oil prospector who, having selected a promising site and drilled a test hole, now waits to see what comes up.

Eventually, Jared began mumbling, speaking in a very low voice as if he were somewhere else but not too far away.

"There are pictures flashing through my mind."

"Images of what?"

"Childhood stuff, my family."

"Uh huh . . . go on."

"Me and Clarence . . . in the Church all dressed up." Jared

looked up at Simon in astonishment. "I'm getting married to Alice!"

"Who's Alice?"

"Just a girl I used to know. She was a really good friend of mine when we were in public school."

"O.K., and what do you make of that?"

"Whaddya mean, what I make of it?"

"Well, how do you understand that information?"

"How do I know?"

"*Try.*" Simon said. Jared bristled.

"Why don't you tell me if you know so much?"

"Look, I'm not trying to harass you, Jared, but I don't think we're there yet. Close your eyes and try relaxing again. Just listen to the tape. Pay attention to your breathing . . . listening to what your unconscious needs you to know about this wedding thing. And I wonder if that was a sign that you have things to accomplish?"

"Like marrying Alice? I haven't even seen her for years."

Simon shrugged, then changed focus.

"Keep your eyes closed, listen to the water and birds. What other important things have you forgotten? Your mind is very wise and is going to tell us what's important."

Simon lit another smoke as Jared focused his thoughts. After a few minutes, he looked up at Simon with an "aha" expression.

"I do remember something – the pinball guy."

"Pinball guy?"

Jared started laughing.

"A guy I used to see in my dreams sometimes when I was a kid. I hadn't thought of him for years, but then there he was in my mind, right in the middle of all that weird stuff in the camp."

"What was he doing?"

"Same as he's always, just being a pinball wizard, but then he stopped his game and talked to me."

"What did he say?"

"He told me that everything that I am, have seen, and done, will do and see is part of the same thing, that our past, present and future is really the same. He said that good and evil are part of the balance, part of everything, and part of us."

Simon rolled his chair closer.

"So what do you think he was trying to help you understand?"

Jared was starting to feel like an itch that only got worse when scratched.

"How do *I* know?" Jared's voice was more irritable than he intended.

Simon locked eyes with him.

"You *know* because this was your experience. You can . . . you must, and you *will* make sense of it."

"Yeah, or maybe I'm just nuts? Miller thinks I'm nuts."

Simon butted out his smoke aggressively in the ashtray and glowered.

"Look, what Dr. Miller thinks, or what I think, doesn't really mean squat with something like this. It's your experience and no one else will ever really understand it, at least in the way that contains most meaning for you. But one thing I do know for certain – a truth is waiting for you. You won't necessarily find it today, but that doesn't mean it isn't there and won't be revealed. There is positive meaning in all this for you, and yes, I don't know exactly what it is, but your mind does, and will let you know when the time is right."

"Well I don't know what it could be." Jared started fidgeting. He was getting tired of this.

Simon lit another cigarette but paid it little attention.

"Let's assume, for a minute anyway, that I'm right and this experience contains positive meaning, but you just don't see it yet. O.K., just for fun, try to imagine what the meaning *might* be. It doesn't have to be right . . . just be creative."

Jared was intrigued with the question.

"Maybe what I saw was a glimpse of positive things to come. Like everybody else, my future will have good and bad."

A smile broke across Simon's face.

"Ah, now we're getting somewhere. Stick with that . . . hey, remember the allegory of the cave?"

"Yeah, why do you ask?"

"Well, do you think the point was for the prisoner to escape from the cave only to return and remain in the dark?"

"No, I think he went back to tell the others about the world of light."

"Exactly. Now how does that story relate to you?"

Jared began to see what Simon was getting at.

"I guess what happened in the camp gave me a look at myself and the world. About how things have been and will be. That we all have the potential for good and evil and we make choices affecting ourselves and others."

"So maybe there's more to this besides punishment, like a positive future that can be created."

"Maybe, maybe so. But what about the stuff with Clarence? What am I supposed to do with that, how do I live with that?"

"I don't know the answer to that, but maybe you need to think of all this in more metaphorical ways. I mean, perhaps the meaning of what you saw isn't literal, and if you look at it differently, you'll understand what you can glean from it. One thing I'm certain of Jared, this experience wasn't meant to destroy you. Something important happened to you, and it likely means a lot of different things. We don't know exactly what right now, but we do know what happened was important, and it certainly means more than you are an evil person. Maybe you've been granted a heads up to use the rest of your life differently. You can choose to see this whole thing as a burden, or you can look at it as a very special gift...a gift with many layers. It may take the rest of your life to finish unwrapping this gift. Would you really want to walk away from your life and never find out what's there?" Simon went to take a drag, and was surprised to find only the filter remaining.

Jared remained deep in thought and Simon waited patiently for his response.

"So maybe this whole experience was a beginning for me, not an ending?"

"Exactly...the start of something important. But thing is, you'll have to stick around in the world to get to the layers."

Someone tapped at the door and Simon glanced at his watch.

"Listen, we gotta finish up; someone else is booked."

Jared looked at the social worker.

"O.K., Simon, just one other thing."

"Yes."

"Thanks Simon, for everything. Can I check in with you once in awhile after I've gone home?"

"I'd be disappointed if you didn't." Simon, his hand on the doorknob, grinned and leaned towards Jared to whisper.

"Truth is, I can't wait to find out what you unwrap."

310

ISBN 1-4120-1419-0